THE
DEVIL'S
RIGHT
HAND

J. D. Rhoades

St. Martin's Paperbacks

"The Devil's Right Hand" by Steve Earle. Copyright © 1978 Chappell & Co. (ASCAP). All rights reserved. Used by permission of Warner Bros. Publications U.S., Inc., Miami, Fla. 33014.

THE DEVIL'S RIGHT HAND

Copyright © 2005 by J. D. Rhoades.
Excerpt from *Good Day in Hell* copyright © 2005 by J. D. Rhoades.

Cover photo © Antonio Mo/Getty Images

Library of Congress Catalog Card Number: 2004056470

ISBN: 0-312-93866-7
EAN: 9780312-93866-6

Printed in the United States of America

St. Martin's Press hardcover edition / January 2005
St. Martin's Paperbacks edition / January 2006

St. Martin's Paperbacks are published by St. Martin's Press, 175 Fifth Avenue, New York, NY 10010.

10 9 8 7 6 5 4 3 2 1

To Lynn, who never stopped believing,

and to my children, Nicholas and Nina

ACKNOWLEDGMENTS

Thanks go to Katy Munger, for reading an early draft, for her excellent suggestions and guidance, for general encouragement, and for her own work; to my editor, Ben Sevier of St. Martin's Press, for crucial tweaks that kicked this book up to a whole new level; and to my agent, Scott Miller of Trident Media Associates, for his enthusiastic representation.

1

"She ain't no damn lesbian," the stocky man said.

"Sure she is," the skinny one said. "Didn't you see that MTV show? Man, Madonna had her tongue right down that girl's throat."

They were sitting in the front seat of a dented pickup truck, pulled back into the woods. From there they could see the trailer the timber company used as an office. It was 5:30 in the morning, and the sky was brightening. A few stray wisps of fog hugged the grass, flowing sluggishly in the humid air. Rusting log trucks loomed in a field behind the trailer, looking like ancient behemoths in the mist.

They had been in place since four A.M. Boredom had finally trumped the need for stealth so they had turned the radio on low. Britney Spears was moaning that she had done it again.

"Man, you got to be crazy," the big one said. "She was goin' with that guy from the who is it, the Backseat Boys. She gave up her cherry for him."

"Well, there y'are, then," the skinny one said triumphantly. "Ever'one knows those guys is all faggots. It was all a cover, man. Like that Richard Gere and Cindy Crawford. All them Hollywood homos cover for one another."

"An' you believe that shit?" the stocky one said. He ran a hand through his thick dark hair. He had kept it trimmed short in prison, thinking it gave him a more menacing appearance. Now it was growing back out, and it was taking some getting used to.

There was a brief flash of headlights through the trees. He reached down and snapped the radio off. "You sure about this now, cuz?" He asked for what seemed like the fiftieth time.

"Sure I'm sure," the skinny man replied. He recited the facts again, with the patience of a specialed teacher repeating a lesson for a slow pupil. He didn't get irritated; it made him feel good to be the one who knew something for a change. All his life, his older cousin had gotten to do everything first. Drink beer, get laid, get arrested. Now it was DeWayne's turn to lead.

"The old man don't hire nobody but Mexicans to do his cuttin' and haulin'. They don't work for nothin' but cash money. They don't pay no taxes that way, see, and neither does the old man. I seen him in the bank the last few Thursdays, gettin' out a big bag of cash. He brings it back here, puts it in the safe for payday Friday."

"I still think we oughta just break in and take the safe out," the stocky one said. "We can find somebody to get it open."

"You wanna bring a stranger in on this?" the skinny one demanded. "Idn't that how you got caught last time? We can trust each other, Leonard, 'cause we're family. But anyone else'll sell you out in a hot second."

"You don't know, DeWayne," Leonard said. "You ain't never done nothin' like this before. Armed robbery is serious shit compared to B and E, man. This DA's got a real serious hard-on for armed robbers. 'Sides, you think that old dude don't have a gun, carryin' around that much cash?" He shook his head and looked out the window, his face glum. "This shit is dangerous."

"You wanna back out, cuz," DeWayne said, "you better do it now. Here he comes." Another pickup, this one at least thirty years old, pulled up in front of the trailer/office. An old man in coveralls got out. He looked to be at least seventy, but his step was sure and confident. He went up the steps of the trailer. He paused a moment on the narrow porch that ran across the front, while he rummaged through a ring of keys. He found the correct one, opened the door and disappeared inside.

"When he comes out," said DeWayne, "he'll have the bag. He takes it out to the job site so he can pay the Mexicans off at the end of the day." Sure enough, in a few minutes the old man came out and walked to the truck. He was carrying a large canvas bag.

The two men got out of their truck. DeWayne let Leonard take the lead. Even though he had let most of his muscle go to fat in his last stay in the joint, Leonard's size still made him intimidating.

"Mornin', sir," Leonard said.

The old man stopped and turned toward them. His eyes were pale green, and made a startling contrast to his skin, which was a light caramel color. "Hep you fellows?" he said in the flat nasal accent of the Lumbee Indian.

Leonard pulled his gun. He was carrying a long-barreled .44, DeWayne a snub-nosed .38. "Let's do this easy, old man, and no one has to get hurt," De-Wayne said.

"Just put the bag down on the ground, and step away real slow," Leonard said.

The old man didn't move. He looked first at De-Wayne, then at Leonard.

"Shit," was all he said.

"What are you talkin' about, man?" DeWayne's voice was high, almost cracking with the strain of adrenaline. He felt the familiar dizzy sensation of things slipping out of his control.

Both of them saw the old man's hand go into the bag. "Don't do it, man . . . ," Leonard shouted as the hand came out holding a small automatic. Both Leonard's and DeWayne's guns barked at once, the sharp cracks muffled by the soggy air. One shot went wide and struck the side of the truck. The other hammered the old man back against the door. The only change in his expression was a grimace of pain, then blankness. The automatic slid from his fingers as he slumped to the ground.

"God *damn* it!" Leonard shouted at the old man. "The *fuck*'d you do that for?" The man didn't answer.

DeWayne rushed forward and grabbed the bag, kicking the automatic farther away with his foot as he did so. He needn't have bothered. The man looked straight ahead, not noticing the bag, the gun, or the rising sun in his eyes. He was dead.

The young paratrooper was full of piss and vinegar, pumped up on the Airborne mystique, and stumbling drunk as well. He looked like he was ready to make an issue out of Keller talking so long to the redhead. Keller didn't see what claim the kid had on the girl, other than the fact she had recently been grinding her crotch on the kid's lap, but he didn't have time to argue. He showed the kid a peek of the 9mm hanging in a shoulder rig beneath his coat. It was enough to make even a drunk kid realize that attitude and training don't make anyone bulletproof. The young soldier did a quick fade into the crowd and Keller turned back to the dancer who called herself Misty.

A lot of people would find it difficult to concentrate on an interview when the interviewee is a redhead wearing only a transparent silk teddy. Keller kept reminding himself he had a job to do and not a lot of time to do it in. Misty helped take his mind off prurient interests by the way she cracked her bubble gum and looked bored. She was no more aware of her clothes, or lack of them, than if she had been in uniform behind the counter at Mickey D's.

"Crystal worked here for a while," she said. It was Saturday night, and the strip club was crowded and noisy. Misty had to shout into Keller's ear to be heard. "She was cute, had a nice figure," she went on "but her heart wasn't really in it, you know? It was like she was half asleep most of the time. Customers want you to be, like, into it. So she left. I don't know where she went."

Keller could see a big guy in a black tuxedo vest and bowtie working his way through the crowd. He wondered for a second how anyone with no visible neck could wear a bowtie. He figured someone had tipped the bouncer off that he was carrying. Keller had all the right permits, but he didn't expect that to cut any ice with the neckless wonder. He flipped Misty a business card.

"If you hear anything," he said, "call me on my cell phone." He had to shout the last phrase, since the music was increasing from the merely deafening to the truly painful. It was time for the next show.

She looked at the card blankly and blew a bubble. "You a bail bondsman?" she said.

"I work for one," he said. He sidled through the crowd toward the door.

Keller stepped out into the humid night and lit a cigarette. A summer thunderstorm had recently blown through, leaving the parking lot scattered with puddles of oily water that reflected back the red and blue neon lights of the club. The sudden cooling brought by the storm had caused the water-logged air to turn to light fog. Keller blew out a long stream of smoke and watched the Friday night traffic sigh past on Bragg Boulevard. A Ford minivan pulled up and a group of young men in sport shirts and khakis piled out. Keller noticed that one of them appeared much drunker than the others, who gathered around him to prop him up. They were whooping and laughing. *Bachelor party,* Keller thought. There was an edge to their laughter, almost hysteria. "We're having fun," the laughter said. "Really. We promise."

There was the sound of footsteps behind Keller.

He turned and saw Bowtie advancing on him. He squared off to face the big man. Bowtie stopped, his red face within a few inches of Keller's. The bouncer squinted, trying to make his small eyes look hard. Keller looked back without expression. Finally, Bowtie spoke.

"You been asking a lot of questions about one of the ladies," he said.

"Yeah," Keller said. Bowtie began to look uncertain. He was obviously used to being placated at this stage of the game. He looked Keller up and down, obviously measuring his broad six feet against Keller's lankier six-two. His jaw worked for a minute, then he said, "You a cop?"

Keller shook his head. "Bail enforcement."

The term obviously threw Bowtie, and the uncertainty was making him angry. His face got even redder and his neck and shoulders seemed to inflate slightly. He was building up his rage for the next stage of the game. Keller interrupted the process. "I'm going to reach into my pocket and get my business card," he said. He did so without waiting for permission. He handed the card to Bowtie, who squinted at it.

"H & H Bail Bonds," he said finally. "What, Crystal in some kind of trouble?"

Keller shook his head. "Her cousin," he said. "Name of DeWayne. They grew up together. He didn't show on a B & E down in Brunswick County. I figured his family might know where he is."

Bowtie stepped back a few inches and deflated his neck and shoulders. "She don't work here no more."

"So I hear. She quit?"

"Naw. I fired her ass. She was, ah, doing private shows after hours. Know what I mean?"

Keller tossed his cigarette on the ground and crushed it out with his boot. "She was hooking."

Bowtie nodded. "I don't need that kind of shit."

Meaning, Keller thought, *that she wasn't cutting you in on the profits. Or letting you sample the merchandise.*

"Plus," Bowtie went on, "she was wasted half the time." He tapped the side of his nose and tried to look knowing. It didn't work. "Know what I mean?" he said again.

"Yeah. Any idea where she went?"

Bowtie shrugged. "Escort service'd be my guess."

Keller sighed. There were at least fifty of those in the Yellow Pages alone. "Don't guess her cousin ever came around." Bowtie shook his head. "No," he said, "she never said nothin' about having a family."

"Okay," Keller said. "Thanks."

"Hey, don't mention it," Bowtie said. "And, ah, sorry about gettin' in your face like that. I gotta look out for the ladies."

"Yeah," Keller said. "You're a real knight in shining armor."

"What?" Bowtie said, but Keller was already walking away.

He walked over to his car and opened the door. The car was a former police cruiser, a late-model Crown Victoria. He had had it repainted to remove the police markings, but it still had a rack in the front seat in which a 12-gauge shotgun rested upright. A cell phone nestled in a hands-free system rose from the floor next to the rack. Keller leaned over and hit the speed dial.

"H & H Bail Bonds," a female voice said after a few rings. It filled the car, directed through the stereo speakers by the hands-free system.

"What are you wearing?" Keller said.

She chuckled softly. "Keller," she said.

As always, her voice saying his name caused a tightening in his throat. "Any luck?" she said.

"I think the cousin's going to be a dead end," he said. "You got anything on the other one, Crystal's brother? They were all raised together. Find one, the other's probably not far away."

"No," she said. "Leonard Puryear missed his last two appointments with his probation officer. The P.O. went out to his house, but the place was empty. They're about ready to violate him. What happened to the sister?"

"I traced her as far as a strip club on Bragg Boulevard, but she's not there. No one knows where she went, but she's probably hooking. Escort service, I'd guess."

"I suppose you could work your way through all of those," she said. "Poor Keller. You always get the tough jobs."

He laughed. "Might be a little hard on the cash flow," he said.

"Among other things," she said. He heard the insectile clicking of computer keys. "Hold on a minute," she said. "If she's hooking, she probably has some kind of record."

He leaned back in the seat and closed his eyes. He saw her in his mind, bent over the keyboard, biting her lower lip like she did when she was concentrating, brushing the long ash-blond hair back from her forehead.

"Got it," she said. "Crystal Leigh Puryear. Known aliases Amber Dawn." She paused. "Jesus," she said. "Amber *Dawn?* Sounds like a feminine hygiene spray." Keller laughed. "Picked up on a solicitation charge two February. Pleaded to disorderly conduct. Last known address—got a pen?"

Keller fished one out of the glove box. "Shoot." She gave him the address. "Best bet's to catch her in the daytime," she suggested. "Saturday night, date night, you know."

"Yeah," Keller said. "Speaking of dating, you thought any about what we were discussing?"

There was a long pause. "Yeah, Keller, I thought about it," she finally said. "I like you, you know that, but I don't think it's a good idea for me to date someone who works for me."

Keller thought for a moment. "I quit," he said.

She laughed. "Nice try," she said. "But I don't date unemployed guys, either."

"Looks like I can't win," Keller said.

"Sure you can," she said. "Just not with me." Her voice softened. "Get some sleep, Keller," she said. "And not in the car. Check in somewhere and put it on the company card. Check out the girl tomorrow and find DeWayne Puryear, preferably by his court date next Thursday."

"Yass, boss," Keller said.

"Pleasant dreams, cowboy," she said and hung up.

Keller leaned back and blew a long breath out through his teeth. He shook his head as if to clear it and started the car.

He considered her advice about getting some rest. He was bone-weary, but he knew from experience that sleep wouldn't come easily. He decided to at least check out the address Angela had given him. Even if no one was there, he could reconnoiter the layout. He had been in this city a number of times before. He had a good idea of where he was headed.

The street was a dead end, lined with small brick houses that had once probably been marketed to young couples in the postwar years as "starter homes." There were no streetlights. Only a few dim porch lights provided illumination. There was a flickering blue glow of television screens behind the shaded front windows of one or two houses, but most were dark. Keller couldn't read most of the house numbers from the street. He snapped the headlights off and slowed to a crawl, giving his eyes a chance to get accustomed to the darkness. Finally, he located Crystal Puryear's address. He parked across the street and rolled down the window.

The house at the end of the street was wooden and looked older than the others, with a more spacious yard and an attached two-car garage. A yellow bulb cast a wan glow over the driveway in front of the closed doors of the garage. A picket fence ran between the street and the overgrown yard, ending at the driveway entrance. There was no light and no sound other than the tick and pop of the cooling engine and the monotonous buzzing of crickets.

Keller sat and looked at the house. One part of his mind automatically mapped out possible approach and escape routes. The other thought about Angela.

She had been right, he mused. Not in her surface excuse about not dating an employee. He could see the real reason when she gently turned him aside from his pursuit of her. She always did so with a soft laugh or a self-deprecating joke about being too old, but the sadness in her eyes told the real story. *Too much baggage*, her eyes seemed to say. *Too much mileage over too many rough roads.* And she was right, he thought. For both of them. He leaned his head back and closed his eyes.

Gravel crunched under his boots as he walked away from the looming bulk of the Bradley fighting vehicle. He had always thought of deserts as soft places, cushioned by sand. This place seemed to be mostly crushed rock and tiny pebbles that always managed to work themselves into your boots. All the sand seemed to come to rest in any mechanical or electronic gear. He looked back and cursed the dead GPS receiver inside the Bradley. He had no idea where they were.

"Shit," he said under his breath. His squad was in the vehicle, most of them asleep. He had to figure out some way to get them home. He unzipped his pants and took a piss on the desert. It summed up his attitude about this place as no words could.

When he was zipping himself back up, he registered the noise of the rotor blades for the first time. It had to be a Coalition aircraft; the raghead air-force had been swept out of the sky weeks ago. He turned toward the sound, waving his arms above his head. "Hey!" he yelled. "Hey . . ."

There was a ripping sound, like the sky being torn open. A bright white bolt like a lance of flame leaped from out of the darkness and struck the Bradley. The boxy metal shape seemed to bulge outward for a split second before erupting in flame from every opening. The concussion knocked him flat on his back. He lay there for a second, staring stupidly at the sky. He saw a metal hatch cover cross his field of vision, whirling across the sky like a UFO. Then he heard the screams. They were burning, but he couldn't get up. His limbs refused to respond to any command that didn't involve curling up into a ball. He could hear himself screaming as well. There was another white flash . . .

He jerked upright in the seat, panting like a distance runner. He flinched as a white tree of lightning arced across the sky, followed by a sharp detonation of thunder. It had started raining again. Keller put both hands on the wheel and waited for his heart to stop pounding. He started the car and drove away.

There was a crowd at the graveside, listen-ing to the preacher's words with the pinched, stoic expressions of people who had been expecting bad news and soon expected to hear worse. The cemetery was well-tended, bordered by woods on two sides and the small white church on another.

Everyone gave a wide berth to the big man in the brown suit. He stared down into the open grave in silence as the preacher intoned the last few words of the service. A few of them looked at the diamond and ruby rings on his fingers and noted the cut of the expensive suit, but no one made comments, at least in his presence. The man had not been a part of their lives for years, but his reputation for random and vicious fits of temper was still legendary.

When the preacher's voice trailed off into a nervous mumble, the big man looked up and looked at him. His eyes were hidden by tinted sunglasses, but after a moment, the preacher looked away and cleared his throat. The big man turned away without a word and walked off toward the line of beat-up cars and trucks in the gravel parking lot. He paused a moment to brush the dust from the cuffs of his pants and opened the door of a large brown 4 x 4 pickup. Letters across the top of the dark-tinted windshield said INDIAN OUTLAW.

He got into the truck and sat down, leaving the door open. The truck's oversized wheels raised the pickup off the ground high enough that the man's snakeskin boots dangled a few inches from the ground like a child sitting in a grownup's chair. He waited.

The group at the graveside had broken into smaller knots, discussing the weather, the tobacco crop, and everything except the recently deceased.

After a few minutes, a young man detached himself from the congregation and walked over to the truck.

"Hey," the young man said. There was no reply.

"Any news on who killed Daddy?" the big man said finally. The Lumbee accent made the last word come out as "diddy."

The younger of the two brothers shuffled his feet in the coarse gravel. "Sheriff said they ain't got no leads."

"Shit," the big man said. He spat on the ground next to his brother's foot. It was an insult that would have resulted in knives being pulled on anyone else.

"Ain't no need to get pissed off at me, Raymond." The younger man whined. "I ain't . . ."

"Someone knew Daddy had a lot of cash. Got any idea?"

The younger man shrugged. "I guess the Meskins knew. Daddy paid 'em off ever' . . ."

Raymond swung his legs into the truck. "We'll go talk to them, then. Get in."

The younger man looked back at the safety of the crowd. "Get in the truck, John Lee," Raymond said. "I ain't gonna tell you again." John Lee took a last look at the church and sighed. He got in the truck. He slumped unhappily in the seat as Raymond pulled away from the church. "I gotta drop by the club," Raymond said. "Then we'll go see what these Meskins can tell us."

· · ·

Interstate Highway 95 stretches 1,970 miles, a gray and black river of asphalt that flows from Miami to the Canadian border. Everything moves on the highway. Truckers ferry livestock, produce, cigarettes, clothing, lumber, bricks, cars, anything that can be shipped in a flatbed or trailer. Tourists stare blankly out the windows of cars, motor homes, and SUVs as they traverse the flat, empty spaces between entertainments. Salesmen study the mile markers for signs that they'll reach their next meeting in time. And, inevitably, drugs and money move on the highway. The FBI, the DEA, and a variety of local law enforcement try to interdict the tons of cocaine, heroin, and marijuana stuffed into the backs of pickups and the wheel wells of compact cars. They catch a few, but mostly they only succeed in angering the African American and Hispanic drivers that they stop in disproportionate numbers.

Raymond's club, the 95 Lounge, was visible from the highway, but a curious traveler had to go a mile up to a little-used exit and double back on a narrow country road to reach it. There was little reason for them to; the club was not advertised on any of the thousands of billboards that grew along the roadside. There was no Texaco nearby, no Cracker Barrel restaurant, no McDonald's or Burger King. The only people who would take the trouble to find their way there were those who knew its real business.

Raymond and John Lee pulled up in the parking lot of the club. It was a low cinder block building painted a dull purple and black. The words 95 LOUNGE were clumsily hand-painted on the front and side of the building in green and white Day-glo letters. There were no windows. A neon sign beside the peeling wooden door announced that the 95 Lounge was "open." There were a couple of battered cars in the parking lot and a new eighteen-wheel truck.

They entered the club, stopping for a moment to let their eyes get used to the gloom. The only illumination was provided by a dim flourescent light behind the bar and a Budweiser sign on the far wall. There were several large booths along that wall. A fat man in a polyester shirt with his name embroidered over one pocket was seated in one of the booths. A skinny woman with bleached blonde hair was seated in the booth on the same side. She was whispering something in his ear. As John Lee stared, her hand slid beneath the table and into the fat man's lap.

"You see somethin' you interested in?" a voice said.

John Lee turned. Billy Ray, the club's manager, was standing behind the bar. He had a malicious grin on his broad copper-colored face.

"Darlene's busy right now, but I don't reckon that

trucker'll take too long," Billy Ray said. "You can have sloppy seconds."

"Shut it, Billy Ray," Raymond said. "John Lee and me got stuff to do." The smile disappeared from the man's face. He sullenly went back to polishing the bar.

John Lee looked back at the couple, who were disappearing out the back door. There was a broken down trailer in the back, he knew. John Lee had never discussed his brother's businesses with him, but he knew the rumors. It was said that some of Raymond's female customers were working off their drug debts in that trailer. John Lee swallowed nervously and followed his brother into the office behind the bar. He sat across the desk from Raymond in a rusted straight-backed chair with a tattered cushion. Raymond flicked his desk lamp on. "You got a pistol?" he said to John Lee.

John Lee shook his head. He felt a sick feeling in the pit of his stomach. "Naw," he said. "I got my deer rifle at home."

Raymond grunted. He turned his office chair around and fiddled with the large, old-fashioned safe behind his desk. With a click, the black door swung open. Raymond reached in and pulled out a large object wrapped in cloth. He set it on the desk and unwrapped it. John Lee stared down at a huge long-barreled revolver that gleamed in the dim light.

"Raymond," John Lee said, "what you planning, man?"

"You and me," Raymond said, "we're gonna find out who killed our Daddy."

"The Sheriff—"

"Don't give two shits about a dead Indian. You know that, and I know that. Anyone goin' to take care of business, it's us. Just like Lowrie."

John Lee, like all Lumbee, knew the name. Henry Berry Lowrie was the Lumbee equivalent of Robin Hood, an outlaw who had taken to the swamps in the 1800s against the Confederate Home Guard and later against the Federals to avenge the murder of his father and brother and the oppression of the Lumbee by whites.

John Lee couldn't take his eyes off the pistol. "You think it was them Meskins?"

"I don't know," Raymond said. "But I aim to find out. And you're coming with me."

"I ain't never killed nobody before, Raymond."

Raymond sighed as if this was some admitted failing on his brother's part. He picked up the gun and stuck it in his waistband.

"Okay," he said. He reached into the safe again and pulled out another pistol, a stubby, ugly automatic. He pulled back the slide and chambered a round before handing the gun to John Lee. "You take this one and back me up. This is your duty, too, little brother. Now let's go."

As they walked back out into the deserted bar, Billy Ray called out to Raymond. "Our friend called," he said. "Our *southern* friend."

Raymond stopped. "What'd he say?"

Billy Ray cast a glance at John Lee. "I told him you were at your Daddy's funeral. He said to give you his sympathy."

"Yeah, right," Raymond said. Paco Suarez didn't get to be the biggest supplier of cocaine on the East Coast by giving himself over to the softer emotions. "He calls again, tell him I'll get back to him as soon as I take care of some family business," Raymond said. "C'mon, John Lee."

They drove for about thirty minutes, with John Lee providing monosyllabic directions. After they got off the main road, the roads grew narrower, but the scenery never changed. They passed field after field of crops growing thick and fat from the dark rich earth where a shallow sea once rolled. Corn, beans, corn, tobacco, tobacco, beans, tobacco. Houses weathered to the same gray as the topsoil stood among the fields, next to metal tobacco-curing barns that gleamed and shimmered in the baking sun. Some landowners had given up the precarious living of farming; those fields grew rows of metal house trailers with postage-stamp-sized dirt yards and old tires thrown up on the roof in a forlorn hope of keeping the roof on in a tornado.

They finally pulled into a narrow dirt driveway

that ran between a double line of rusting single-wide trailers. About halfway down the line on the left, there was a break in the regular spacing of the trailers. The soil in the gap created had been denuded of grass and pounded flat by years of trampling. A group of young Latino men sat playing cards at a picnic table under a spreading live oak in the middle of the common area thus created. They looked up warily as the truck pulled up. One of them stood and walked over to the driver's side window.

"You know who I am?" Raymond said.

The man nodded. He was short and broad, with a dark-brown pockmarked face and a thin Fu Manchu mustache. He looked to be in his midforties, in sharp contrast to the other, younger men. He spoke formally, like a man who had learned his English in school rather than on the street. "We were sorry to hear about your father," he said in his heavy accent.

Raymond looked the man up and down. His eyes flickered to the other men who were beginning to gather around the truck. Still others were coming out of the trailers.

John Lee cleared his throat. "Hey, Raymond," he said. "Maybe we better—"

"Shut up," Raymond replied. He turned back to the man by the truck window. "Y'all know anything about who mighta done it?"

"'Ey, bitch," one of the other men piped up from the crowd. He stepped forward. He was massively built, with ropes of muscles straining the sleeves and chest of his T-shirt. His arms were covered with elaborate gang tattoos. "We already talk about all this to th' cops," the tattooed man said. "Why we got to answer you?"

"I say anything to you, greaseball?" Raymond snapped. There was an angry murmuring from the crowd around the truck and the circle of men tightened. John Lee tried to slide down in the seat.

Raymond made a sudden movement and the long-barreled pistol was in his hand, pointed at the chest of the older man by the window. The man flinched slightly, then straightened and looked Raymond in the eye.

"There is no need for this," he said. He turned slightly, back toward the man who had spoken, and rattled off a long sentence in Spanish. His eyes never left Raymond's face. There was a high-pitched, angry reply. The man by the window responded sharply, then added something with a sly grin. There was a ripple of nervous laughter from the crowd. The tattooed man's face grew dark with anger, but he turned away and stomped off.

The older man turned back toward Raymond. "I was the one who found your father's body," he said. "The rest of the crew," he gestured at the men around the truck, "Was with me. We always go in together in my truck. No one here killed him, I am sure of it. We all leave work together the night before, and we all go in together the next day."

"Somebody knew he had a lot of cash on him," Raymond said.

"That was our pay," the mustached man said. "We were going to get that money the next day anyway. If one of us stole it, he would be stealing from the rest of us, and from our families back home. No one here would protect him for stealing that."

Raymond thought that over for a moment, then nodded. "Okay," he said. "So who else might've known about the money?"

The man thought for a moment. "There was a man who came looking for work," he said finally. "An Anglo." He smiled thinly at Raymond. "I didn't like him."

Raymond ignored the jibe. "You get a name?"

The man shook his head. "No. He talked with your father, not me. I told your father afterwards I didn't like his looks. He laughed and said he wasn't hiring anyway. He had a full crew. He took down the man's name and phone number, but that was just to get rid of him."

"Anyone else know him?"

There was a moment's hesitation. "He said he was a friend of Julio's," the mustached man said.

Raymond looked around. "Which one's Julio?"

There was another stirring in the crowd and the men looked at each other. "He's the one who just left," someone said. "The one you call greaseball."

"Go get him," Raymond said. No one moved. Raymond pulled back the hammer on the big revolver. Someone detached himself from the back of the crowd and hurried off.

In a few minutes, the tattooed man came stalking back, a can of beer in his right hand and a sneer on his face.

"This feller who came looking for a job," Raymond said. "You know him?"

Julio shrugged. "I don' know, man," he said. "I know a lot of people. How come you askin'?"

"Because I think that might be the man that shot my Daddy. And if he is, I mean to kill him for it."

Julio's face split in an ugly grin. "Well, shit, *vato,* whyn't you say so in the first place? Yeah, I knew him. I met him in the joint. Little guy. Name of Dwayne somethin'."

"You tell him Daddy carried a lot of cash?" Raymond's face bore no expression, but there was a dangerous note of tension in his voice.

The grin left Julio's face. He raised his hands in front of him, as if to push away the trouble he saw coming. "Whoa, man," he said. "This Dwayne fucker, man, he said he was needing some cash when he got out. I tol' him I don't know for sure, but

I was working for an old man who paid in cash an' I was going back when my ninety days was up. Thass all I said."

Raymond thought for a minute. He looked at the mustached man. "You," he said, "would you recognize this Dwayne guy if you saw him again?"

The man looked unhappy, but nodded slightly.

"All right then," Raymond said. "Get in the truck."

There was another rustle and murmur in the crowd. The mustached man didn't move.

With his free hand, Raymond reached into the pocket of his suit and pulled out a roll of bills. "You need work, now that Daddy's gone. I need somebody who can eyeball the sumbitch and tell me if he's the right one. You'll be gone a couple days, then you'll be right back here."

The man's eyes went back and forth from the roll of bills to the gun in Raymond's other hand that remained pointed at him. "Always it is the same," he murmured. *"Plomo o plata."*

"What?" Raymond said.

The man looked up at him. "Silver or lead," he translated. "Always the same choice."

Raymond nodded. "That sounds about right."

The man sighed. "The money first," he said.

Raymond thought for a second. "Half now, half when you show me."

The man hesitated, then shrugged his shoulders. "All right. But I need to leave it here."

Raymond smiled and tossed him the roll of bills. The man turned and motioned a slim young man with a ponytail out of the crowd. The two conferred for a moment in Spanish, then the moustached man handed the bills to the man with the ponytail, turned and walked to the passenger side of the truck without looking back. John Lee opened the door and slid to the middle of the seat as the man got in. Raymond started the truck and began backing out. The crowd of men watched him go.

They drove in silence for a few minutes before John Lee spoke up. "I'm John Lee," he told the man. "This here's my brother Raymond. You here from Mexico long?"

The mustached man smiled without humor. "Oscar Sanchez," he said. "And I am from Colombia."

"Well ain't that a coincidence." Raymond's smile was equally humorless. "Some of my best friends is from Colombia."

Sanchez sighed and leaned back in the seat. He closed his eyes and appeared to go to sleep.

"How much we get?" DeWayne said. He was standing by the window of the tiny motel room, occasionally using the barrel of his pistol to nudge the curtain aside enough to peer out into the parking lot. Except for their truck, the lot was empty.

"Damn it," Leonard replied, "Y'made me lose count." He glared at the piles of cash on the burn-scarred table. "And quit peekin' out the damn window every ten seconds."

DeWayne sighed. "Well, you was almost done," he said. "Where'd you lose count at?"

Leonard picked up the joint that lay smoldering in the ashtray and took a long drag. His dark, lined face screwed up in an exaggerated mask of concentration. "'Bout twenty-seven hundred," he said, his words coming out high-pitched and strangled-sounding as he held in the smoke. "Figger about three thousand for the whole shootin' match." He chuckled slightly at his own inadvertent pun and let the smoke out in a long stream.

DeWayne closed his eyes and leaned his head against the post of the window. "Three thousand," he repeated. "We killed that old man for three thousand bucks."

"Aww, man," Leonard said. "We didn't mean to do it. Ain't nothin' but a thing, cuz." He put the joint to his lips, took another long pull, held it. "Here," he croaked as he held the joint out.

"I don't . . . ," DeWayne began. Then he shrugged. "Fuck it," he said. He sat down in one of the mismatched chairs. "We gotta figger out what we're gonna do now," he said. He took a drag on the joint and coughed.

"Well," Leonard said thoughtfully. "I could use a beer. And maybe some pussy."

"God damn it, Leonard—" DeWayne began.

"Easy, cuz," Leonard said. He gave his cousin a lopsided grin and took the joint from him. "Look, we've had a coupla hard days, right? We're both stressin'. We got the money, sure it's not as much as we thought it was gonna be, but it's more than we had. So let's enjoy it, man. Life's too damn short."

"Don't it bother you we just killed somebody, Leonard?" DeWayne said.

The joint was almost gone. Leonard put the roach out in the cracked ashtray. "Sure it bothers me," he said. "But that old fucker brought in on hisself. He'd a done what we told him, he wouldn't be dead. Ain't nothin' gonna change what we did. All you can change is how you look at it."

DeWayne digested this for a moment as Leonard stood up. Leonard put his hands at the small of his back and arched, wincing slightly at the snapping and popping sounds. "Gettin' too old for this shit," he grunted. He scooped a handful of bills off the counter and went to the door. "There's a Short Stop across the street," he said. "I'm gonna go get us some beers. Then we're gonna get in the truck, drive on up to Fayetteville, and get you laid." The lop-sided grin was back. "You're gonna be amazed at how it changes the way you look at things." He walked out.

DeWayne sat for a minute, the thoughts coming slowly to him. He wasn't used to reefer, and the thoughts seem to struggle upwards in his brain.

Fayetteville, he thought. *Who do I know in Fayetteville?* Then it came to him. *Crystal,* he thought.

After a few minutes, Leonard came back in, carrying a paper bag under one arm. He had a Budweiser Tall Boy in the other hand.

"Leonard," DeWayne said. "Crystal still living in Fayetteville?"

"Yeah," Leonard said. "Shakin' her ass in some titty bar on Bragg Boulevard, last time I heard." He took a long pull on the beer. "Momma and Daddy don't even mention her name anymore."

"She might let us hide out at her place for a while. I been there once."

Leonard pulled a beer out of the bag, popped the top, and handed it to his cousin. "Not a bad idea," he said after a moment. "Bet she'd introduce us to some of her friends, too." He grinned like a satyr. "Shit, we play our cards right, we might not even have to pay for pussy. Now you're thinkin' right, old son."

2

Keller walked out into the motel parking lot, blinking against the bright light of day. The previous night's thunderstorms had blown away, leaving the world exposed to the hard glare of the sun. The heavy, waterlogged air soaked up the heat until walking across the parking lot was like swimming through soup.

As he approached his car, he saw a white police cruiser parked crossways behind him. There was a big cop leaning against the car, his arms crossed over his chest. His sleeves were rolled up to accentuate his massive forearms. His partner was standing beside Keller's Crown Victoria, peering through the window with one hand shading her eyes. She was a tall woman, with the lean build of an athlete.

Both cops' eyes were hidden behind the inevitable mirrored sunglasses. The female cop turned as Keller approached.

"This your car, sir?" she said. There were a few wisps of light brown hair coming untucked from beneath her blue cap, but that was the only hint of softness about her. Her lips were compressed into a thin line when she wasn't speaking. When she spoke, her voice was the officious bark of a drill sergeant. She made sure that the word "sir" contained not a speck of actual respect or courtesy.

Keller took a deep breath. "Yes, ma'am," he said. "Is there some kind of—"

"Mind telling us why there's a shotgun in the front seat?"

He kept his voice mild, inwardly cursing himself for choosing not to bring the shotgun in with him. The desk clerk at the last place he had stayed had seen him carrying his gun into the room and had spent most of the evening coming by and calling on various flimsy pretexts to make sure Keller had not killed himself with it. "It's not against the law to have a shotgun, is it?" he asked.

The big cop straightened up. His lips stretched over his teeth in a rough approximation of a smile. "Smart-ass, huh?"

The female cop looked annoyed at the interruption. "Mind if we look in the car, sir?"

Keller did mind, but there was no way to win the

argument without a lengthy discussion, part of which would probably take place at the police station. It was a discussion he was sure he would win, eventually. Still, that would take time, possibly a lot of time. Keller wanted to get back to work. He took the path of least resistance.

"Sure," he said. He was still smiling. He took his keys out and opened the doors.

The search was quick and sloppy. Keller noticed that the male cop seemed to take particular pleasure in leaving the contents of the glove compartment scattered over the front seat so Keller would have to put them back himself.

"Why do you have these metal rings welded to the floor of the back seat, sir?" the female cop asked.

Keller's smile was beginning to pain him. "I work bail enforcement," he said. "Sometimes they don't want to stay in the car. The rings are for the handcuffs."

"What about the police scanner?" she said.

"Like I said," Keller replied, "I work as—"

"A bounty hunter," the male cop said. He pronounced it like a curse.

"Whatever," Keller said. There was no overt insolence in his voice, but the lack of deference seemed to anger the male cop. He got out of the front seat of Keller's car and stood up.

"You got a—" he began. The female cop interrupted him. "Can you open the trunk, sir?" she said.

Keller's shoulders tensed, then he shrugged. He popped the trunk. The male cop walked around to the back and whistled in amazement.

"Marie," he said. "Come look at this." The female cop walked around to the back of the car. "Holy shit," she said. She reached in and pulled out a length of heavy chain. Heavy leg cuffs were soldered to each end. She held it up and looked over at Keller.

"It's all legal," Keller said.

"We'll decide that," the male cop said.

Keller's temper had reached the limit. "Bullshit," he said. "There's not a damn thing you can make stick here. I've got permits for the handguns. The handcuffs and restraints are all legit. All my licenses are up to date. So if you're going to arrest me, do it. But stop jerking me around."

"All right, smart-ass," the male cop said. "Hands on the car and spread your legs." Keller shook his head in frustration, but complied. The male cop frisked him quickly while the other one, Marie, stood back to give herself a clear field of fire if Keller decided to try anything. Keller felt the male cop's hand at the small of his back, heard him chuckle as he withdrew the 9mm from Keller's waistband.

"Looks like carrying a concealed weapon to me."

"I told you, I've got a carry permit—" he was cut

short by an explosion of pain across his lower back. The cop had pulled his nightstick in a cross-body draw that would have done credit to a samurai. He whipped the nightstick in a short arc and smashed Keller across the kidneys. Keller arched his back in agony and dropped to his knees.

"And resisting arrest," the cop said. Keller heard his high-pitched giggle. He tried to roll over on his back to stave off another blow, but he felt a sudden weight on him. The female cop had thrown her body across his. One of her hands grabbed one of Keller's wrists. He heard the clink of metal as she took the cuffs off her belt. "Stay down," she muttered. "You can't win. Just stay down." Keller tried to stand, then suddenly realized that she had placed herself between him and another blow. He relaxed and allowed himself to be handcuffed with his hands behind his back. When she was done, she rolled off and yanked Keller awkwardly to his feet. Her grip was very strong.

Keller looked at the male cop. The man's image seemed to swim in a red haze before Keller's eyes. The cop's own eyes were dreamy and far away and there was a slight smile on his face.

"When this is over," Keller said through pain-clenched teeth, "I'm going to take that fucking baton away and shove it up your ass."

The cop's smile widened. This was what he had

been waiting for. He drew back his hand for another shot. Keller had no way to protect his head; he knew the next blow would shatter his skull. The female cop interposed her body between them again. "Get in the car, asshole," she said. She put a hand on Keller's head to guide him through the open door of the police cruiser. Without taking his eyes off the male cop, Keller slid into the back seat.

The brown truck pulled into the parking lot of the timber company office. The trailer was still surrounded by a web of yellow crime-scene tape that appeared to have been strung mostly at random. The three men got out of the truck and approached the steps. Raymond took a curved Hawkbill knife out of his pants pocket, opened it, and sliced through the tape. They walked up the steps and stood before the locked trailer door. There was a moment of silence. "John Lee," Raymond said. "You got the keys?"

"Oh, um, yeah," John Lee said, embarrassed. He fumbled for a moment in his pocket, then unlocked the door.

The interior of the trailer office was small and cramped. A metal desk sat facing the doorway and took up most of one side of the room. There was a gray metal filing cabinet behind the desk on their right. Raymond went around the desk and tried to open the cabinet. It was locked. He rattled the handle in frustration. "You got a key to this, John Lee?" he said.

John Lee shrugged. "Sorry, Raymond," he said. "Daddy always kept that one hisself."

Raymond slammed his hand against the cabinet in frustration. He turned to Sanchez. "He ever tell you where he kept the key to this?"

Sanchez shook his head. "No," he said.

Raymond turned back. He hit the cabinet again, as if he could convince it to open by beating it enough times. He withdrew the pistol from his belt and drew back the hammer. He carefully pointed it at the latch on the filing cabinet.

"Wait," Sanchez said. He reached into his pocket and withdrew a small plexiglass key ring. He laid it carefully on the table. There were two keys on the ring, one smaller than the other.

Raymond looked at Sanchez, his eyes narrowed. "You trying to be funny?"

Sanchez looked back without expression. "You didn't ask if I had a key. You asked if your father had ever told me where his key was."

"God damn it," Raymond snarled. "You knew what I meant."

"Me?" Sanchez spread his hands. "How was I to know?"

Raymond made a strangled sound deep in his throat and pointed the pistol at Sanchez. Sanchez didn't move.

"I was your father's foreman," he said. "He trusted me with a lot of things. If you kill me, there are many things you will never know."

Raymond slammed the pistol down on the desk. John Lee flinched. "Then tell me, asshole!" Raymond yelled. "Quit playin' games! I need me some goddamn help here!"

Sanchez' face clouded with anger. "You have never asked. You have never asked me for anything, least of all help. All you have done is wave your *pistola* around and shout orders." He looked at John Lee. "The two of you are out to avenge your father. All right. It is a matter of honor. A man understands such things. A man might be willing to help. A stupid 'greaseball' who must be ordered around—" he shrugged. "Such a one will only do what he is told, no more."

Raymond stared at him for a long moment. "I ain't gonna beg you," he said finally.

Sanchez shook his head. "That is not what I ask." They continued to stare at one another, neither one willing to be the first to look down. It was John Lee who finally spoke.

"Mr. Sanchez," he said, "will you help us find the man that killed our Daddy?"

Sanchez smiled. "*Si,* I will help you," he said.

"And call me Oscar." He pointed at the desk. "When the man Julio talked about came around, he left a phone number where he could be reached. I saw your father write it on the pad on the desk."

Raymond looked down at the desk blotter. It was covered with ink stains, coffee rings, doodles, and hastily scrawled notes.

Finally he located something. "DeWayne Puryear," he read. "That sound familiar?"

Sanchez nodded. "That is the name that he gave."

"There's an address and phone number here," Raymond said.

Sanchez turned around and walked out the door. He was already waiting in the truck when Raymond and John Lee followed him.

Like most of the people who wore the black robe, Judge Harold T. Tharrington was a former prosecutor. The District Attorney had handpicked Tharrington to run for election to the bench. He had run without opposition; none of the other prosecutors would dare to buck the bosses' choice. For their own part, the lawyers of the defense bar declined to take the salary cut that came with going on the state payroll. Defendants paid better, and often in cash.

Tharrington looked over his glasses at Keller, who was standing before him. He was a short, balding man with a round face and a fussy demeanor. He clearly found Keller's presence in his courtroom distasteful.

Keller had spent the previous day and night sharing a jail cell with a pair of Jamaicans. The two men had totally ignored him. They spent the time playing a seemingly endless game of cards and arguing in low, incomprehensible voices. The argument and the fact that the lights had never been turned off in the cells had made it impossible for Keller to sleep. His eyeballs felt raw and gritty. He hadn't been allowed to shave. His hands were shackled in front of him and his ankles were fastened together with a short length of heavy chain. His lawyer stood by his side.

The lawyer's name was Scott McCaskill. He was an imposing figure, a full six and a half feet tall. He had thick snow-white hair brushed back until it resembled a lion's mane. His face tended to remind people of someone they'd seen on TV, someone playing a senator or president. He had represented Keller several times before. Part of the secret to his success was his massive presence that seemed to draw all attention in the room to him and away from his raggedy-assed client.

"Your Honor," McCaskill intoned in a voice so deep that it almost rattled the water glasses, "my client has no prior record. He is a bail bondsman licensed by the State of North Carolina. He served his country with distinction in the armed forces and was decorated for bravery in the Persian Gulf. In addition, we are confident that these charges are the result of a misunderstanding and will be resolved in his favor at trial."

The judge picked up a sheet of computer printout and studied it. "Your client," the judge observed, "has been remarkably lucky to have no record of convictions. The PIN check provided by Officers Jones and Wesson shows a remarkable string of charges that were either dismissed by the local prosecutor or resulted in 'not guilty' verdicts at trial. Can you explain this?"

McCaskill shrugged and smiled. "The nature of Mr. Keller's business is such that the people he returns to custody are often, shall we say, less than happy with their situation."

"Two of them apparently ended up dead," the judge said.

"For which incident a jury returned a verdict of not guilty by reason of self-defense," his lawyer replied smoothly.

Tharrington put the printout down and looked at Keller again. Keller was beginning to feel like a piece of livestock being haggled over at the market, but he kept his face neutral.

"I'm concerned here, counselor," he said, "that your client is a violent man. He was apprehended with a shotgun in his car. He was carrying a weapon concealed on his person—"

"For which—" McCaskill began, but fell silent

when Tharrington raised a hand. "I realize he claims to have a carry permit for that weapon. He has not been able to produce it."

"That's because Officer Wesson took it. Sir," Keller said.

"Which brings us to my greatest concern," Tharrington said. "The contempt and disrespect shown to law enforcement. It's bad enough that Mr. Keller apparently fancies himself some sort of bounty hunter, despite having no official standing as a sworn law enforcement officer. But for him to assault a real officer and threaten him with further violence—"

"Sir," Keller said. "Officer Wesson assaulted *me*." He ignored the lawyer's hand on his shoulder urging him to keep quiet. "He struck me with his baton while I had my hands on the car. Officer Jones can confirm that."

Tharrington looked behind Keller. "Officer Wesson," he said. "Is Officer Jones present in the courtroom with you?"

Keller didn't trust himself to turn around and look, but he could hear the smooth confidence in Wesson's voice. "No sir," he said. "She had, ah, other duties to attend to. And your honor, I was forced to use my baton to subdue Mr. Keller when he attempted to reach for the firearm I was taking from him."

"And is it not true, Mr. Keller, that you threatened

to take Officer Wesson's baton away from him and beat him with it?"

"No sir," Keller said through clenched teeth. "I told him I was going to take it away from him and shove it up his ass."

Tharrington reddened. He picked up his gavel. "Bail is set at fifteen thousand dollars. Cash." He nodded to the deputy Sheriff standing at one end of the bench. "Take him back to the holding cell."

"Your Honor," a soft female voice said. "I'll be supplying Mr. Keller's bail. But may I request that the court change it to a secured bond rather than cash?"

Keller looked around for the first time. She was standing at the back of the courtroom, dressed in a floor length black trenchcoat that contrasted starkly with her white-blonde hair. Her jeans were black as well and she wore a white blouse buttoned up to the neck, despite the outside heat. Her hands were covered with black gloves. One hand rested on the silver handle of a dark cherrywood cane.

"And you are . . . ?" the judge asked.

She walked down the center aisle of the courtroom with a pronounced limp, leaning on the cane for support. "Angela Hager, your honor," she said. "H & H Bail Bonds. I'm Mister Keller's employer."

The judge tapped his chin with his pencil. "Hager, Hager . . . ," he said thoughtfully. "You look familiar . . ."

She arrived at the bar and looked up at the judge. She brushed her hair from her eyes with her free hand. "My husband was Jeffery Hager."

The judge dropped his pencil. "Yes, of course," he said. "I—I remember the case. You—ah—you seem to be doing well."

"Thank you," she said. "Now, about the bond. I can supply a cash bond, but it's less paperwork if I don't have to transfer that much cash. The IRS, you know." She smiled slightly. "I assume H & H's credit is still good with this court?"

The judge didn't answer at first. He was staring in fascination at the narrow band of puckered scar tissue that peeked above the high collar of the blouse. She waited patiently, still smiling. Finally the judge realized that he was staring and his gaze broke away as he began randomly shuffling papers on the bench.

"Yes, yes," he said. "Certainly. Fifteen thousand," he said to the clerk. "Secured by H & H."

"Thank you, your honor," Angela said. She approached the low desk to the side of the bench where the court clerk was organizing the forms she would have to sign. She didn't look at Keller until she finished signing. Then she stood up and smiled at him. "I've got to get back," she said. "There's no one in the office. I had to lock up to come down here and get you. Will you be okay?"

"Yeah," Keller said. "I'll pick up my car from impound. I've got some more leads to run down. I'll keep in touch."

She patted his shoulder. "Back to work, cowboy," she said, then walked out.

The judge picked up his gavel, prepared to adjourn court. "Your honor," Keller's lawyer spoke up. "There is still the matter of Mr. Keller's vehicle and, ah, its contents, which were impounded."

The judge seemed to have recovered his composure. "He can have the vehicle back," he said. "Not the weapons or the restraints."

The lawyer tried again. "Those are the tools Mister Keller needs to conduct his business, if your honor—"

"Well, that's the problem, isn't it?" the judge snapped. He stood up. "Adjourn court, Mr. Bailiff," he ordered.

"This court stands adjourned," the bailiff called out. "God save the State and this honorable court."

"Mister Keller," a voice said.

Keller turned. Officer Marie Jones was sitting in a red Honda Accord in a parking space in front of the courthouse. The driver's side window was down. Her uniform blouse had been replaced by a white T-shirt with a Gold's Gym logo on it. Her police cap was gone but her light brown hair was still pinned up. She still wore the mirrored shades.

"You need a ride?" she said.

Keller approached the vehicle. "My car's in the impound lot," he said.

"I know," she said. She leaned over and opened the passenger side door. "Get in. I'll take you over there." Keller got in. She pulled away from the curb without speaking. She was dressed in a pair of black workout shorts and tennis shoes. Keller looked her over. Her body was lean and muscular, the body of a swimmer or long-distance runner.

After a few moments, she spoke up. "I'm sorry about Eddie," she said. "Officer Wesson, I mean."

"That would have meant a lot more if you'd been there to tell what really happened."

She sighed. "No one told me about it. I went off duty and went to the gym."

"Would you have told the truth if you'd been there?"

"Of course I would have," she snapped. Keller looked at her for a long moment. She thought for a moment, then shook her head. "I don't know. I mean, yeah, I guess." She sighed. "Fuck, I don't know." She sounded weary.

"What is he, your boyfriend?"

Jones yanked the wheel suddenly, steering the car over to the side of the street and slamming on the brakes. She turned to Keller. "Get out," she said. Her voice was absolutely flat.

"Whoa, whoa." Keller said. "I'm sorry, I—"

"I am so *sick* of that bullshit!" She slammed her open palm on the steering wheel. "From Eddie's wife. From my ex. From every asshole in the station. The ones that don't assume I'm fucking Eddie assume I'm some sort of dyke because I'm *not* fucking him. Well, fuck them, and fuck you too." She grabbed the wheel with both hands. She rested her head on the steering wheel for a moment, getting herself under control. Her knuckles were white.

"You're right," Keller said softly. "I was out of line. It was a stupid thing to say. I'm sorry."

She took a deep breath and straightened up. She looked straight ahead for a moment, took another breath, blew it out. She turned to Keller.

"I sit for the Sergeant's exam next month," she said. "I've got a kid that my ex keeps threatening to take away every time I make a fuss about the back child support. You think I need that kind of problem?"

"Not meaning to add to your load, but you've got another problem. Wesson's a psycho," Keller said. "He's apt to turn on you."

Jones shook her head. She pulled the car back into traffic. "He's really an okay guy," she said.

"He's just been having some problems at home. He's wound a little too tight these days, I guess."

"Officer Jones," Keller said. "Your partner's more than wound too tight. I've seen that look in people's eyes before. He's getting ready to cut loose. And when he does, he's going to kill somebody. And maybe get himself killed as well. Or you."

She shook her head again. "He's my partner," she said. "I'm supposed to look after him."

"You're supposed to look after each other," Keller said. She didn't answer. Keller could see he was getting nowhere, so he changed the subject. "How'd you find out about the hearing?" he asked.

"Your boss got me on my cell phone," Jones said. "I tried to get here, but I ran into her in the parking lot and she told me it was all over, that you'd been turned loose." She looked at Keller. "Do you mind if I say something?"

Keller shrugged. "Depends on what it is, I guess."

Marie laughed. "Fair enough. It's just that your boss—Angela, is it?"

"Yeah, Angela Hager."

"She's pretty, but she's kind of spooky-looking. What's the deal with the gloves?"

Keller leaned back in the seat and looked out the window. "She's got some pretty bad scars. Burns. She doesn't like people staring at them."

"How'd she get burned?"

Keller looked at her. "Her husband founded H &

H bail bonds. He was a big shot, knew everybody, liked to throw his money around. He also used to beat her up. Finally, she had enough and took out a warrant on him. He went into court and denied everything. He had been a major supporter of the DA in the last election, so they dismissed all charges without even a trial." Keller looked out the front window. "Jeff Hager went home, kicked in the front door, and broke both her legs with a baseball bat so she couldn't run. Then he set the house on fire."

"Damn," Jones whispered. "He do any time for it?"

"No," Keller said. "But only because he shot himself in front of her."

"How'd she get out?"

"Dragged herself out of the house on her elbows."

Jones gave a low whistle. "That is one tough lady."

"Yeah," Keller said. They were pulling up to the chain-link fence that surrounded the impound lot. As Keller moved to get out, Jones took off her sunglasses and turned to him.

"Mister Keller," she said. "When this comes to court, I'll tell what happened. All of it."

"That's not going to help your career much," Keller said.

"I know," she said.

Keller looked at her. She obviously meant it. Her jaw was set and she stared at him defiantly, as if daring him to question her resolve. He noticed that her eyes were blue, the sharp, hard blue of the sky on a clear winter day. Finally, he shrugged.

"It'll be a moot point anyway," he said. "The DA'll make a lot of noise about jail time, then when it gets close to trial, they'll offer to dismiss everything in exchange for me agreeing in writing not to sue the department for excessive force."

"And you'll agree." Her voice was flat.

He looked away. After the idealism she showed in her offer to testify, he hated what he was about to say. "It's not like I'm giving up much. With your help, I may win the resisting, but they're scared shitless of the publicity that they'd get from a civil suit. So they'll make damn sure I go down on something. Even if they have to make something up."

"Pretty cynical," she said.

He shrugged. "Yeah, it is," he said. "But I've seen it happen. If it happens to me, I lose my bondsman's license. I weigh that against the possibility of winning a civil suit against the Fayetteville police. Even if I take it to a jury, who do you think they'll believe?" He thought for a moment about the judge's description of him as a violent man. "I've got better things to do with my time than take on lost causes. Even my own." He closed the car door. He was walking toward the small guardhouse at the entrance to the impound lot when he heard her voice. "Mister Keller."

He turned. Her hand was out the window, holding a small piece of paper. He walked back and took it. It was a business card, the type cops gave to victims and witnesses who might need to contact them. The police switchboard number was scratched out and another number written in blue ink.

"That's my cell phone number," she said. "In case you change your mind. Or, you know, if you want to, like, talk about anything else."

He smiled at her. "That's not going to do a lot to help your career, either."

She didn't smile back. "Yeah. Well." She didn't go on. She'd replaced the mirror shades, so it was impossible to read what was in her eyes.

"Okay," Keller said. "I'll keep it in mind. And my name is Jack."

"I'm Marie," she said. She looked like she was about to say something else, but she stopped. She put the car in gear and backed out of the gravel driveway. Keller put the card in his shirt pocket as he watched her go.

3

"**What about the neighbors, what they** gonna say, hey little sister got carried awayyyy," DeWayne sang in a loud, slurred voice. He reached over to crank up the volume on the cassette deck.

DeWayne's buzz had been veering back and forth all day from catatonic stupor to manic lunacy. It was the fifth or sixth time that he had played the song, stopping it at the end to rewind and play it again so he could sing along and play air guitar on the solos. It had been getting on Leonard's nerves since the second run-through.

"Damn it, DeWayne," he said, "shut up for a second and pay attention." DeWayne lurched back in the truck seat with his eyes closed, playing air guitar along with Stevie Ray. His back arched orgasmically as he launched into the chorus. Part of the beer in his left hand spilled on his shoulder as he mimed the solo. "Hey, hey . . . ," he wailed. "Look at little sisterrr . . ."

"*DeWayne!*" Leonard bellowed. He reached over and turned the stereo off.

DeWayne's eyes snapped open. "'Eyyyy, man," he whined. "The fuck'd you do that for?"

"I got no idea where we are, man." Leonard said. "You been to Crystal's, I ain't. You gotta tell me where to go."

DeWayne straightened up and look around blearily. He squinted as if to bring the road into better focus. "I'm gettin' hungry," he said.

"One thing at a time, cuz," Leonard said. "We gotta—"

"Wait, turn here, man!" DeWayne yelled. "Turn right, turn right!"

They were almost past the turn. The tires screeched as Leonard instinctively obeyed. The truck rocked up slightly on two wheels.

"Whoo!" DeWayne shouted. He laughed and drained the last of his beer. "It's down here at the end."

In the daylight, it was apparent that the neighborhood was struggling against becoming decrepit. It was losing. Some of the houses were in good repair, others had sagging roofs and trim that was badly in need of fresh paint. There were small clumps of skinny, half-bare trees in some yards. In others, the owners had apparently given up on even mowing the weeds that grew around the stumps where the trees had once been.

A red Corvette was parked in the driveway in front of the house at the end of the street. It was the newest, brightest object visible. There were still a few flakes of the original white paint clinging to the picket fence in front of the house. The rest had weathered to gray.

Leonard picked up the bag with the money in it and got out. DeWayne followed. The two men got out of the truck and walked toward the white house, with DeWayne leaning on Leonard's shoulder for support. He was singing again: "Heyyyy, hey, look at little sisterrrr—" All of the shades were drawn. Had it not been for the car parked out front, the house would have appeared deserted.

Leonard pushed the doorbell button beside the door. There was no sound of a bell inside and no answer. He knocked. He knocked harder. No answer. Leonard began knocking steadily, monotonously, like a man pounding nails in Hell. Finally, a slurred female voice responded, "All *right,* God damn it, I'm coming." There was a creak of footsteps. DeWayne stuck his face up to the peephole in the door and grinned maniacally. "Oh, Jesus fucking Christ," the voice said. It sounded very weary. There was a rattle of a chain, the solid snick of a heavy deadbolt, then the snap of the door lock. The door opened a crack.

"The hell do you two want?" the girl said.

"C'mon, Sis, let us in," Leonard whispered. There was a heavy sigh and the door swung wide. The two men stepped inside. DeWayne wrapped his arms around the girl and lifted her up off the ground in a bear hug. "Put me down, asshole," she said, the words muffled against his shoulder. There was no anger in her voice, just a kind of weary amusement. DeWayne put her down and stepped back.

She was a tiny woman, a little over five feet. It was the breasts that men noticed first, an unfortunate fact that had shaped most of her adult life. They seemed overly large for her thin body and thrust against even the shapeless cloth robe she wore, demanding attention. Her hair, cut short and parted in the middle, was dyed a dark reddish-brown. The hair was rumpled, as if she had just gotten out of bed. Her facial features were small and regular, but just enough out of proportion to one another that she missed beautiful by a narrow margin and had to settle for cute. Her mouth was drawn in a perpetual affected pout that she thought was sexy, but served only to give the impression of a sulky child. The year since they had seen one another had not been kind to her. Leonard noticed her pallor, the bags under her eyes, the slight trembling as she took a cigarette out of the pack on the hall table and lit it.

"We need a place to stay for a couple days, Sis," Leonard said. "Can we come in and talk about it?"

"You are in," she said, then sighed. "Okay, c'mon. I think there's some beers in the fridge." She turned and walked back into the house. DeWayne and Leonard followed. A short hallway led toward the living room. A door to the right about halfway down the hallway opened into the kitchen. Leonard dropped the bag on the floor across from the kitchen door.

"Look like you're sleepin' late, Crys," DeWayne said. "Livin' a life o' leisure, huh?"

"Fuck you, DeWayne," she said. She sat at the kitchen table, which was piled with newspapers. She gestured at the fridge. "Help yourselves."

There was no beer in the refrigerator, and no food other than a jar of mustard and a can of cat food with a plastic lid. Finally, DeWayne located a half-empty bottle of Popov Vodka in the freezer. He made a happy noise and sat down at the table across from Crystal. He took a drink straight from the bottle.

She looked from one to the other with a mixture of resentment and resignation. "Well?" she said. "What's all this about?"

Leonard explained the situation to her. Her expression never changed. He finished by saying, "So we just need to lay up here for a couple days, till we can figger out where to go. Okay, Sis?"

She blew out a long streamer of smoke. "Yeah,

okay," she said finally. "But y'all gotta be careful. This is a quiet neighborhood. People work nights, sleep days. You start raisin' hell," she looked at De-Wayne, "and you're gonna have the cops all over this place."

DeWayne gave her a lopsided grin and took another pull from the bottle. "No problemo, sweet thing," he said.

There was a muffled beeping noise from the handbag hung over one of the kitchen chairs. "Shit," Crystal said. "What time is it?"

Leonard looked at the clock over the stove. It was stopped. "Ahhh, about five-thirty," he guessed.

Crystal swore under her breath. She pulled a small black beeper out of the purse and looked at the screen. She shook her head. She picked an old-style rotary phone up off the floor next to the table and dialed.

"Yeah, it's me," she said. She listened for a moment. "I can't tonight," she said. "I got company." There was a burst of angry speech on the other end. "No, no, it's not—I'm not—" she was having trouble getting a word out. Finally, the voice on the other end said something that caused her eyes to widen. "Okay," she said. "Okay, I'll be there as soon as I can. I just got up. I will. I will, I promise." She hung up the phone and looked off into the distance for a moment, chewing her lower lip. "I gotta go," she said, and stood up. "I gotta go to work."

Leonard and DeWayne looked at each other. "Hey, Crys," DeWayne said finally, "if your boss is givin' you any trouble, we can, you know . . ."

"No, no," she said. "It'll be alright. It's okay. They're just—shorthanded."

"At a *titty* bar?" DeWayne said.

Her eyes narrowed and snapped around to bear on DeWayne. "You mind your own damn business, DeWayne, you hear?"

Both of the men put up their hands. "Easy, Crys, take it easy," Leonard said. He used the soothing tone of voice he had developed through years of intercession between his sister and their cousin. Crystal got up and walked out of the kitchen.

"The fuck's eating her?" DeWayne wondered. Leonard shrugged. "Whatever," he said. "We need to get us some food. And we're outta beer." He stood up, put his hands in the middle of his back and stretched. "Gettin' too old for this shit," he muttered. He walked into the living room, with DeWayne following.

The old farmhouse was in the middle of what John Lee referred to as "Bum-fuck Egypt." It fronted on a narrow two-lane road and was surrounded on the other three sides by tobacco fields. An enormous oak tree dominated the front yard. A row of crepe myrtle obscured the lower half of the screened-in porch that ran along the front of the house. The crepe myrtle was beginning to bloom, with long strings of flowers, some bright red, some pink, bowing down the branches with their weight. The thick greenery had been allowed to grow long, so that the screen door in the center seemed to peek out from a flowered jungle.

As the truck pulled into the driveway, an old man came to the door. He was of medium height, with white hair that stuck out in unruly tufts from beneath an ancient gimme cap from a long-defunct seed company. The cap was as lined and creased as the hand that rested on the jamb of the screen door, holding it half open as the man waited. In contrast, the old man's bib overalls seemed brand new, with a knife-edged crease in the pants.

"Stay here," Raymond muttered. John Lee nodded once. Sanchez looked worried.

Raymond got out of the truck and walked toward the old man, smiling like a door-to-door salesman. "Hep you?" the old man said as he approached. His voice was neutral, but his eyes flickered warily between Raymond and the two men in the truck. A Latino traveling with a pair of Indians was an unusual sight outside of the realm of manual labor. People tended to stick with their own kind. Raymond was too well-dressed for picking cotton or priming tobacco.

"Nice farm," Raymond said, still smiling.

"Ain't mine no more," the old man said. "Got too old to work it. Had to sell ever'thing but the home place."

Raymond nodded. "That's too bad." The old man said nothing. "DeWayne around?" Raymond asked.

The old man's face seemed to close up, as if steel shutters had suddenly dropped down across it. "He ain't here. He an' Leonard done took off somewheres. Ain't seen him in a couple weeks."

Raymond had arrived at the door. He slowed down rather than stopping, crowding the old man until he stepped back out of the doorway. Raymond replaced the old man's hand on the door with his own. The old man looked at the rings on Raymond's fingers and back to his eyes, which were obscured behind his tinted glasses. The old man swallowed nervously. "He ain't here," he repeated in a smaller voice. Raymond continued to shuffle forward, forcing the old man to retreat farther into the cool darkness of the screened porch. "We kinda need to talk to him," Raymond said. "It's about a job he applied for." He put a hand on the old man's shoulder and turned him slightly, guiding him into the house. John Lee and Sanchez saw the door close behind them.

"What is he doing?" Sanchez asked.

John Lee shrugged. "Gonna ask him where this Puryear guy might've gone, I reckon."

Sanchez shook his head. "I don't like this," he said. "What will he—"

"Don't worry," John Lee said. "Nobody's gonna do anything. Just relax."

Sanchez looked at the house. His brow furrowed. "Your brother is a dangerous man," he said. "He is a *narcotraficante,* a smuggler, no?"

John Lee's eyes went cold. "Where'd you hear that?"

"Your father, he worried about this," Sanchez replied. "Sometimes I heard him talking on the phone about how worried he was."

"And what the hell business was that of yours?" John Lee said.

"I have sons," Sanchez said. "In Colombia. I know what it is to worry. I felt bad for him."

"Well, he don't worry no more," John Lee said. "And you don't worry neither. You just mind your business."

"If I was minding my business," Sanchez pointed out, "I would not be here." John Lee had no answer for that.

They sat in silence for a long while. Sanchez watched the front door. It was late afternoon and the shadows were beginning to deepen beneath the trees.

There was a sound from inside the house, a wordless cry of pain. Then a sharp bang.

Sanchez jumped, sitting up straight in the seat. He looked around frantically. *"Que? Que pasa?"* he said. "What is happening?"

"Nothing," John Lee said, but his own agitation robbed the words of all calming effect. He drew his pistol from beneath the seat. He slid over to the driver's side door and started to open it. There was another cry, then a sound like someone crying. John Lee stopped, half in and half out of the open door of the truck. A louder wail came from the house, an unmistakable sound of pure agony and despair.

"Do something!" Sanchez cried. He reached for the door handle. John Lee swung the pistol to bear on Sanchez. "You stay there!" he said. His voice shook, but Sanchez heeded the message of the gun rather than the sick look on John Lee's face. The two men stared at each other, each straining their ears, wanting to hear what was happening and desperately afraid of what the next sound would bring. The silence roared in their ears for what seemed like hours. Another flat bang, then the faint sound of a voice. It was pitched high and fast, with a note of desperation. Then there were two more bangs and the silence closed down again.

After a few minutes, Raymond came out of the house. He was folding a torn piece of paper. He put the paper in his jacket pocket. John Lee and Sanchez noticed the pistol was stuck in his waistband.

John Lee slid back over to the middle of the seat as Raymond got in. Sanchez was staring at him, eyes wide.

"What happened?" John Lee asked.

"Nothin'," Raymond said. He drew the gun out of his waistband, laid it on the seat between himself and John Lee. "Found out he has a sister in Fayetteville. We'll try there." He patted his jacket over the pocket. "I got her address."

"How did you get the address?" Sanchez demanded. "What did you do?"

Raymond smiled. "I asked. Nicely. But I had to ask a few times." He started the truck.

Sanchez shook his head. "No. This is not right. This is not what I agreed." His accent had become thicker with agitation.

Raymond put the truck back in park and looked at Sanchez. His face was expressionless. "You want out, you can get out here."

Sanchez looked at the pistol on the seat. He swallowed hard. After a few moments, he looked into Raymond's eyes. He saw there what would happen to him if he got out of the truck. He shook his head again. "No. I stay."

Raymond smiled again. "That's what I thought," he said. He started the truck and drove off.

DeWayne leaned over the mirror with the intense focus of the truly wasted. He stuck the rolled up twenty into his left nostril and slowly hoovered up the first of the thick white lines laid out on the mirror. Then he switched nostrils and did the other one. He straightened up, threw his head back, and howled like a dog.

"God Damn it, DeWayne," Crystal's voice came from the next room. "I told you to keep quiet."

"I feel good, da-da-da-da-da-da-da," DeWayne sang. "I knew that I would, y'all—"

"Hey, James Brown," Leonard said. "Shove that mirror over here." DeWayne obliged him, placing the small bag of cocaine on the mirror. "Man," he observed. "This is some good shit."

Crystal came out of the bedroom, dressed in a plum-colored low-cut dress. Her mouth dropped open in shock at the sight of DeWayne and Leonard demolishing her stash. Her face turned red with anger. "What the hell do you two think—"

"Easy, Crys," Leonard said. He pulled the fat roll of bills out of his shirt pocket and waved it at her. "We gotcha covered," he grinned.

She looked at the cash, suspicion and avarice warring for possession of her face. "How much of that do you still have left?" she demanded.

"Less you know, little sister," DeWayne said, "the—ahhhh—less you know." He giggled.

"More'n that in this here bag, darlin'," Leonard promised, holding up the money bag. "Think you could get us some more o' this good toot?"

"Yeah," Crystal said, her eyes still fixed on the bag. She tore her eyes away and smiled at him. "I gotta run a couple of other errands first though."

"Ain't you gonna be late for work?" DeWayne said. "You been in there an hour."

She laughed. It was a bitter, humorless sound. "They'll wait," she said. "They always do." She held out her hand and Leonard counted off several bills into it with the flourish of a king rewarding a favorite courtier. "We need some more beer, too," he said.

Crystal nodded. "I'll be a couple hours," she said. She picked up her purse and walked to the door. "For Chrissakes, try to stay quiet." As she walked out, she pulled a cell phone out of her purse. Leonard went to the window to watch her go. He saw her talking on the phone as she walked to the car.

"We oughta eat somethin'," DeWayne suggested. "How 'bout we order a pizza?"

Leonard thought it over. It seemed reasonably safe. "Yeah, all right," he said. He picked up the phone.

"And see if they'll bring us some more beer," DeWayne suggested. "I don't feel like waitin' two hours for Crystal to get back. I got a thirst."

Leonard sighed. "They don't do that, DeWayne," he said. "You can't get no one to deliver beer."

"Shee-it, cuz," DeWayne replied. "One thing I know, people'll do damn near anything if the money's right."

Leonard picked up the phone.

Keller pulled over and parked halfway down the block on the dead end street. He noticed a rusted pickup truck parked in front of the white house. The truck had not been there when he had checked the house out before. He didn't recognize the truck or the license plate as any of the ones that Angela had supplied him with as being registered to DeWayne Puryear. The truck could have belonged to any resident of the street. Still, Keller felt his heart quicken. There was no logic to it, he knew, but some instinct made the hair stand up on the back of his neck. He took a second to savor the anticipation. The takedown was just moments away. The adrenaline began to course through him, singing in his bloodstream. It was the reason he did the job. He reached for the cell phone. As he picked it up, it buzzed softly. He silently thanked the reflex that had caused him to turn the ringer off and set the phone to "vibrate." The sudden quivering sensation, however, made the phone feel like some small and frightened animal in his hands.

"Keller," he said softly into the phone.

"Where the hell have you been?" Angela's voice demanded. Her voice sounded strained. There was none of the usual banter.

"Sorry," he said, still almost whispering. "Turned the ringer off. And I had to run a few errands." He looked at the truck. "I need you to run a plate for me."

"In a minute," Angela said. "You need to hear this. DeWayne Puryear's parents have been killed."

Keller tensed. "When?"

"A few hours ago. Both of them, shot in the back of the head. Execution style. It was on the radio."

"They think he did it?"

"No." her voice was shaky. "I know a couple of people on the sheriff's department down there, so I made some calls. I got a couple of details that weren't on the news." He heard her take a deep breath. "They think the father had been tortured. The fingers on his left hand were broken, like somebody bent them back till they snapped."

Keller winced. "Any idea why?"

"There was some money stashed in a coffee can under the sink, so that's not what they were looking for."

Keller thought for a moment. "DeWayne? They think someone else is looking for him?"

"They know he's on the run. And they know H & H

made his bond." She took a deep breath. "The person I talked to was real interested in where *you* were."

"Wait a minute," Keller said. "They think *I* had something to do with this?"

"They said they just wanted to talk to you. See if you knew anything."

"I hope you told them that I wasn't going to commit murder over a ten percent recovery fee for a fifty-thousand-dollar bond."

"They never outright accused you. There was nothing for me to deny. Like I said, they claimed they only wanted to talk to you."

"Damn it," Keller said. "This I don't need." He drummed his fingers on the steering wheel. "You tell them where I was?"

Her voice was hurt. "Of course not." She paused. "Keller, something's screwy here. There's somebody else out there who wants to find DeWayne Puryear. Somebody willing to torture a seventy-year-old man to find out where he is and then kill him. I want you off this job. Call the local cops and let them handle it. It's not worth it."

He looked back at the pickup truck. "It is to me."

"You just said you weren't going to kill someone over five grand. Now you're telling me you want to die for it?"

"I took the job. I want to finish it."

"What are you, the Mounties all of a sudden? You always get your man?"

"Yeah," Keller said. "That must be it."

"Damn it, Keller," she said. "Call the cops and let them handle it."

"I'm not exactly fond of the local constabulary right now. Besides, if the cops bring him in, you still going to pay me for it?"

There was a brief pause. "Would you take it if I did?"

"No."

Angela made an exasperated sound that sounded almost like a growl. "Jesus," she said. "It's not the money. You've just got the worst case of testosterone poisoning in human history. You ought to have your head examined, Keller, you know that?"

"I tried that," he said. "It didn't work. You going to run that plate for me?"

He heard her sigh, heard the click of computer keys. "Go ahead."

He gave her the license number. He heard the keys clicking again, then silence as she waited. He wished she would say something. She didn't. Finally, she spoke.

"Vehicle is a 1987 Ford pickup registered to one Leonard Puryear," she said. Her voice was flat.

"DeWayne's cousin," Keller said.

"Yeah. Where's the truck?"

"It's parked at that address you gave me. Crystal Puryear's house." He smiled. "Jackpot."

She sighed. "Yeah. Jackpot."

"Maybe it's a family reunion," he said. He wished she would make a joke back.

"Yeah," she said. "Except for Mom and Dad." There was a short pause. "Just be careful, Jack," she said.

"I will," he said, but she had already hung up.

Keller glanced over at the stubby black shotgun nestled in the rack by the seat. Rearming himself had not been a problem. Fayetteville was a military base town. There were a hundred pawnshops where a man with a valid credit card could buy enough guns to outfit a platoon. It had taken Keller only an hour or so to find a weapon that suited him, a Mossberg 500 "Cruiser" model combat shotgun with a shoulder rig, no stock, and a barrel short enough that it flirted with the edge of legality. Keller had modified the weapon by covering the hard plastic pistol grip with a rubberized one; other than that, the lethal little shotgun had been good to go. Though Keller always carried a handgun, he preferred a shotgun for takedowns. There was something about the unmistakable sound of a pump shotgun being cocked that made even the most hardened criminal think twice. A handgun carried more ammo and had a faster rate of fire and reload, but

Keller was going to try to stay out of any situation where that would be a factor. "Wanted dead or alive" was a concept that had long passed out of vogue.

Handcuffs and restraints had been another problem. There were a couple of stores in town that sold police gear, but they had gotten sticky in the last few years about selling to people without law enforcement or government credentials. Keller didn't have the time or the cash to persuade them that bail enforcement would fit the mold, despite the lack of official standing. He had settled for stopping by a hardware store and purchasing a roll of duct tape. Crude and messy, but effective. He sighed. At least they hadn't thought to pull the police scanner out, or they hadn't had time. The numbers pulsed fluorescent green across the front screen of the scanner slung beneath the dash, running rapidly through the frequencies he had obtained for the local cops. There was only the occasional squawk of static and brief burst of clipped chatter as the various cars checked in with the dispatcher. It was a quiet night.

He considered his options. He didn't know for certain if DeWayne Puryear was inside. Besides, he didn't know the interior layout of the sister's house. The possible addition of Leonard Puryear was another wild card. He decided to wait and see if DeWayne would come out where Keller could take him in the open, preferably alone. He leaned back in the seat and crossed his hands over his chest. He watched the house through half-closed eyes. To a casual observer, he would have appeared to be asleep.

Angela was right. There was something screwy going on here. He should cut and run. But he knew he wasn't going to.

For years, Keller had felt like an observer in his own life, as if he had been severed from himself and was watching someone else go through the motions of getting up and walking through each day. He thought of a poem he had heard in high school. *We are the hollow men,* the poem read, *we are the stuffed men, headpiece filled with straw*. . . . It hadn't made much sense to him in school, especially since his English teacher had read it in a rich, fruity voice that was supposed to be dramatic, but succeeded only in making the class snicker. Now, he wished he hadn't tuned out and wished he could remember more of the poem. Only two things made him feel anything anymore: being with Angela and the takedown. Since it looked like the first one wasn't going to happen, the second one was really all he had left. He sat motionless, like a predator by a waterhole, and waited.

He had been sitting like that for almost an hour when he saw the brown pickup in his rearview mirror. The big truck was crawling down the street like a tank rolling through an unknown town. Keller could see the outlines of three men in the front seat, but it was too dark to make out their faces. The truck pulled down to the end of the street and parked across from the Puryear vehicle. No one got out.

"That's the address," Raymond said. "Sanchez, that look like the truck the feller was drivin'?"

Sanchez shook his head. "I can't tell," he mumbled. "I didn't get a good look at what he was driving. Only the man."

Raymond drummed his fingers on the steering wheel. "John Lee," he said. "Get out and look it over."

Sanchez got out first and John Lee followed. Sanchez stood by the front fender as John Lee walked across the street and peered in the driver's side window. After a few moments, he came trudging back, head down.

"Can't see nothin'" he said. "'Course, I ain't real sure what I'm supposed to be lookin' for."

Raymond was silent for a moment. Another set of headlights appeared at the entrance to the street. A dented blue Chevy Nova rattled its way down the street toward the three men. There was a white triangular sign perched on top of the car on the driver's side. The sign was lit from within so it looked like the sign on top of a taxi, but running length-

wise to the car. The sign read DOMINO'S PIZZA. FREE
DELIVERY. The Nova pulled up and double-parked
beside the truck. A thin young man in a red, white,
and blue uniform got out, holding a large vinyl
pizza delivery case.

"I got an idea," Raymond said.

Keller had been watching the scene unfold
before him. He hadn't moved, because he was still
unsure of what was going on. He saw two men get
out of the brown truck. One of them stayed there
while the other walked over and examined the
Puryear truck. Keller heard another car engine and
saw a flash of headlights. It was a pizza delivery
car.

As the delivery boy got out, Keller saw a big
curly-haired man in a suit get out of the driver's side
and approach. In the dim light of the car sign, Keller
saw the man approach the pizza guy. There was a
brief conversation, and some money changed
hands.

"Looks like we got perfect timing," Ray-
mond told the tall kid in the deliveryman's uniform.
The kid backed away slightly as Raymond advanced.
He looked suspiciously from the big Indian dude to

the other two leaning on the truck. "Huh?" he said. Then he saw the wad of bills in the Indian dude's hand and relaxed slightly. It no longer looked like a potential robbery to him. He had been robbed twice already, and neither time had the crooks approached him with money in hand.

Raymond gave the kid his most amiable grin. "Guy who ordered this is a friend of ours," he said. "Tell you what, why don't I get this, and we can take it in. He's expectin' us."

A look of doubt crossed the kid's pimply face. "I don't know," he said. Raymond began pulling off bills. The kid looked back into his car at the stack of pizzas still to be delivered. "Twenty-two fifty," he said. Raymond paid him and threw in a five-dollar tip.

"Wow," the pizza guy said. "Thank you, sir, and have a good night." He got back in his car. As he drove away, Raymond motioned to Sanchez.

Keller saw the pizza car drive off. The curly-haired guy called a shorter, Latino man over and spoke to him for a moment. The Latino nodded, but from the slump of his shoulders and the way he trudged toward the front door, pizza in hand, he didn't appear happy. As the Latino rang the door-bell, Keller eased the shotgun out of its rack.

· · ·

"About damn time," DeWayne said as the doorbell rang. He looked out the small window next to the door and saw a Mexican standing on the front steps holding a pizza. He opened the door.

The Mexican looked him in the face for a moment, then thrust the pizza forward. "Twenny-two fifty," he stuttered.

"You bring the beers?" DeWayne said. The Mexican smiled and shrugged. "Twenny-two fifty," he repeated.

"The beers," DeWayne said. "*Cervezas? Dos* six packs *de* Budweiser?"

Another smile and shrug. *"No comprende."*

DeWayne sighed. "Damn it," he muttered. "Cain't get decent service anywhere." The smell of the pizza reached him and his mouth began to water. "Ah, what the hell," he said. "Not your fault if the order guy didn't tell you about the beer." DeWayne reached over beside the door and picked up the canvas bag full of cash. He reached in and rummaged around, finally coming up with a fifty-dollar bill. He handed it to the Mexican guy, grinning at the look on the guy's face. "Keep the change," he said magnanimously. Before the guy could say anything else, DeWayne took the pizza and closed the door.

. . .

They watched Sanchez as he came back across the street. "Well?" Raymond snapped when he reached them.

Sanchez nodded slightly, his head down. "It is him." He looked back up, his face solemn. It was the face of a man pronouncing a death warrant. "And he has a bag full of money."

"Did he recognize you?" Raymond said. Sanchez shook his head.

Raymond opened the door of the truck. He took out his pistol and handed another one to John Lee. Both men held their pistols down along their legs. "Come on," Raymond said. "It's time."

"I will wait here," Sanchez said.

"I don't think so," Raymond said. "We need you to get him to open the door again. Go back and knock. Tell him you gave him the wrong change or something. We'll be on either side of the door."

"Wait," Sanchez said. There was a note of pleading in his voice.

Raymond smiled. "Don't worry, buddy-ro. We'll be doin' all the hard stuff."

"And then you will kill me," Sanchez said. "Like you killed the old man. So there will be no witnesses."

Raymond's face hardened. "You don't know

what you're talkin' about," he said. "I tell you one thing, though, Sanchez. You don't get a move on, I *will* shoot you."

Sanchez bowed his head. He turned back toward the house, shuffling like a man walking in his sleep. He was muttering something underneath his breath.

"*Dios te salve, Maria,*" he was saying, "*Llena eres de gracia.*" Hail Mary, full of grace . . .

Keller saw what looked like an argument between the three men standing in the street. Suddenly, the argument seemed to resolve, with the Latino turning and heading back toward the house. The other two men followed. He held the shotgun across his lap, waiting to see what developed. He eased the driver's side door open and set his foot on the asphalt, ready to move. *As soon as I figure out what the hell's going on,* he told himself.

"You go knock on the door," Raymond said. "He knows you, sorta. When the sumbitch opens the door, step back. We'll take it from there."

Sanchez didn't look up. "*Santa Maria,*" he murmured. "*Ruega por nosotros pecadores . . .*" Holy Mary, pray for us sinners.

Raymond looked over at John Lee. "What the fuck's he talking about?" he whispered.

John Lee shrugged. He looked as nervous as Sanchez. Raymond briefly regretted not bringing a couple of professional hitters along, but dismissed the idea after a second. This was a family affair.

They had reached the front steps. Raymond and John Lee moved to opposite sides of the door, out of sight of anyone inside. They raised their pistols. Sanchez reached up and took a deep breath. *"Ahora y en la hora de nuestra muerte."* Now, and in the hour of our death. He knocked on the door.

In the dim yellow glow of the bug light on the porch, Keller saw the glint of guns in the hands of the men on either side of the door. He realized at that instant that he had waited too long. He swore under his breath and got out of the car. He held the shotgun across his chest and began to run.

The knock on the door was loud inside the house "Who the hell could that be?" DeWayne said. With a mouth full of pizza, it came out as "oof ell at mee?"

"I'll get it," said Leonard. He got up and walked down the hallway. He peered out of one of the narrow side windows that framed the door. "It's some Mexican dude."

"Aw right!" DeWayne crowed. "He musta come back with the beer. Let 'im in, cuz."

Leonard opened the door.

Keller was at the foot of the walkway leading to the house when he saw the door swing open. He saw the curly-haired man beside the door reach out and yank the Latino off the narrow stoop. The curly-haired man stepped into the Hispanic's place. Keller saw a look of surprise cross the face of the man who answered the door. There was a bang and the face disappeared as the heavy-caliber handgun punched the man back into the shadows behind the doorway. The last thing Keller saw of it was the mouth opened in a silent "O" of amazement.

"Police!" Keller yelled. It wasn't true, but people instinctively knew what it meant, unlike "Bail enforcement!" which people had to think about. *"Put the gun down!"*

The man in the doorway ignored him and moved forward into the house. The man on the other side of the door turned, his face registering the same shock as the guy who had just been blown backwards into the hallway. He raised the pistol in his hand. "Put it *down!*" Keller bellowed. The man looked stupidly at him, the gun in his hand still moving upwards toward Keller. Keller's reflexes took over. The shotgun in his hands roared. Keller couldn't recall having pulled the trigger. The blast of the gun was followed by the crack of the man's body as it met the wall of the house, slammed back by a full load of #4 buckshot. Keller reflexively jacked another round into the chamber and swung the shotgun to bear on the Latino who had knocked on the door. That one was panting in fear and crawling away on his hands and knees. He stopped crawling and vomited into the grass. No target. Keller swung back to the man he had shot. He had slid downwards into a sitting position, his back against the building. His entire front was chopped meat. He stared at Keller. He shook his head as if trying to shake off a hallucination. When Keller failed to vanish, he only looked more bewildered.

The front door yawned wide open, inviting Keller into the darkness beyond. He heard screaming from inside. He swore softly and moved into the darkness.

DeWayne heard the door open, then the pistol shot. There was a muffled scream, then the sound of something heavy hitting the floor. Instinctively, he leaped to his feet, picking up the flimsy coffee table as he rose. In the room's dim illumination, he saw a large man with curly hair come through the doorway from the hall. DeWayne saw the dark skin and thought at first it was the Mexican pizza guy. This man, however, was much taller and broader and dressed in a suit. He was holding a pistol in his hand. DeWayne heaved the table at him. The impact spoiled the man's aim and knocked him on his ass. The first shot went wide and blew out the curtained picture window behind the couch.

A high pitched rhythmic sound came from the hallway, like some great mechanical bird. It was Leonard screaming. "Leonard?" DeWayne said. The curly-haired man was picking himself up. He had lost the tinted glasses. DeWayne saw his eyes for the first time. They were a pale green. As the stranger raised his gun, DeWayne remembered the old Indian man they had killed. He looked down the barrel of the upraised gun and saw his death there.

Keller advanced down the hallway, his shotgun at the ready. He heard a crash, saw a confused tangle of movement in the dimly lighted room. *"Freeze, God damn it!"* he yelled.

Raymond heard the voice behind him, real- ized that it wasn't John Lee come to back him up. He whirled and fired almost in the same motion. The dark figure in the hallway dropped to the floor. When Raymond turned back, DeWayne was gone.

DeWayne didn't know who the voice from the hallway belonged to, and he was too terrified to care. When the big Indian turned away and fired, he hurled himself toward the kitchen. He scooped his own gun off the kitchen table as he passed. He fumbled with the door, almost sobbing with frustration as his fear-numbed fingers refused to work. Finally, he was able to yank the door open and stumble into the backyard.

The tiny backyard was overgrown with weeds. A rusting metal shed, barely six feet tall, sagged in one corner of the yard. DeWayne ran toward it, hoping to hide out inside. He yanked at the shed door. It was padlocked. Behind him, the kitchen door slammed open. DeWayne shrieked in panic and fired blindly back toward the sound. Glass shattered in the window. The figure silhouetted in the doorway didn't fall, but it did pull back.

As the man in the living room had turned, Keller had instinctively dropped and sought cover. The only thing to get behind was the body of the man from the doorway. Now Keller lay full length on the floor, trying not to look at the eyes of the dead man. The body was close enough to touch. There was a sticky wetness under him and the familiar sharp metallic smell of blood. Keller realized that he was lying in a huge smear of it where the man had tried to drag himself down the hallway, his life flowing out of him and onto the floorboards. There was too much blood gone for any man to survive. Keller looked into the man's eyes. Those eyes were becoming more inanimate with each passing second. The man had lost the strength to scream. At first Keller thought that a blessing, but the pitiful sight of the man's mouth moving, trying to form words was worse. Finally a word came out, expelled like a sob on the man's dying breath.

"Who . . . ?" Keller didn't see any need to answer. There was no one left to hear. Keller heard faraway sirens drawing closer. Someone had called the cops. There was a shot from outside, then the sound of glass shattering. Someone swore from inside the kitchen.

Keller took stock of the situation. Behind him were the cops. Before him, there were two men with guns. He wasn't sure where they were. For that matter, he wasn't completely sure who they were.

"Fuck this," he said out loud. He started backing down the hallway, sliding on his belly, the shotgun held out in front of him.

He felt a sudden touch of metal on the back of his neck. "Stop there," a voice said in a soft Spanish accent.

"We didn't mean to kill him," DeWayne called out. "I swear it, man. We didn't know he was carrying a gun."

The figure behind the door made no answer. De-Wayne crouched deeper in the shadows beside the shed. "You can even have the money back, man, it's in the bag in the hallway. Just let me go get some help for my cousin."

"Your cousin's dead," came the voice from inside the house. "I kilt him."

DeWayne put a hand to his forehead. "Okay, man," he said. "Okay. So we're, like, even, right? An eye for an eye?" There was no answer.

His eyes were more accustomed to the darkness now. There was a chest-high chain-link fence at the back of the lot, where the yard of the house behind backed up to this one. He began edging his way back, then leaped up and turned toward the fence. He threw one leg onto a narrow metal tube running along the top of the fence and tried to vault over. The metal tube collapsed under his weight. He landed atop the metal points of the chain link. De-Wayne screamed as the crudely twisted ends of wire gouged him. He dropped the gun. The Indian came running out, firing on the run. The muzzle flash of his pistol lit up the yard. DeWayne rolled off the fence and the bullets passed over him. DeWayne sobbed in fear and rage as he scrambled to his knees. His hand closed over something hard and metallic. His gun. The shadowy bulk of the big man was approaching the chain-link fence. DeWayne raised the gun and pulled the trigger again and again, barely aiming. He fired in blind panic, the muzzle flashes ruining his night vision. "Leave me alone, you sumbitch," he screamed. "Just leave me the fuck alone!" Then he was no longer firing. The firing pin clicked on the empty chamber. DeWayne tensed, waiting for the bullet that would tear out his heart or shatter his brain. It never came. There was silence. His night vision began to return slowly. The big Indian was lying on the ground. DeWayne leaped to his feet.

"Ha-haaaaa!" he crowed in triumph. "I killed you! I killed you!" He heard the sound of approaching sirens. He threw down the gun and ran.

4

"I'm not moving," Keller said.

"Good," the man behind him said. "Now slide the shotgun away from you, backwards. I am tired of having guns pointed at me."

Keller shoved the shotgun away from him across the floor. It slid in the pool of blood, leaving a ripple in the rapidly congealing liquid.

"Now," the voice said. "Tell me who you are and why you are here."

"My name's Keller," he replied. "I work for a bail bondsman down in Wilmington. DeWayne Puryear disappeared a few weeks ago and my boss got a little worried about him showing up for court." He paused. "And who are you," he said, "if you don't mind my asking?"

There was no answer. Keller could hear the man's harsh breathing. Then the man chuckled. It was a strained sound, the sound of barely tethered hysteria.

"Right now," he said. "I am a man with a bag of money and a gun. Soon I will have a big truck. It is the American dream, no?" Keller felt the gun pressed more firmly into the back of his neck. "No moving until I am gone," he said. The pressure of the gun was suddenly gone. Keller heard the sound of footsteps. After a moment, he heard the sound of a large truck starting up and driving away.

Keller got slowly to his knees. His shirt clung to his body, sticky and heavy with blood. His pants were soaked as well. The smell of it filled the air, mixed with the acrid stench of gunpowder. He fought down the urge to retch. The sirens were much closer now. He staggered to his feet and stumbled toward the door. He stopped there for a moment, hanging on, taking deep breaths to clear his nostrils of the slaughterhouse reek inside. After a few moments, he straightened up. He walked, then ran down the walkway to his car. He passed the first cop cars on the way out, watching in his rearview mirror as they screeched to a stop in front of the house.

He turned the corner, went down a few blocks, turned another. He had no idea where he was going. After a few random turns, he spotted an abandoned gas station. The doors and windows were boarded up with graffiti-covered plywood. But it was the tall hedges on three sides of the building and the drive-way that led to the back of the building that got Keller's attention. He whipped the car into the driveway and pulled behind the building.

There was a jumble of old tires and parts piled haphazardly in the narrow alleyway. Keller got out and pulled a gym bag from the backseat. Quickly, he stripped off the bloody shirt and pants and ex-changed them for the pair in the bag. He toweled the residue of blood off his face as best he could. He knew he was probably missing some, but at least the smell wasn't so bad anymore. He leaned against the car for a moment.

Puryear, he thought, *he's back there.* It was crazy to go back. He knew it. But he could almost feel the nearby presence of his quarry. The siren promise of the takedown sang again in his ear, overriding everything. He got in and started the car.

Every nerve in DeWayne's body was de-manding that he lie down on the pavement and curl up in pain, but he knew that would only attract atten-tion. He held himself upright by sheer force of will as he staggered down the street. The distant sirens had come closer and closer, then stopped. He won-dered what they would make of what they found at the house. The sudden thought of his cousin made him stop. He crossed his arms across his torn stomach, leaning over in pain. He felt the heat of tears on his face. Leonard was dead. He had told himself at first that the Indian dude had been lying, but De-Wayne knew in his heart that he wasn't. And it was his fault. He never should have gotten them into this mess. He stumbled along, weeping, no longer caring how he looked. He wondered how they would break the news to Crys. And his aunt and uncle. The thought made him cry even harder. They had been good to him, and he had fucked everything up.

After a few minutes he reached the main road. He was going to have to pull himself together, unless he wanted to spend the rest of his life in prison. Or worse. The thought of being strapped to a gurney in Central Prison while a doctor injected him with poison stiffened his resolve. He straightened up and wiped his eyes. A big car was slowing down. At first he was terrified that it was a cop car, but there were no lights on the top or radios on the dash. The car pulled to a stop and a man got out. He was a big guy, dressed in jeans and a T-shirt. He had shoulder length blonde hair. Definitely not a cop, DeWayne thought with relief.

"Hey, pal," the man said. "You okay?"

"I just racked up my bike," DeWayne lied.

"Need a ride to the hospital?" the guy asked.

"Naw," DeWayne said. "I could use a ride home, though." He wasn't sure where he was going to say home was; the important thing was just to get out of the area.

"Sure," the guy said. "Hop in." DeWayne turned toward the car. Suddenly he noticed something about the blonde guy.

"Dude," he said. "Did you just have a wreck too?"

"Why do you say that?" the guy said as he came closer.

"Because you've got blood on you." DeWayne said. "It's, like, even in your hair."

"Sorry, DeWayne," the guy said. "Didn't have time to shower."

"Hey," DeWayne said, "how do you know my—" He never got to finish the sentence before the guy slugged him across the jaw. Everything went blurry. When DeWayne's vision cleared, he was shoved face-first over the hood of the car with his hands pinned behind his back.

Keller bound DeWayne's hands with the duct tape. DeWayne had struggled briefly at first until Keller had smacked his face against the hood. After that, he was docile. Keller pulled his prisoner to his feet and marched him toward the back of the car. He unlocked the trunk.

"Hey," DeWayne whined. "You ain't no cop." He seemed offended.

"That's right, DeWayne," Keller said. "I work for your bondsman. You forget your court date? Down in Brunswick County?"

DeWayne stared at him. "You gotta be kidding me, dude," he said. "You're picking me up on a fuckin' B & E? That was, like, a million years ago."

"Three weeks, actually."

"Like I said. Man, I ain't gettin' in no trunk. I'll suffocate."

"I drilled air holes. I do this for a living, DeWayne. A lot of guys have ridden in there, and I haven't lost one yet. Now get in, or I'll stuff you in. Your choice."

"Awww, maaaan," DeWayne whined. Keller took that as the choice. He grabbed DeWayne by the back of his belt, grunting with effort as he lifted the smaller man off the ground. Keller used DeWayne's waist as a fulcrum to tip him over and into the trunk headfirst. He stuffed DeWayne's legs in next and slammed the trunk lid. "Hey!" DeWayne yelped. "Hey, man, lemme out!" There was a drumming of feet on the inside of the trunk. Keller cursed. Normally, he would have the prisoner shackled down, but he didn't have his gear. Keller slammed his hand down on the lid and the noise stopped.

"Quiet," Keller snarled, "or I'll plug the air holes. I mean it, asshole." There was silence.

As Keller drove away, he picked up the cell phone and dialed Angela. "I got him," he said.

"Any trouble?" she asked.

He thought of lying or minimizing what had just happened, but he needed help. "Yeah," he said. "Whoever was after DeWayne got there before I did. There were three guys. Two Indians and a Latino. One of the Indians drew on me." He thought about the man he had left lying beside the door. He took a deep breath. "I'm pretty sure that one's dead. I don't know about the other one. I saw him shoot someone, probably DeWayne's cousin. The Latino guy drove off."

There was a brief silence, broken only by the crackle of static in the cell phone. "You still there?" he said.

"Yeah," she said after a moment. Her voice sounded choked. "Yeah, I'm here."

"Listen," he said. "I need you to get on the phone. Talk to some of your contact people. Anybody you know who can find out what the hell is going on. Call me back."

Another brief silence. Then simply, "Okay," and the line went dead.

Keller drove carefully, keeping slightly under the speed limit. He was heading south on 301 near the Coliseum when the police car fell in behind him. He swore under his breath and reduced his speed slightly, hoping the car would pull around and pass him. The only response was an explosion of flashing blue lights. He gritted his teeth and pulled over on the shoulder.

"Not a word, DeWayne," he yelled back, not sure if he could be heard from inside the trunk. "Not a fucking peep, you understand?" He reached into the glove box and pulled out his license and registration. He rolled the window down and heard the crunch of heavy shoes on the gravel shoulder as the cop approached. "License and registration," a familiar voice said. Keller's stomach tightened as he turned and looked at the cop. It was Eddie Wesson.

Wesson grinned. "Out of the car, smart-ass," he said. "Hands behind your head."

Keller got out slowly, his hands in the air. He looked back at the cop car behind him. Marie Jones stood at the left front fender, one hand on her gun. "Eddie," she said. "Why don't you let me—"

"Shut up," Wesson said. He grabbed Keller by the back of the shirt and slammed him against the car, face first. Keller felt the bone of his nose crunch against the roof support. Wesson yanked him off the car and slammed his knee into the back of Keller's leg, propelling him to the ground. Wesson put his knee in the small of Keller's back and leaned on him with his full weight. Keller gritted his teeth against the pain.

"Cut it *out,* Eddie!" he heard Marie yell. Wesson ignored her. He yanked Keller's wrists behind his back. Keller heard the snap of the handcuffs as Wesson secured him. Wesson gave the cuffs an extra squeeze to tighten them to the point of pain. Then he heard another sound.

DeWayne Puryear was hammering his feet against the trunk lid. "Hey!" he yelled. "Help!" Wesson stood up and drew his pistol. He pointed it at Keller on the ground. "Give me an excuse, asshole," he snarled. He turned to Marie. "Get the trunk open," he said. Keller, his face to the ground, heard the snap as Marie unbuttoned her holster and drew her own weapon. He turned his head to try to talk to her. "The guy in the trunk is DeWayne Puryear," he said. "Bail jumper from down in—" his words were cut off by a grunt of pain as Wesson kicked him in the ribs. "I didn't ask you anything, asshole," Wesson said. Keller could see Marie's shoes as she walked past him to get the keys out of the ignition. She walked back to the rear of the car and opened the trunk.

"Oh, Thank you, Jesus," he heard DeWayne say. He sounded hysterical. "He's crazy, officer! I was mindin' my own business when this sumbitch grabs me off the street and stuffs me in the trunk. I ain't done nothin' I swear it, I was just—"

"Okay, okay," Marie said. "Just calm down, sir." Keller looked. She had helped DeWayne clamber out of the trunk and was guiding him back to the side of the police car.

"Get that tape off his wrists," Wesson ordered.

"I don't know, Eddie," she said. "What if he's—"

"Just do it, Marie," Wesson snapped.

Marie holstered her weapon and produced a small knife from her belt. She began sawing through the duct tape binding DeWayne's hands behind his back. DeWayne was still babbling thanks.

"Don't do it, Marie," Keller said. He was rewarded with another kick in the ribs.

Finally, Marie sawed through the last of the duct tape and DeWayne's hands were free. He threw his arms around Marie in a bear hug. "Thank you, pretty lady," he said, his voice choked with tears of gratitude. She tried to push him off. "Sir," she was saying, "Sir, you need to let—"

DeWayne sprang back from her. He was holding her pistol clutched in his hand. Keller heard Wesson's shoes grinding on the gravel as he tried to turn, simultaneously with the report of the gun and the wet smacking sound of the bullet striking Wesson.

"Eddie!" Marie screamed. Wesson's limp body thudded into the ground behind Keller. There was brief scuffle of gravel as Wesson's body twitched and writhed in its death throes. Keller kept his eyes fixed on DeWayne, willing himself not to look back. Marie leaped toward DeWayne, but he had already swung the pistol back to point at her face. She drew up short, her hands in front of her. Her mouth moved soundlessly. DeWayne was panting like a long-distance runner, but his hands were steady.

"Don't do anything stupid, lady," he said. He motioned with his head toward Wesson lying beside Keller on the ground. "This gets easier every time I do it. It ain't like I want to do it, but the way I figger it, I ain't got nothin' to lose now, y'know? Now get your hands up. Behind your head."

Slowly, like a person moving in a nightmare, Marie complied.

"Now down on the ground," he ordered. She sank to her knees. Her face looked blank and dead in the harsh glare of the headlights. DeWayne backed away from her, then turned the gun toward Keller. He smiled for the first time, but the smile was a rictus, devoid of pleasure or humor. The blue lights of the police car still flashing behind him gave the scene a surreal, nightmare quality. DeWayne looked like a funhouse clown turned insane. Keller looked down the barrel of the gun.

Burning, they were burning. He could hear the screams as they died. Keller tried to stand, stumbled, then crawled toward the Bradley on his hands and knees. The gravel beneath him cut into the palms of his hands and shredded the knees of his uniform. Twenty feet away from the burning hulk, the heat pushed him back like a force field. He sobbed in frustration. The screams were abruptly cut off, drowned in the hammering series of explosions as the ammo inside the Bradley cooked off. The sky was filled with white flashes and streaks of red and yellow. Keller sank to the ground. Helpless. Useless.

"Do it," Keller snarled up at DeWayne. "Get it over with." He looked into DeWayne's mad eyes for a long moment. The gun held steady on Keller, then wavered. Then DeWayne stepped back and lowered the gun.

"I cain't do it," he said. His shoulders sagged as if under a great weight. He looked over at where Marie knelt on the ground. "I cain't shoot you while you're just layin' there helpless." He shook his head. "Reckon I still got that much good left in me." He edged past where Keller lay on the ground. Keller attempted to turn his head to watch where DeWayne was going. He couldn't see, but he heard DeWayne's voice. "But this is for lockin' me in a fuckin' car trunk." Keller caught a glimpse of a heavy boot headed for the side of his head, looking absurdly large. There was a blinding flash of white light and an explosion of pain in Keller's skull, then darkness.

There were three of them, two majors and a light colonel. They were sitting behind the table, looking immaculate in their class-A uniforms. They made him wait a long time at attention before speaking. "Sergeant Keller," the youngest of the two majors began. "We have investigated your claim of casualties caused by so-called friendly fire. The conclusion of this board of inquiry is that your vehicle became separated from the rest of the unit and came under attack by an Iraqi antitank platoon."

"No sir," Keller said flatly. "It was a helicopter. I heard."

"Sergeant," the major on the other end of the table spoke up, "we've checked thoroughly. There were no Coalition air assets reported in the area at the time of the attack."

"Then either someone was as lost as I was," Keller replied, looking the major in the eye, "Or someone is lying. Sir." The major looked down and shifted uncomfortably in his chair, but the colonel in the middle purpled.

"Or maybe, Sergeant," he said in a gravelly voice, "You fucked up, got out of your assigned area, and led your squad into an ambush." He stood up. "You've got a good record so far, Sergeant," he said. "Don't throw away your career."

Keller stared at him. He couldn't control the hysterical laugh that bubbled up unbidden from his chest. "My career?" he said, almost choking with the laughter. "My career?" he laughed harder. Then he noticed that the three officers' faces were changing, melting like candle wax. As Keller stared, flames erupted from their eyes and mouths. They fell to the floor, burning. The air was filled with the stench of burned flesh and hair. They were scream-

*ing. Keller tried to go to them, but he couldn't move
his feet. He looked down and saw that his feet had
sunk up to the ankles in the floor. He began screaming as well.*

"Honey," a voice was saying, "Honey, wake up."
There was a hand on Keller's shoulder, shaking
gently. He tried to reach up and grab the hand, but
his right arm wouldn't respond. He opened his
eyes.

He was in a hospital bed. He noticed that his vision was obscured by a mass of bandage across the
bridge of his nose. The entire front of his face was
throbbing with pain.

A middle-aged black woman in a nurse's uniform
was standing over him. As Keller's eyes focused on
her concerned, kind face, she stopped shaking him.
Her hand remained on his shoulder. "Bad dreams?"
she said. Keller nodded. She withdrew her hand,
patting him on the shoulder as she did so. "Well,
you're all right now. You're safe."

Keller tried to raise his hand again, but couldn't.
"Then why am I handcuffed to the bed?"

The nurse's mouth drew into a disapproving line.
"Not my idea, believe me. There's some police outside that want to talk to you as soon as you wake up.
I say you're going to see a doctor first. You want
some water?" Keller nodded again. She poured him
a cup from a plastic pitcher at the bedside and he

took it with his free hand. She patted him on the shoulder again and went out the door. There was a brief conversation outside, ending with the nurse's raised voice saying "I *said,* after he's seen a *doctor.*" He heard her heavy footsteps going away. No one entered.

After a few minutes, the door opened again and a man in a white coat came in. He was short, no more than five-two or-three, with dark skin and jet-black hair ineptly combed, giving him an absentminded look that was enhanced rather than contradicted by his round wire-rimmed glasses. A curlicue of elaborately embroidered lettering above the pocket of his white coat identified him as Dr. Ahmad.

"Good morning," he said in a precise, almost British accent. "I am Doctor Ahmad. And how are we feeling today?"

"Like someone tried to kick our head in," Keller said.

"Ha ha," the doctor said, pronouncing each syllable as if he had learned to laugh from a language textbook. He withdrew a small penlight from the pocket of his white coat and leaned over. He shined the light into first one eye, then the other. "Are you experiencing any blurred vision, slurred speech."

"I'm fine," Keller said.

Ahmad leaned back. "Your nose was broken," he said. "I've called for a plastic surgery consult—"

"I'm fine," Keller repeated.

Ahmad looked annoyed at the interruption. "We've been hesitant to give you anything for the pain until we determined whether there was any skull fracture or closed-head injury. That danger seems to have passed. You're quite lucky."

"Yeah," Keller said. "Lucky." He raised his right hand a few inches and the handcuff chain clinked. Ahmad looked at the cuffs and swallowed nervously. "Yes. Well," he said. "There are a couple of policemen outside who wish to talk to you." The nurse reentered the room, holding a small cup of water in one hand and a small paper container in the other. "Of course," the doctor said, "if you would like some pain medication, I can tell them to come back later."

"No," Keller said. "I don't want anything that'll make me sleep."

"He has bad dreams," the nurse said. Keller felt a flash of annoyance and embarrassment, as if she had informed the doctor that she had caught him picking his nose.

"Ah," the doctor said, nodding as if that explained everything. He picked up the clipboard from the foot of Keller's bed and made a note. "That sort of thing is not unusual after a frightening experience like yours. It's called—"

"Post-traumatic stress disorder," Keller said.

"You've heard of it," Ahmad said, making another note.

"Yeah," Keller said. There was an uncomfortable silence. "Okay," Ahmad finally said. "I can still tell the men outside that you're not to be disturbed. If you wish."

Keller thought for a moment, then sighed. "No," he said. "Let's get it over with." He looked at Ahmad. "Thanks, Doc."

Ahmad smiled for the first time. "Don't mention it." He and the nurse left the room. After a few moments, two men came in.

They were the classic Mutt-and-Jeff cop team. The older one was small and wiry, with a pockmarked face and a bad comb-over. He had a short, brushy moustache that was saved from being Hitlerian by only a quarter inch of extra length. His face was furrowed with lines of weariness as if his feet hurt. The other cop was taller and broader, with a flushed face and short, brush-cut blonde hair. The bigger cop leaned back against the wall and folded his arms. The older one pulled up a chair beside the bed.

"Detective Barnes," he said. He gestured at his partner. "This is Detective Stacy." Stacy didn't respond. Neither did Keller.

"We want to ask you a couple of questions about the shooting of Officer Wesson," Barnes said.

"How's Marie?" Keller said. "Officer Jones, I mean."

The two detectives looked at each other. "You know Officer Jones?" Barnes said.

"A little," Keller said, inwardly cursing himself for letting slip that he knew her first name. Now they'd never let it go. "We'd met before."

"She's doing okay, I guess," Stacy said. "For someone who fucked up and got her partner killed," he added.

Keller started to sit up. "That's not what happened," he said. "She was doing what Wesson told her to do."

"You seem awful interested in Jones's welfare," Barnes observed mildly.

"I just don't want to see her get blamed for this. Wesson was a fucking maniac. He hated me so much he couldn't see straight. He ordered Jones to let my prisoner go. That's why he got killed."

"You were seen leaving the courthouse yesterday with Officer Jones. In her car," Barnes said.

"She gave me a ride to the impound lot to pick up my car," Keller said. "She felt bad about Wesson roughing me up."

Stacy had been standing with his arms across his chest, his face growing redder and redder as Keller and Barnes talked. Finally he couldn't contain himself any longer.

"Eddie Wesson was a friend of mine, you son of a bitch," he growled.

Keller looked at him. "Doesn't surprise me."

Stacy leaned over the bed, grabbing a rail in each meaty hand. He brought his face within inches of

Keller's. "Let me tell you what I think," Stacy said. Keller noticed for the first time that his eyes were red. There was beer on his breath. "I think you and Eddie were both banging her," Stacy said. "You didn't like her doing it with Eddie. So you and your little buddy Puryear engineered this somehow to get rid of Eddie." Stacy's face twisted in a sickening leer. "How was she, anyway? I bet she can really move that tight little ass when she gets going. How about it, Keller? She one hot piece?"

Keller looked him in the eye. "Your mom was better."

Stacy's face grew slack for a moment. Then he screamed in rage and grabbed the front of Keller's hospital gown with one hand. He yanked Keller up off the bed. He balled up his fist and pulled it back.

"What the *hell* you think you're doin'?" a voice bellowed from the doorway. The nurse Keller had seen first came charging into the room like an avenging angel. "You *put* my patient down!"

"Back off, bitch," Stacy snarled. "Police business."

"Uh-huh?" the nurse said, standing with her hands on her hips. "I *seen* your kind of po-lice business. What's the matter, a man got to be cuffed an' in a hospital bed before you can take him on?"

"Well," a deep voice said from the doorway. "This is an interesting scene."

Scott McCaskill stood slightly inside the door.

Despite the hour, the attorney was dressed as if he was entering a courtroom. He strode into the room, his eyes riveted on Stacy.

"Interrogating another prisoner, Stacy?" he said mildly. "I'm sure you've read him his rights first."

"Don't need to," Stacy said. "He's not in custody."

McCaskill gestured at the bed. "He's handcuffed to the bed."

"And this man was getting ready to hit my patient," the nurse said.

McCaskill cocked an eyebrow. "Really," he said. "So I think we can safely assume that anything my client has said will be inadmissible in court." He gave Stacy a nod of the head that was almost a bow. "Thank you, Detective Stacy," he said. "You always make a defense lawyer's job so much easier." Stacy looked like he was about to go for McCaskill, but Barnes stood up. "C'mon, Stace," he said. His voice sounded tired. "Let's let Mister McCaskill have a word with his client." Stacy stepped back from the bed. He gave Keller a murderous glare. "This isn't over, asshole," he said. Keller opened his mouth to reply. McCaskill silenced him with a hand wave. The two detectives left.

McCaskill sat down, looked at the nurse. "I know you, I think."

She smiled at him. "I reckon you do. I'm Robbie Duke's Aunt Emma."

McCaskill snapped his fingers. "Of course." He

stood up and shook her hand. "How is Robbie?"

Her smile broadened. "Graduates from Fayetteville State next semester," she said. "We got you to thank for that. You hadn't got him out of that trouble, things would have turned out real different. Once we got him away from those boys he was runnin' with, he straightened right out."

McCaskill shook his head. "No, he has you to thank for that. Tell him I asked after him, would you?"

"I surely will," Emma said. She turned to Keller. "You need anything before I go?" Keller shook his head. She left.

McCaskill sat back down. "My daughter wants me to thank you."

Keller thought for a moment. "I don't think I know her."

"You don't," McCaskill said. "But with all the work you and Angela are throwing my way, we're going to be able to send her to Europe for her senior year."

"Hilarious," Keller said. He lay back against the pillows and closed his eyes.

McCaskill smiled. "Tell me what happened."

Keller started to describe the traffic stop. McCaskill silenced him with a raised hand. "Start with the house," he said. His tone was mild, but his eyes were sharp.

Keller took a deep breath. He didn't know how

much Angela might have told him. He decided to play it straight. "I had information that a bail jumper named DeWayne Puryear might be holed up there. Three guys got there before I did. One of them was a Latino, maybe a Mexican, I don't know. The other two looked to be Indians. Lumbees. One of the Indians shot the first guy that answered the door. I think the one that got shot must have been Puryear's cousin Leonard. They hang out together. When I yelled at them, the other Indian, the one standing beside the door, drew on me." Keller paused. "I shot him." He looked at McCaskill. "I didn't have any choice." McCaskill looked at him silently, without expression.

Keller stopped. It was an old trick shared by cops and lawyers, creating a silence that the person being interrogated felt obliged to fill. Keller took a deep breath. "Anyway, the other Indian guy apparently tried to shoot it out with Puryear. I guess DeWayne must have got lucky."

"Why do you say that?"

"Puryear's always been a small timer. He's got no record of violence. The other guy, the shooter—well, I don't know. There was something about him. He moved like a pro. DeWayne must have gotten lucky."

McCaskill took a small notebook out of an inside pocket. He flipped it open. "They've got two bodies down at the morgue, one ID'd as Leonard Puryear, the other one a John Lee Oxendine."

"Leonard's the cousin I told you about."

McCaskill nodded. "Here's where it gets interesting. Oxendine's father was killed in an apparent robbery a few days ago. And Oxendine's brother Raymond is upstairs in ICU. Somebody shot him in the gut, but he's going to live." Keller thought of the man he had seen shoot Leonard Puryear. "Big guy, curly hair?"

"Haven't seen him," McCaskill said. He looked pointedly at Keller. "Have you?" Keller was silent for a moment, thinking it over. "Because right now," McCaskill went on, "the cops have nothing tying you to any of the deaths at the house. Raymond Oxendine isn't talking. Naturally, neither are the two men downstairs in the morgue. But if you tell the police what you know about who shot either of them, that puts you at the scene. With a gun in your hand."

"You think I should keep my mouth shut."

McCaskill smiled thinly. "As an officer of the court, of course I'm not telling you not to cooperate with the police."

"It was self-defense," Keller said.

"And I'm sure I could be successful with that defense. At trial. Pretty sure, at least. After all, I've done it for you before."

Keller closed his eyes. "Just get me out of here," he said.

"Thanks to Detective Stacy's little display, I'm

reasonably sure I can manage that," McCaskill said. Keller heard him stand up. He opened his eyes.

"What about Officer Jones?" he said.

McCaskill looked puzzled. "What about her?"

"It sounded like she's getting hung out to dry over Wesson's death. I don't want that to happen. It was Wesson who fucked up, not her."

McCaskill patted him on the shoulder. "She's not my client, Keller. You are. She's not my problem, and not yours."

"Jesus," Keller said. "I keep forgetting what a cold bastard you are."

"Of course I am," McCaskill said. He smiled. "It's why you and Angela keep calling me. I'm exactly who you want on your side."

5

The first thing Raymond was aware of was the slow, steady beep of the heart monitor. The sound percolated downward into his conscious mind like water seeping into the earth. There was the low hum of machinery and the sharp smell of some kind of antiseptic. He opened his eyes without moving.

The room was tiny, almost a cubicle, crammed with gleaming white and chrome machines that surrounded his bed like sentinels. Each of the machines trailed long wires or tubes that ran under the crisp white sheet and attached at various points to his body. The room was in semidarkness, lit only by the green and red lights of the machines and a soft glow that appeared to come from one wall of the room.

Raymond turned his head slightly. As his eyes came into focus, he realized that the glowing wall consisted of a heavy sliding door of metal and glass. The door was half opened, with a thin gauze curtain for an illusion of privacy. The glow came from the fluorescent lights beyond the curtain. There was a shadow cast by the lights, a human figure standing beyond that veil. For a moment, Raymond thought back to Sunday School lessons about the Temple in Israel. There was a veil there, hiding the Holy of Holies, where God dwelt. His head spun for a moment as he thought he might be about to come face to face with . . . The curtain parted and the illusion shattered. A short redhead in a nurse's uniform entered. She was carrying a plastic bag that appeared to be full of some kind of fluid. The shadow was revealed as a large man in a police uniform with his back turned to the room. He was standing guard, Raymond realized. More clarity returned and he felt the cold circle of metal around his wrist. He was cuffed to the bed.

As the nurse approached he closed his eyes, pretending to be still unconscious. As he listened to the sounds of the nurse performing whatever errand had brought her in, he wondered what had happened to John Lee. He wondered how much the cops knew. Enough, he figured, or he wouldn't be cuffed to the bed. Finally, he heard the nurse leave. He opened his eyes again. He began looking around for something he could use as a weapon when they took these damn cuffs off.

Keller was dozing lightly when Dr. Ahmad reentered the room. "You are being discharged," he said. "We performed a CT scan of your skull. There is no sign of permanent injury or skull fracture."

"You said discharged," Keller said. "Not released." For emphasis, he rattled the handcuff that still secured him to the bed rail.

Ahmad looked down at his pad and began writing. "That is not my decision," he mumbled.

"It is, however, the decision of the Fayetteville police," the voice of Scott McCaskill boomed from the doorway. He entered the room, followed by the slouching figure of Detective Barnes.

Barnes's normally sour expression was even more pronounced. "Detective Barnes and I," McCaskill said with a smile, "have had an enlightening conversation with the District Attorney's office, as well as the city's legal counsel on civil matters. We've decided that there's no evidence connecting you with any real crime."

"Yet," Barnes said, half under his breath. He had an expression on his face as if some small animal had shat in his moustache.

"If you turn up anything, Detective," McCaskill said, still smiling, "anything *real,* that is, I'm all ears."

Barnes muttered something else that Keller didn't catch and took a small key out of his pocket. He unlocked the cuffs without looking at Keller. After he was finished, he pocketed the cuffs and key, turned on his heel, and left.

Ahmad finished writing and tore a page off his clipboard. "Here are your discharge instructions," he said, "and a prescription for the pain. You may want to take it easy for a few days. Avoid excitement."

"An excellent suggestion," McCaskill said, looking significantly at Keller. "In fact, a week or two off might be a good idea. Some place far away, like a beach in Florida." He winked at Ahmad. "Just what the doctor ordered, eh?"

Ahmad looked up and blinked. "I don't believe I said anything about Florida."

"Just an expression, Doctor, just an expression," McCaskill said, patting him on the shoulder. Ahmad still looked confused as he left.

This is one cool ride, DeWayne thought. He was headed south on I-95, going slightly under the speed limit. He had the windows rolled down and Steve Earle cranked on the CD player.

About the time that daddy left to fight the big war
I saw my first pistol in the general store
In the general store,
when I was thirteen
Thought it was the finest thing I ever had seen . . .

He could feel the vibrations of the big engine through his boots on the pedals. The dude that had been chasing him had obviously done some serious modifications to the engine. DeWayne wished that he could really open it up and see what that engine could do, but he didn't dare take the chance. He had gotten lucky with the two cops and the bounty hunter. If he had learned anything from his life, it was that luck like that never lasted.

So I asked if I could have one someday when I
  grew up
Mama dropped a dozen eggs, she really blew up
She really blew up,
I didn't understand
Mama said the pistol is the devil's right hand.

The police scanner under the dashboard crackled. DeWayne leaned over and turned it up. A garbled voice on the other end checked in with the dispatcher. DeWayne squinted as he passed an exit sign. A highway patrolman was three exits ahead, a good ten miles. DeWayne figured he'd better get off the main road. He wasn't sure that anyone was looking for this car, but he wasn't taking any chances.

There was a cluster of businesses at the top of the ramp: a shabby-looking motel, a discount cigarette outlet, and a Handi Mart convenience store. Only the last one was open, its bug-spattered floodlights creating an island of harsh brilliance in the darkness. DeWayne swung the car into the empty parking lot of the convenience store. There was nobody inside except the guy behind the counter. DeWayne could see him through the window, flipping through a magazine. DeWayne looked at the gas gauge. About a quarter tank. He took a deep breath. He needed money and gas. A cigarette and a beer wouldn't hurt, either.

The devil's right hand
the devil's right hand,
Mama said the pistol is the devil's right hand

DeWayne reached for the gun on the seat beside him.

He had tried to argue with the nurse about the wheelchair, even though he knew from the start it was a losing battle. "I know, I know," she had cut him off when he tried to protest that he could walk. "You a big, strong man. But you fall down and break your leg leavin' this hospital," she said, "it ain't your silly ass they're going to blame. It's me, and I got two years left 'til my profit-sharing plan vests, and I ain't losin' that over you, hear? Once you get to the front door, you can do anything you want. Right now, sit your butt down in that chair for Emma like a good boy, okay?" Keller sat. They made the elevator ride down in silence.

Angela stood up as they came off the elevator into the lobby. She stood there and looked at him as he stood up. He walked over to her.

"You all right?" she said.

"Yeah."

She reached up and touched the bandage on his nose, lightly. "Does it hurt?"

"A little."

"Damn it, Keller," she said, her voice breaking, "you scared the shit out of me." She threw her arms around him. He took her in his arms and hugged her tightly to him. After a few moments, she pulled away, wiping her eyes. Keller looked back at the nurse who was standing with the wheelchair. "Looks like my ride's here," he said.

The nurse smiled. "I see that." She looked at Angela. "This your man, honey?"

Angela looked at Keller. "No," she said, a small smile playing over her lips. "I'm his boss."

"Good for you," the nurse said. "Get him trained right."

Angela laughed out loud at that. "No, I mean he really does work for me." Her smile turned a little sad. "We're just friends."

"Uh-huh," the nurse said. She sounded unconvinced. "Well, y'all have a good day." She backed into the elevator and closed the doors.

"Ready to go home?" she said.

"I need you to find out something for me first," he said.

"What?"

As they walked to the parking lot, he told her about Wesson's shooting. She listened in silence to the end. By that time, they were sitting in Angela's car.

"So what do you want me to do?" she said. Her voice sounded strange to Keller.

"Internal Affairs will be investigating. They always do in a cop shooting. I need you to make a few calls to your friends in the department. Find out what's going on, when the hearing is. I need to be there to tell what really happened."

Angela shook her head. "Why are you doing this, Keller?"

He was getting angry. "I don't know why I have to keep explaining this, especially to you. She didn't do anything wrong. She's getting screwed by her own department. And I can do something about it."

Angela shook her head. She was silent for a few

minutes. A couple of times she opened her mouth as if to say something, then shut it. She looked as if she was debating something with herself. Finally, she sighed. "Jack, this is why I won't go out with you."

He was baffled. "What does this have to do with you not wanting to go out with me?"

She turned and looked him in the eye. "For some reason, you think it's your job to rescue the world. So now you've found yourself another damsel in distress."

"Don't tell me you're getting jealous now. Jesus, your timing is worse than mine."

"That's not what this is about!" she snapped.

"Then what is it?" he demanded.

Angela looked away for a long minute. She took a deep breath. Finally, she said in a quiet voice: "That look in your eyes you get when you talk about her. I've seen that look. It's the same way you look at me. You treat me like I'm someone who needs big, strong Jackson Keller to pull her out of the fire." She turned back to him. "Well, Jack, I have news for you. I may have been fucked over, beaten up, and set on fire, but I don't need help. I can rescue myself. And so can she."

Keller threw up his hands. "I can't figure you out, Angela. One minute, you've got your arms around me like you never want to let me go, the next you're telling me what an idiot I am."

She looked at him soberly. "I never said I didn't

care about you, Keller. Like I said, you're a good man. You're kind and strong, and let's face it," she gave him a sad smile, "you're easy on the eyes." The smile vanished and she looked away. "There've been times when I've wanted to take you up on your offer. But we both know what it would mean. There's no way either of us could just casually date." The smile this time was almost bitter. "We are not casual people. It would be way too easy for me to fall for you, Keller. And I don't know what being in love with you would do to me. I'm afraid I might end up feeling the same way you do. And that would destroy me, Jack. It would make me the same scared, dependent person I was with—with my husband."

Keller put his hand on her arm. "I'm not that guy, Angela."

There were tears in her eyes. "But I'm that woman, Jack. At least I know I can be. I have been. And I'll spend the rest of my life alone before I'll be her again."

He thought about that as she started the car. They didn't speak for a long time. Finally she said, "I'll make a few calls. In the morning."

"Thanks," he said. She just nodded.

There were two cops, a little guy with a mustache and a big guy. Raymond closed his eyes as they entered, but he wasn't fast enough. "Forget it,

Chief," the big cop said. "We know you're awake."

Raymond opened his eyes. "I got nothing to say."

"You don't want to find out what happened to your brother?" The big one said. Raymond didn't answer.

The short cop, the one with the bald head and the moustache, pulled up a chair and sat next to the bed. He took a piece of paper from his file folder and laid it on Raymond's chest. It was a color photograph of John Lee sprawled against the wall next to the door of the house. His eyes were wide open in shock. His shirt across his chest was shredded and the flesh beneath looked like chopped meat. Raymond closed his eyes.

"Someone shot your brother with a heavy-gauge shotgun," he heard the big cop say. "We didn't find a gun on or near him, so we figure he was unarmed. That sound right, Chief?"

"Quit calling me Chief," Raymond said.

"Stace," the bald cop said, "Zip it, okay? Go sit down outside or something. You've done enough this evening."

There was a short pause. Even with his eyes closed, Raymond could feel the tension in the room. Finally, he heard a rustling of curtains as the big cop left. He felt something else being laid on his chest. He opened his eyes.

The bald cop had laid another photograph in front of him. This was in black and white. The numbers along the bottom identified it as a police mug shot. The picture showed a man with shoulder-length curly blond hair brushed back from a high forehead. His eyes looked pale in the camera. His square jaw was clenched as if he were gritting his teeth.

"This guy look familiar to you?" the bald cop asked.

"I never seen him before," Raymond said.

"His name's Jackson Keller. Works for H & H Bail Bonds out of Wilmington." The bald cop picked up the picture. "He's a bounty hunter. We think he was after a guy named DeWayne Puryear. We found DeWayne's cousin Leonard dead just inside the house." He stood up. "You get into some kind of argument with him? Maybe you had some sort of personal beef with one of the Puryear boys and Keller got in the way?" Raymond turned his head away from the side of the bed where the cop was sitting. He watched the green lights and numbers flicker on and off on the machines beside the bed.

"Sorry about your father," the cop said. "Must be tough losing a father and a brother the same week."

Raymond turned back to look at him. "You don't care nothin' about my Daddy. Or my brother."

The cop obviously sensed an opening. He sat back down. Raymond cut him off before he could say anything else. "No one cares. I know damn sure you don't." He looked at the ceiling. "I got nothing more to say. Get my doctor."

The cop didn't move. "We got two dead in that house, Raymond, and no guns in anyone's hands but yours. It's only a matter of time before we get a ballistics match between the bullets we dug out of Leonard Puryear and the gun we found next to you. So you're not getting out of here. The guy that killed your brother goes free. And one of the guys who killed your father does, too." Raymond must have looked shocked for a second; the cop smiled slightly. Raymond silently cursed himself for letting his composure slip.

"Robeson County Sheriff's been looking for the Puryear boys in connection with your father's death," he said. "You got no other connection we can see. But it's the end of the line for you, Raymond. If anyone gets the guy that killed your father, it'll be the cops."

Raymond continued to stare at the ceiling. "I got nothing to say," he repeated. "Now get my doctor. I need somethin' for pain."

"Get him yourself," the cop said. He picked up his file folder and walked out. Raymond found the nurse-call button fastened to a cord on the side of the bed. He held it in his hand for a moment, then set it back down. His gut throbbed like someone had fed him burning coals, but he needed his head clear.

His life was over, he knew. When they matched up those bullets, they'd try to lock him up. He had al-

ways told himself that any real man would die rather
than submit to that. He knew he was going to die
soon, and violently. He had known all along he
would probably end like that. It had been something
he had come to accept about the life he had chosen.
But there was some family business to take care of
before he rested. He remembered the face of the man
that the cop had showed him. Puryear and Keller, he
thought. He had to kill them. Then he'd come back
after the cop who had called him "Chief." They
would kill him then, most likely. But he would die on
his feet like a man, having done what a man would
do. He closed his eyes. There would be blood. Blood
and fire, like the end of the world.

A snatch of song came back to him, a hymn he
had heard in church. It seemed like a thousand years
ago, but he remembered the end down through the
years. The song had been about the story of Noah. *No
more water,* the song had ended, *but the fire next time.*

"The fire next time," Raymond whispered to
himself.

The counterman's eyes widened when he
saw the gun in DeWayne's hand. DeWayne set down
two six-packs of Budweiser and a carton of cigarettes.

"Open up the register, buddy," DeWayne said.

"And turn the gas pumps on"—he looked at the plastic badge on the kid's cheap polyester shirt—"Todd."

The guy didn't move, except to start trembling. He was a skinny guy, and young. He didn't look to be more than sixteen or seventeen. His hair was cut short and there was a silver earring stuck in a fold of flesh above his left eyebrow.

"Man," DeWayne said. "Don't that thing hurt?" Todd opened his mouth, but no words came out. He shut it. "Ya don't talk much," DeWayne observed. "I like that. Now do what I say an' give me the damn money."

The kid never took his eyes off the gun. He fumbled a few times getting the register open. He pulled a few bills off the top. DeWayne impatiently reached over the counter and grabbed for the bills. "The gas pumps now," he said. "Hurry up." The kid walked over to the black plastic controls for the pumps and stood there for a minute. His hands gripped the side of the console and he stared down at it as if trying to figure it out. DeWayne could see the kid's hands still shaking. "C'mon, God damn it," he muttered. "I ain't got all fuckin' night." The kid's shaking got worse. DeWayne saw a tear fall onto the control box. "P-p-please, Mister—" the kid sobbed. "D-don't shoot me."

"Oh for Chrissakes." DeWayne said. Why the hell couldn't anyone do what they were told? He marched around the counter and shoved the kid out of the way. The kid collapsed in a corner and pulled his knees up to his chest. It took a few moments for DeWayne to figure out how to turn the pumps on. He turned back to tell Leonard to go pump the gas while he kept the gun on the kid. That was when it hit him. Leonard wasn't there. Leonard would never be there, never again. DeWayne had pushed the fact out of his mind while he concentrated on his escape, but now it burst on him like a flood. The control panel in front of him went all blurry. It was like he was going blind. It was then DeWayne realized his eyes were full of tears. He smashed the pistol butt down on the console, again and again. He whirled around, screaming like an animal in the narrow confines of the area behind the counter. He swept a rack of cheap cassette tapes onto the floor, followed by an upright rack containing the latest edition of the *Weekly World News* and another rack of snack crackers. The kid screamed at DeWayne's sudden explosion of rage and covered his head with his hands. DeWayne whirled on him with the gun. The kid looked up in sudden panic.

"I ran out on him," DeWayne rasped. "That sumbitch killed him, and I ran."

"It's all right," the kid croaked. He was obviously baffled, but desperate. "It'll be okay . . ."

"Like *hell* it is!" DeWayne screamed. He

slammed the gun down on the counter. "You don't know *shit*!" DeWayne shouted down into the kid's face. "He never ran out on *me! Never!*"

"Please, mister," the kid sobbed. "Please . . ."

When they were kids, DeWayne had been a strange child, prone to tantrums that no one could explain or control. His aunt and uncle blamed it on his mother having run off, leaving six-month-old DeWayne in their care. As he got older, the tantrums matured into fits of berserk rage in which DeWayne would throw fists, bottles, anything handy. Once he had tried to slash another kid's throat with a box cutter over a half-pint of milk spilled in the school cafeteria. He was twelve at the time. DeWayne had bounced in and out of juvenile court more times than he could remember and had been suspended so many times that the entire school seemed to breathe a sigh of relief when he dropped out. The only one who could calm him down was Leonard, who would wrap DeWayne up in his big arms and silently hold him until the storm passed. Leonard never asked what was wrong, never made any comment at all when the incident was over. He just set DeWayne down, gave him an extra squeeze, and walked away. DeWayne had always depended on that, depended on Leonard's quiet, unquestioning solidity to anchor him and keep him from flying off completely. Now, that was gone. DeWayne felt that familiar, sick giddiness, like he'd been on a roller coaster too long. He staggered slightly as he raised the gun.

"Please!" the kid shrieked. A dark stain appeared at the crotch of his jeans as he wet himself. When DeWayne saw the slowly spreading stain and the puddle that was collecting under the kid's ass, he began to laugh. It began as a slow bubbling chuckle with an edge of hysteria. The laugh picked up speed and depth as the kid's face showed the dawning realization of what he had done, and quickly exploded into a full-out belly laugh that left DeWayne clutching his stomach with one hand as he held the gun on the kid with the other. He slid slowly to the floor on the other side of the area behind the counter, laughing, his gun hand never wavering. The kid looked uncertain for a minute, then angry, then he started to laugh along, forcing it out as if to placate the man with the pistol. The falsity of the sound sobered DeWayne immediately. "Okay," he said, "you can cut it out." The kid stopped, his face again frozen in a mask of fear. DeWayne reached up and pulled the carton of cigarettes down off the counter. He ripped it open with one hand and took out a pack. He ripped the cellophane off the pack with his teeth and opened the pack, tapping a cigarette out and withdrawing it with his teeth. He offered the clerk one, but the kid shook his head.

"Good for you, bubba," DeWayne said. "These things'll sure as hell shorten your life." He looked over at the kid. "I kilt two men tonight," he said. "Maybe three," he added, thinking of how the blonde dude had looked after DeWayne had kicked him in the head. "One of 'em was a cop. So I reckon it don't much matter if I kill you. I'm gonna die if they catch me. They either gonna shoot me down like a dog in the street or they're gonna strap me down a few years from now and shoot a load of poison into me. What's one more dead guy to me now? And you can tell the cops I been here. And what I looked like, and what I was drivin'. Don't think I want to give up that ride just yet."

"I won't say anything," the kid whispered. "I promise."

DeWayne snorted in derision. "Right," he said. "Boss comes back, all the money's gone from the register, you got a tank o' gas not paid fer, and two sixes of beer missin', plus a carton of smokes. An' you're not gonna say anything about where they've gone? Don't bullshit me, Todd."

"Please," the kid begged, "please don't kill me."

"It's not like I want to, kid," DeWayne said with real regret in his voice. "I ain't got to where I enjoy it. Not yet, an' I suppose that's a blessin'. But it's like I said. I can't take no chances. I coulda shot a couple other people tonight. I didn't do it. Now— I'm thinkin' maybe I oughta done it." The kid began to sob uncontrollably then. DeWayne's earlier frenzy had worn off. All he felt now was tired, bone-weary. The kid's wailing was beginning to get on his nerves. Besides he had to get moving. He raised the gun. It felt like it weighed a thousand pounds. As he took aim, an idea came to him.

"Kid," he said. Todd sobbed harder. "Kid! Damn it, look up!" Finally, Todd raised his tear-streaked face. He looked like a three-year-old.

"You got a girlfriend, bubba?" DeWayne asked. After a moment, the kid nodded. "You got a picture of her?" Todd looked at him dumfounded for a moment, then pulled out his wallet. "Slide that over to me," DeWayne said. Todd did. DeWayne picked it up and flipped it open. A picture of a young blonde girl stared up at him. She was seated in a porch swing, looking at the camera with a bright smile. DeWayne stared at the picture for a long moment and sighed. There was a whole world in that picture that De-Wayne would never see. "She's a cutie pie there, Todd," he said. "What's her name?"

"S-s-Sandy," Todd said.

"Y'all got it on yet?" he asked.

"Th-that's—n-none of your—" Todd stammered.

"Thought not," DeWayne grinned. "So where's she live?" DeWayne said. There was no answer. He looked up. Todd was staring at him with an expression of horror. DeWayne raised the gun again. "Answer the question, Todd," he said.

Todd shook his head. "No," he said. "No way. You'll hurt her."

"I ain't never hurt a woman before in my life that didn't deserve it," DeWayne said. "But I tell you my plan. When the cops get here, you tell 'em a pair of wild-ass screamin' niggers in a pickup truck come in here with bandanas on and robbed you." He gestured toward the parking lot with his head. "I got a police scanner in my vehicle yonder. I hear anything different, like a good description of me or my car, I pay Miss Sandy here a visit right quick. If I'm gonna spend the rest of my life in the joint waitin' to die, I figger I'm gonna need one last bit of pussy to tide me over, know what I mean? But if you do like I say, she'll be okay and save that nice cherry just for you. Or," he said, raising the gun again, "I could just kill you and not worry about it. So what's it gonna be, Todd?" He pulled back the hammer.

"Seventy-one-oh-three   Black   Oak   Church Road!" Todd screamed. "Oh, *God* please don't . . ." DeWayne stood up. He scooped up the beer and cigarettes and walked toward the door.

"Mister?" the kid said. DeWayne stopped and turned back. The clerk gestured toward the ceiling. DeWayne looked up. A small video camera was mounted on the wall behind him, pointed at the sales counter. "There's a videotape of you in here," the kid said. "It won't matter what I say."

"I hope you know how to get the tape out," De-Wayne said. The kid nodded and reached under the counter. DeWayne raised the gun again in case the kid wanted to try anything. He tensed when he saw the black object in the kid's hand until he saw it was a small videotape.

"Thanks, bubba," he said as he walked over and took the tape. "I knew you was a smart one. Now you and that pretty little thing have a nice life together, y'hear?"

He walked out.

"Shit," Angela said as she hung up the phone. She stared at the North Carolina map on the wall of her office for a few moments, gnawing at a fingernail. She was seated behind the desk.

"Anything?" Keller said. He came in and sat in one of the wooden chairs in front of the desk.

Angela shook her head. "Internal Affairs has the whole thing locked down tight. My usual contacts either don't know anything or won't tell me."

"Told you. It's a whitewash. They're trying to cover up for Wesson. And Jones is the sacrificial lamb."

Angela shrugged. "Sorry, Keller. Not much more I can do. You able to get in touch with Jones?"

He shook his head. "She's either not home or screening her calls. I left a couple of messages, but—"

"Maybe she doesn't want to talk to you."

Keller nodded. "Probably. She's caught enough

flak by being associated with me. But I'm the only witness. I need to let her know that I can help her out."

"Keller," Angela said. "Maybe she *wants* to take the fall, you ever think of that?"

Keller shook his head stubbornly. "No way. I don't buy it." He got up and walked to the office door. He leaned against the jamb. The firm's tiny waiting room had a plate glass window that fronted the street. Keller stared for a few moments through the large gilt letters that read H & H BAIL BONDS. Finally, he said, "Wesson's funeral is this afternoon. She'll probably be there."

"No," Angela said. "No way. Keller, those guys will probably shoot you on sight."

"I'll be fine," he said.

Angela threw up her hands. "Jesus. You never give up, do you?"

"It's why you hired me."

6

Eddie Wesson was buried on a hot, humid
summer afternoon, surrounded by fellow officers in
dress uniforms complete with gold braid and white
gloves. Keller could see the crowd through the bars
of the cemetery's heavy wrought-iron fence. He sat
in his rental car across the street from the gates of
the cemetery. A line of cars and pickup trucks
stretched along the curbside, dominated by a long,
black limousine directly in front of the gates. A TV
van idled nearby, its antenna raised and pointed
toward the station, feeding the hunger of the news-
room for more news, faster. A trim young brunette
in an expensive-looking blouse stood by the van,
holding a microphone down by her side. A cameraman and sound technician lounged against the van

with the loose-limbed slouch of soldiers after a long patrol. The woman jumped as shots cracked out, muffled in the heavy, humid air. It looked like they were giving Wesson the full treatment, complete with salute. The technicians knew the signal and hoisted their gear into action positions as the reporter adjusted her earpiece. Keller drummed his fingers on the steering wheel and waited.

People began filing out the front gate, most in dress uniforms. A gray-haired cop with more braid than most was immediately taken aside by the reporter, who stuck her microphone in his face. The older man's reply was brief. Keller picked out the widow by her black dress and the folded flag she carried across her chest with one hand. She held the hand of a bewildered-looking little girl with the other. An older couple stood to either side of her, ready to offer support. The rest of the cops broke up into smaller groups and milled around on the pavement talking to each other. They didn't actually ignore the widow, but no one made a direct attempt to talk to her as she and the child got into the black limousine. Their only connection to her had just been put into the ground. She was not part of their world anymore. The camera lens tracked them into the darkness of the vehicle's interior. Then Keller saw Marie.

She was dressed like the rest of them, in her formal blues, and was again wearing her dark glasses. She walked up to a small knot of officers who were chatting about something, as nonchalantly as if the funeral had never happened. All conversation, however, ceased as Marie walked up. They stood in their circle, not looking at her or at each other. Finally she turned and walked away, her shoulders slumped. Keller swore under his breath and started the car. The brunette reporter detached herself and her team from the crowd and trotted after her. Marie made a go-away gesture with her hand without looking around and walked faster. The reporter persisted, following behind her at a trot and holding the microphone in front of her like a baton being passed to a runner. Finally Marie whirled, and said something short and brutal that caused the reporter to reel backwards, the technicians crashing into her from behind. The reporter turned to shove the sound guy away, cursing. The cameraman was laughing. He continued to film the collision and its aftermath until the reporter made a savage slashing motion across her throat. Marie continued her march down the street alone. Keller pulled out and followed.

Her car was parked at the end of the street near the corner. Keller pulled over and rolled down his window. "Marie," he called to her.

She turned around. Her face hardened. "Shit," she said. "It's you."

"I need to talk to you," Keller said.

She opened the car door. "You're not helping me, you know," she said savagely.

"I can," he insisted. "I'm the only one besides you who knows what really happened. I'm the one who can prove Wesson's death isn't your fault."

"Oh, great," she said, tossing her cap onto the front seat. "That'll make me *real* popular."

"Like you are now?" Keller said.

She sat down in the car, but left her feet on the pavement and her legs outside. "I can make it back from this," she insisted. "It'll blow over. But not if I keep getting seen with you."

"It's not going to blow over, Marie," Keller said. "I've seen this shit before. You're getting shafted." He took a deep breath, hating what he had to say. "You're gone, Marie. It's over. But you don't have to go quietly."

Marie looked up the street. Cars were beginning to pull away from the curb. She swung her legs into her car and closed the door. "C'mon," she said. "I can't be seen with you. Follow me."

"Where are we going?" Keller said.

"My place," she replied. He backed up slightly to allow her to get out, then followed.

Marie Jones lived in a small one-story house with a two-car garage in a development full of nearly identical one-story houses with attached two-car garages. The houses were clustered around cul-desacs off a central street, in an attempt to make neighbors out of the strangers who moved in, stayed a few years until the next transfer, then moved out. Each house had a concrete-slab driveway where the cars were actually parked. The garages had no room for actual vehicles; they were full of lawnmowers, bikes, tool benches, and boxes of things that the families in the houses never actually got unpacked because they were of little use, but never discarded because they were too valuable. Keller parked behind Marie's car in the driveway after she got out to move a plastic Big Wheel from the center of the drive onto the neighbor's lawn next door. He followed her inside.

Inside, the house was small and neatly kept. The front door opened up into a small livingroom with a couch, a recliner, a TV/VCR combination sitting on an old footlocker, and a pair of low, plastic bookshelves. A few plush toys were scattered here and there.

"Wait here," Marie said. "I need to change out of these blues before I keel over from heatstroke." She went off down the hallway, leaving Keller alone.

Keller sat down on the couch. After a few moments, he got up and walked slowly around the living room while he waited. He stopped to look at the pictures that completely filled one wall. In one of the photographs, a much younger Marie was standing, holding a rifle confidently on her hip. She was standing next to a smiling gray-haired man. Another photo showed her cradling a soccer ball in one hand, standing next to the same man. In this picture, the man was in a police uniform. They were both smiling. In another photo, obviously a professional portrait, she was dressed in an army class-A uniform, looking serious against a cloudy silver background. A series of smaller pictures in a collage frame showed her in a variety of situations with a young child: a hospital bed holding an infant, holding a baby in her arms in front of a Christmas tree, bending over to push a laughing toddler in a swing. There was no sign of the father.

Keller heard Marie reenter the room. He continued looking at the pictures. "This your dad?" he said over his shoulder, pointing at the picture of her with the gray-haired man.

"Yeah," she said around a hair clip held in her teeth as she pinned her hair up.

"He was a cop, too."

"Yeah," she said. "Thirty years. He's retired now."

Keller turned around. Marie had changed into a baggy sweatshirt and a pair of running shorts. Her face was drawn and pale and there were dark circles under her eyes.

"Where you from?" he asked.

"Portland, Oregon," she said.

"Miss it?"

She shrugged. "Sometimes."

Keller gestured back at the picture. "Bet your dad loved the idea of his little girl joining the force."

"I'm not a little—" she began, then caught herself and grinned. "Sorry. Conditioned reflex. But yeah, he nearly had a stroke. He got over it."

He looked again at the picture of Marie in her class-As. He noticed another, smaller frame hanging next to it. Instead of a photograph, the frame held a small badge. It was a wreath surrounding an iron cross with a target in the center of it.

"Expert rifleman," he said. "Impressive."

"Thanks," she said. "Dad always wanted a boy to take hunting with him, but he only got daughters. So he taught me to shoot." She grimaced. "For all the good it did me. I ended up in the MPs. Germany." She walked back over to the easy chair and sat down. Keller tried not to stare at her legs. "You were in Saudi, I hear."

"Yeah. And points north."

She smiled a little sadly. "Closest I ever got to a war was directing traffic at Oktoberfest."

"You were lucky," he said. She looked at him strangely and he realized that he had spoken with a bit more heat than he had intended. He looked back at the wall. "Cute kid."

"Thanks," she said. "He's with his grandparents for the weekend."

"Not with your ex?"

Her lips tightened. "You didn't come here to talk about my kid."

"Right." Keller sat down on the couch.

"You said I didn't have to go quietly," she said. "What did you mean?" she said.

"Has anyone come to you and actually said, 'keep your mouth shut, let it blow over, and we'll take care of you'?"

She shook her head and looked at the floor. "No."

"They need someone to blame for Wesson getting killed. Good cops don't let punks like DeWayne Puryear gun them down."

Her voice was bitter. "Good cops don't let punks take their guns away, either."

"You didn't want to get close to him. You tried to argue Wesson out of it. He pulled rank. He did it to show me he was the boss and if I said black, he could say white and that was that. If he hadn't let that blind him, you wouldn't have gotten near enough to Puryear for him to have been able to get your gun."

She shrugged. "So?"

"So, right now Wesson's being treated like a god-damn hero and a good cop can't even get the time of day from the people who are supposed to be her backup. I don't like it. I bet you don't either."

"How do you know so much about it?"

"Like I said. I've been there. I've had the people I trusted to be watching my back turn on me."

She stood up suddenly. "I need a drink," she said. "You want one?"

"Yeah, okay," Keller said. "Whatever you've got."

She went into the kitchen and came back with a pair of rock glasses half filled with ice and a half-empty bottle of Jack Daniel's. She set the glasses on the coffee table in front of Keller and poured each one half full. Keller noticed that her hand shook slightly as she poured. She sat back down in the recliner and drained off half of her glass before Keller had gotten his to his lips. He took a sip. Marie raised the glass again and he heard the edge of it rattle against her teeth as her hand shook again. He set his glass down.

"It's not going to help," he said.

She looked at him. He could see the whites all around her eyes. "What?" she said.

"The booze. It helps blot out what happened, but the only way to get to that place is to get too plastered to think. And it doesn't last. You sober up eventually. And you'll still have the dreams."

"You don't know me. You don't know shit about my dreams," she said. Her voice shook.

"I think I do," he replied. "You're back there on that roadside. Staring down the barrel of that gun. And you're not just afraid you're going to die. You *know* it. You've just seen someone you know, someone you've lived and worked with, cut down. And you're next. You know you are. There's no way you're going to survive. Am I right so far?" She was looking at him with an expression of pure panic on her face. Her breath was coming in short gasps. He couldn't stop himself from going on. "You push it down, pretend it doesn't bother you because that's what it takes to do your job, but it keeps coming back at you. Whenever you stop for a minute, whenever you let down your guard, whenever you lie down at night, you're back there again. On that roadside."

Marie's face went slack. Keller snatched the glass from her limp hand, catching her as she slipped off the chair toward the floor. He guided her down to the carpet. Her body shook feverishly.

"G-G-God," she whispered against his neck. "I was s-s-so *scared!*" He wrapped his arms around her. She clutched him back with the hysterical strength of the drowning. She sobbed into his chest like a child, her whole body convulsed with grief. He pulled himself up to a sitting position against the recliner and rocked her gently, stroking her hair with one hand. "It's okay," he whispered. "I know. I know how it feels. It's okay." He held her like that for a long time as she cried herself out.

Gradually, as she ran out of tears, she quieted. Keller became uncomfortably aware of her body pressed against him. Her breasts pressed into his chest. He became even more aware of how her hands had stopped clutching at him and had become gentler, almost caressing. She turned her tear-streaked face up to him. Her lips were slightly parted and her eyes were glazed. Her hand dropped lower, finding unerring proof of the effect she was having on him. She moaned. The edge of hysteria in her voice made it almost into a whimper.

Keller swore to himself. He had experienced this himself in the aftermath of combat, a surge of pure sexual heat that was the body's response to nearly being snuffed out. It was as if the genes within the body, realizing their fragility, desperately tried to take one last chance to reproduce. He knew that what she was feeling had nothing to do with him. He could have been any warm male body. It was wrong to take advantage of her in the aftermath of her emotional catharsis, he knew that. But her lips under his were warm and yielding, tasting slightly of the whiskey. Her hand stroking him was gentle but insistent. He reached down and pulled her hand away. She made a petulant sound and tried to grab him again. He pinned her hand and gently kissed her on the forehead. She looked at him for a moment as if he had lost his mind. Then she leaned her head against his chest and her body relaxed. She fell asleep as quickly as if she had been blackjacked. Keller sighed. He shifted her body slightly to try to get his arms under her. He stood up, with difficulty, cradling her in his arms. He carried her into the bedroom and laid her on the bed. He found a blanket in the closet and threw it over her. She grumbled a bit in her sleep, but pulled the blanket tighter around her. He stood by the bed for a few moments, watching her breathe. He thought about Angela's words to him.

You think it's your job to rescue the world, she had said. *So now you've found yourself another damsel in distress.* He sighed and shook his head. He walked back out into the living room and stretched out on the couch.

It was dark when he awoke. He sat up, checked his watch. Eleven-thirty. He heard the sound of the shower running. He rubbed the sleep out of his eyes. His back felt cramped from sleeping on the couch. He hadn't realized how tired he was.

After a few minutes, she came out into the living room. She was dressed in a short, white silk robe that belted at the waist. Her hair was still wet from the shower. She sat on the recliner. They looked at each other for a while, neither one speaking.

"Hey," she said finally.

"Hey," he said. "Sleep good?"

She smiled. "Yeah. I, uh—I guess I needed that."

"It's a start. Some things take a while to get over."

"You sound like you know what you're talking about."

He nodded. "Yeah. I've been there."

"You keep saying that."

"I know."

"You get over it?"

He shook his head. "No. Not yet."

"And it's been how long?"

"Ten years."

Marie shook her head. "Jesus." They were silent for a minute. She turned to him. "Look, um, Keller, the way I acted . . ."

"Don't worry about it. You needed to let it go."

"Did you ever lose it like that?"

"No," he grimaced. "It's probably why I'm still so fucked up."

"Hmm," she said. "But anyway, that's not what I meant. Not the crying. The—the other thing."

He looked away and cleared his throat. "Don't worry about that, either, he said. "Stress reaction. Happens a lot to people who—"

"I don't act like that, Keller," she interrupted. "Ever."

"I didn't think so," he said. "Like I said. Stress."

She looked down for a second, then back at him. "What I want to know is—damn it!" She shook her head angrily.

"You want to know why I didn't take you up on it."

She bit her lip. "It's not like I wanted you to—I mean, I did at the time, but I'm not—I mean . . ."

She looked at him with narrowed eyes. "You're not queer or anything, are you?"

He barked out a laugh. "I think you know better," he said. "You had a pretty good grip on the evidence." Her face reddened with embarrassment and Keller immediately felt contrite. "Look," he said. "You know how confused you are right now? Imagine how you'd feel if we *had* done it."

This time it was her turn to laugh. "Okay," she said. "Point taken." She gave him a crooked smile. "A regular Sir Galahad, you are."

He shook his head. "It would have been unfair. Like you say, you weren't yourself. I'd only want it if . . ." He stopped.

"What?" she said.

"Nothing."

She stood up and walked over to stand in front of him. "You'd only want to make love to me if I was myself, is that what you were going to say?" she said softly.

He looked into her eyes. His mouth felt dry. "Yeah."

She looked uncertain for a moment, then took a deep breath. "So what about now?"

He could only nod.

"That may be the nicest thing anyone's ever said to me," she said. She reached up and unbelted the robe. She was naked underneath. She moved forward and seated herself across his lap, straddling his hips.

"I'm feeling a lot better now," she whispered as she kissed him. He hesitated for a moment, then kissed her back, his hands sliding around her to caress up and down her back. She moaned deep in her throat. This time, there was no hysteria, no pain in the sound. She reached down to undo his belt. He raised his hips slightly as she hooked her thumbs into his waistband and yanked his jeans and underwear down to his knees. She moved farther up on him as he grasped her buttocks in his hands and pulled her down. She gasped as they fit together. "Go slow," she whispered. "Please—go slow." He did as she asked, entering her slowly, gasping at the feel of her inner muscles gripping him. She threw her head back for a second and groaned as she slid farther down onto him. Then they were joined together, fitting like puzzle pieces. She opened her eyes to look into his as they began to move.

They took it slowly for a long time, each trying to prolong the exquisite sensations as long as possible. Then control fell away from both of them and they moved faster, their gasps and moans filling the room. He buried his face in her shoulder and clutched her to him tightly as she screamed in climax. He groaned and came as well, feeling as if he was emptying himself into her, all the rage and pain and fear leaving him in one long rush.

They stayed like that for a long while, him still buried deep inside her, her head on his shoulder. Then she looked up. She opened her mouth to say something, but he stopped it with a kiss. They got up and walked together into the bedroom.

"Hey," Raymond called through the curtain. *"Hey!"*

The cop outside poked his head in the door. "Yeah?"

Raymond lifted his hand. The chain on the handcuff jingled as his arm reached the limit of its tether. "Ain't I s'posed to get a phone call if I'm under arrest?"

The cop gave him a nasty grin. "Doesn't look like there's a phone in your room here."

"I want to talk to a lawyer. You keep me from doin' it, my civil rights are violated. Maybe you even have to let me go. You think about that."

The cop's smile vanished. He withdrew into the corridor. Raymond could hear the crackle of the cop's handheld radio and a few muttered words. He lay back against the pillow and waited. His gut ached like a bad tooth, but he had carefully stashed his painkillers. After about a half hour, a young black guy came in, dressed in the blue coverall of the maintenance staff. He was carrying a white plastic phone in one hand. Without a word, he plugged the phone into a wall jack behind the bed and placed the phone on the bedside table. "You dial nine to get a outside line," he mumbled. He didn't look at Raymond as he left.

The cop stuck his head back in. "You got fifteen minutes to make your phone call. Then I'm coming back in and unplugging it. You ain't going to spend the whole night calling nine hundred numbers on the county's dime."

"I don't want you listenin' at the door," Raymond said. "Move off down the hall."

The cop's face reddened. "Listen, you son of a bitch, you ain't givin' me orders."

"I got a right to talk to my lawyer in private." He showed the cuff again. "I ain't goin' nowheres with this thing on."

The cop's jaw worked for a moment. "I'll be right down the hall," he said. "Don't try anything." He backed out into the hall again.

After he was sure the guy was gone, Raymond picked up the phone. He dialed a number he knew by heart, but it wasn't a lawyer that he called.

7

"Fuck," DeWayne said.

He was looking at the back end of the Crown Vic, which stuck halfway out of a ditch at the side of a two-lane country road. Too many beers, too little sleep, and DeWayne had drifted off behind the wheel. His first warning of any danger was the sound of the car's tires ripping through the soft grass and earth of the shoulder. By then it was to late to keep the car out of the ditch. He had sat there for a few moments, too stunned and dazed to realize what had happened. Then he clambered out of the car, toting the paper sack containing the remaining beers and the rest of his cigarettes. He stuffed the pistol inside the bag.

"God *damn it!*" DeWayne fumed. "What the fuck

am I s'posed to do now?" A soft glow over the nearest hill rapidly brightened, then resolved into a pair of headlights. DeWayne briefly considered hiding in the woods, then realized that it was too late for that. The car slowed as it approached. DeWayne tucked the bag tighter into his armpit and waved. The car stopped in the opposite lane.

It was a metallic blue Trans Am with tinted windows. As DeWayne approached, he could hear the pulse of rap music from inside, loud enough that DeWayne could feel the pounding of the bass in his chest, even with the windows rolled up. As the driver's side window came down, the music got even louder. DeWayne couldn't see the driver clearly, beyond a glimpse of blonde hair and a pale blur of face in the green glow of the instrument panel.

"Need help?" a female voice called over the beat.

"Yeah," DeWayne said. "My car—a deer ran in the road. I ran into the ditch. I need a lift."

"Hop in." DeWayne ran around to the passenger side and got in. The interior was as dimly lit and smoky as a nightclub. He smelled the sweet reek of pot smoke as he closed the door. A joint smoldered in the ashtray.

"Whatcha got in the bag?" said the girl behind the wheel. She was a skinny blonde who looked no more than eighteen or nineteen. Her blonde hair was cut short and framed her pale face. Her slightly receding chin and pronounced overbite robbed her of any prettiness she might have had. Still, DeWayne thought, not a bad body, although he would have liked a little more in the tit department. She was dressed in a thin tank top and denim shorts.

"Got some beers," DeWayne said. "Want one?"

Her pale blue eyes showed a muted flicker of interest. She was stoned out of her mind, DeWayne realized. This night was looking better and better. "Sure," she said.

He reached into the bag and fumbled for a full can. The condensation on the cold beers, however, had rendered the bag as flimsy as tissue. It ruptured and spilled its contents onto the floorboard. De-Wayne swore as he fumbled among the cans and cartons.

"Hey," the girl said. "Is that a gun?"

DeWayne picked up the pistol and pointed it at her. "Yeah," he said. "Don't try anything. Just drive."

The girl showed no reaction. "You a bank robber or something?"

Jesus, DeWayne thought, *was she simpleminded?* "Or something, yeah. Now . . ."

"Cool," the girl said. "I never partied with no outlaw before." She smiled, showing her buck teeth. "You got any money? I know where we can get some rocks if you got some cash."

"I got a little," DeWayne admitted.

"Awesome," she said. She put the car in gear. "I'm Debbie," she said as she pulled off.

DeWayne blurted out the first name he could think of. "I'm Leonard—ah, Lenny," he said.

"You wanna party, Lenny?" she said. She picked up the joint from the ashtray, tried to puff on it. It had gone out.

"Honey, I love to party," DeWayne grinned. He took the joint from her fingers and put it between his lips. He punched the cigarette lighter.

"Awesome," she said again.

Keller awoke with the morning sun streaming through the bedroom blinds. Marie was lying on her side next to him. He slipped an arm around her. She murmured something and snuggled back against him. He lay like that with her for a few moments before the pressure in his bladder became too demanding.

When he came back from the bathroom, she was sitting up in the bed, blinking. She looked up at him and an expression of surprise flitted across her face. Then she smiled, a little shyly.

"Hey," she said.

"Hey," he said.

She looked at the clock. "Wow," she said. "I never sleep this late."

He sat down next to her on the bed and put his arm around her. He tried to kiss her on the mouth, but she turned her head slightly and caught it on her cheek. She turned back to him, put a finger over her lips. "Dragon breath," she explained. "Not you," she added hastily, "me."

He laughed. "I don't mind." He kissed her again, this time on the mouth. "Mmmmm," she said. She broke the kiss. "Thanks for last night," she whispered. "And thanks for staying. It—well, let's just say it's been a while."

"I could tell."

She pulled away and pulled the sheet around her defensively. "What," she said, looking down at the floor, "you're saying I'm out of practice? It wasn't good?" She gave a short, abrupt laugh. "I didn't hear any complaints."

"No, no," he pulled her close again. "But it was like you were making up for lost time."

She thought that over for a moment. "I'm trying to decide if that was a compliment."

"It was."

She smiled and relaxed against him again. She reached up and kissed him on the chin. "Maybe you just better quit talking. It's not your strong point." She turned to him and let the sheet fall. "Besides, I have some more lost time to make up for."

Afterward, they lay together in a tangle of limbs and sweaty sheets. Marie stretched like a cat and smiled. "Hungry?"

"Yeah," he replied.

She jumped up and threw her robe on. "Wait here," she said. "I'll whip something up."

"Breakfast in bed?" Keller said.

She laughed. "Not hardly. I'll call you when it's ready."

Keller lay back on the bed and closed his eyes. He had almost drifted back into sleep when he heard a sound, a rattle and buzz that sounded oddly familiar. As he struggled to place the noise, it came again. It sounded as if some huge insect was buzzing against the floor. Keller sat up and looked over the edge of the bed. His jeans lay in a heap on the floor, his belt still drawn through the loops. It was his cell phone in its holster on one of the loops that was vibrating with its silent ring. Keller considered not answering. Then he sighed. He plucked the phone from the holster and flipped it open. "Keller," he said.

"Where are you?" Angela's voice sounded tense. Keller fumbled over his answer, but she cut him off. "Never mind," she said. "The Highway Patrol found your car."

Keller sat up. "Where?"

"In a ditch in Bladen County."

"Anybody in it?"

"No," Angela said. "But they did find a gym bag full of bloody clothes."

"Damn," he said.

"Keller, they'll be testing those. They're probably doing it now. And when they get a match on the blood—"

"They'll know I was at the Puryear house," he said.

"I've already gotten a call, Keller," she said. "They want you to come down to the station and talk to them."

"Who's they?"

"A Fayetteville detective named Stacy."

"Yeah," Keller said. "I'll bet he wants to talk."

"What do I tell them, Jack?" she said.

Keller looked around the room. He saw Marie's uniform cap on the top of the dresser. Her badge lay next to it, glinting in the morning light that came through the blinds.

"Tell them you don't know where I am," he said. "It's the truth. And call McCaskill."

"I already did," she replied. "He's in court. I had to leave a message. Jack, if they think you're running . . ."

"I'm not running," he said. "I just don't want to talk to them right now. I'll be fine."

Marie's voice came from the other room. "Breakfast," she called out. Keller gritted his teeth, wondering if Angela could hear. Her tone when she finally spoke made it clear that she had.

"Yeah," she said. "You'll be fine." He started to

say something, but she had hung up. Keller shook his head and snapped the phone shut. He stood up and pulled his jeans on.

Marie was seated at the table in the kitchen, a bowl of cereal in front of her. There was another bowl across the table from her. "It's just corn flakes," she said. "But the strawberries are fresh." She smiled, a little apologetically. "I'm not much of a cook."

"This is good," he said as he sat down.

"Who were you talking to?" she asked. He started to say something, then he saw in his mind's eye the golden badge sitting on Marie's dresser.

"Just checking in at work," he said. "Seeing if there was anything new on DeWayne Puryear."

"Was there?"

"No."

Marie shook her head. "Don't worry about him anymore, Keller," she said. "He's our problem now. He shot a cop."

Keller cocked an eyebrow at her. "Our problem? I thought you were suspended."

She looked down at her cereal. "Yeah. Well. You know how it is. Once a cop, always a cop."

"Yeah," he said. "I know."

She looked at him and sighed. "You're not going to give up on this, are you?" she said.

"I need to find him," he said.

She got up and carried her cereal bowl to the sink. "Okay," she said, not looking at him. "It wasn't like I had anything to do in the next few days anyway."

"What do you mean?"

She turned back to him. She crossed her arms across her chest and looked at him levelly. "I mean I'll help."

Keller was silent for a moment. The words stirred an unaccountable feeling of dread in him. *I work alone,* he wanted to say. What he did say was, "You don't have to."

Her mouth was set in a hard line. "That son of a bitch shot my partner. I want his ass in custody as bad as you do."

Keller had no answer for that. "So where do we start?" she said after a long pause.

He thought for a minute. "The sister," he said. "She's the only family connection we have."

Marie nodded. "She was held for a while, charged with harboring a fugitive. I heard she made bail."

Keller stood up and carried his bowl to the sink. "We'll start with her house, then."

What this Debbie lacked in looks, DeWayne
thought, she made up in enthusiasm, at least once he

had used some of his dwindling money supply to get her a supply of rocks. He lay back on the bed, feeling as if all of the fluid had been drained from his body. Debbie sat at the other end of the bed, naked. She was preparing another hit of the rock cocaine, using the pipe she had constructed out of a beer can. She had punched a hole down at one end and made a bowl out of tinfoil, taping the bowl in place with electrical tape. She lit up with a disposable plastic lighter, cranking the flame up all the way so it sputtered like a tiny flamethrower. Debbie applied the flame to the bowl and drew deeply on the smoke. She threw her head back, her eyes closed in ecstasy, and held the smoke in her lungs. DeWayne looked away, feeling a little queasy. He had never heard anyone say anything good about crack. It seemed to keep Debbie happy and horny, though, so he put up with it.

He focused on the TV behind her. It was another one of the things about Debbie that DeWayne found disquieting. She always had to have something playing: radio, CD player, TV. It was as if she was afraid of silence. Even when they were doing it, she had to have the TV on. He was sure she wasn't watching it as they did it, though. Pretty sure.

Debbie reached the end of her lungs' endurance and blew a long stream of smoke out her nostrils. She lowered her head and looked at DeWayne. Her eyes were bright and glassy. "Meeee-ow." she leered at him. She started crawling up the bed toward him, her small breasts swinging beneath her.

"Aww, c'mon, honey," DeWayne said, trying not to make it sound like a whine. "I'm spent."

She stuck out her lower lip. "You ought to try you one of these rocks," she said. "It'd put lead in your pencil." She began rubbing her cheek against his thigh, just above the knee. DeWayne closed his eyes. She was starting to get to him again. Suddenly, the TV caught his attention.

"Hey," he said, "turn that up."

"Huh?" she replied, but he was crawling past her. She squealed in protest as he almost knocked her off the bed. The room was so small that DeWayne could lean off the end of the bed and reach the volume control.

The eleven o'clock news was on. Over the shoulder of the pretty young anchorwoman, DeWayne could see a little box. In the box was the face of the guy who had stuffed him in the trunk.

". . . in connection with a shootout in Fayetteville that left two men dead, another critically wounded, and which may have been connected with the later shooting of a Fayetteville police officer."

The newscaster's face dissolved to a videotape of the Crown Vic being pulled out of the ditch by a wrecker. Everything in the picture was lit up in the fluorescent green glow of a night vision camera.

"Police now say they have located a vehicle belonging to Jackson Keller, a bail bondsman operating out of Wilmington. Clothing found in the vehicle bore traces of blood that matched one of the victims, one Leonard Puryear."

The car vanished off the screen and was replaced by an old photograph of Leonard. Quick tears stung DeWayne's eyes as he looked into his cousin's face.

"Hey," Debbie said, leaning into him from behind. "Ain't that your name?"

"Shut up," DeWayne said.

The newscaster went on. "Also killed in the gun battle was John Lee Oxendine of Robeson County." Leonard's face slid to one side of the screen. The other side was filled with a face that DeWayne didn't know. "Authorities state that Oxendine was unarmed at the time and was most likely an innocent bystander."

"Bullshit," DeWayne muttered.

Both faces vanished to be replaced by the pretty newscaster, her face a study in vapid concern. Keller's face was back in the box looking over her shoulder. "Police also say Keller is wanted for questioning in the deaths of Puryear's elderly parents a few days ago."

DeWayne's mouth dropped open. He felt a sick feeling in the pit of his stomach. "What the . . .," he whispered.

"Keller had reportedly been searching for another member of Puryear's family in connection with a bail violation. When asked if Keller was a suspect in the deaths, police had no comment, other than to say that anyone sighting Keller should immediately notify the Fayetteville police department." The camera pulled back to reveal the second anchor, a distinguished-looking man with gray hair. He was shaking his head with a look of grim resolution on his craggy face.

"These so-called 'bounty hunters,'" he said in a deep, measured tone. "They're loose cannons. Something needs to be done."

The female anchor matched his serious expression and nodded in unison with him. "You're certainly right, Tom."

The camera panned to the man. The serious expression melted away to be replaced by a smile that must have cost a fortune. "Coming up, will this warm weather give way to some much-needed rain? Stay tuned, as the news continues."

"That son of a *bitch!*" DeWayne exploded. He leaped up from the bed.

"What's going on?" Debbie said frantically.

DeWayne paced back and forth in the narrow confines of the bedroom like a tiger in a too-small cage. "Son of a bitch," he snarled. "Son of a bitch."

"Hey. Lenny. Or whatever," Debbie said pleadingly. "You're scaring me. What happened? Please, just tell me what happened."

DeWayne stopped and looked at her. His eyes

were wild. "That son of a bitch," he repeated. "That guy Keller. They just said he killed my folks. The folks who raised me."

She looked puzzled. "Did they say that? I didn't hear."

"Oh, they didn't come right out and say it," De-Wayne said. "They won't till they catch him and charge him. But he did it. He did it to try to get to me."

She pondered that for a moment. "Wow," she said finally. "That sucks. What an asshole." She reached for the pipe again. "You sure you don't want a hit?" she said. "It might make you feel better."

He briefly considered backhanding her to shut her stupid mouth. But she seemed to be looking at him with real concern as she held out the improvised pipe. And he could surely use something right now to make all this hurt go away.

"Yeah," he said, reaching for the pipe. "Okay."

In the daylight, Crystal Puryear's house seemed sad and worn. The sunlight revealed the dirt-caked windows, the warping trim, and the peeling paint that had never been applied all that well to start with. It was nearly noon, but the shades were still drawn. Only the Corvette in the driveway gave any sign that anyone even lived there. There was still a ragged shred of yellow crime-scene tape knotted around one of the posts of the porch.

They had come in Marie's car, but it was Keller who led the way up the walk. He slowed as he approached the doorway, tensing as he recalled the gun battle in the yard. He glanced over at the ground by the door where John Lee Oxendine had lain with his chest blown apart by Keller's shotgun. He thought he could see a reddish tinge of bloodstain on the paint, but it might have been his imagination. He stopped for a moment, causing Marie to almost bump into the back of him.

"Jack?" she said. "You okay?"

"Yeah," he said. He took a deep breath and stepped to the door. The plastic button of the doorbell was gone, leaving only a pair of rusty wires sticking out of the jamb. Keller knocked. There was no answer, no movement within the house. He knocked again and waited. There was no response. Keller tried the knob.

"Hey," Marie said. "We don't have a warrant."

"That's okay," he said. "I'm not a cop." He turned the knob. The door was unlocked.

"Who the hell leaves a door unlocked in this neighborhood?" Marie said.

"Someone who doesn't care what happens to them," Keller said grimly. He drew his gun and entered.

The hallway was dim, but he could see a flicker of light from the living room at the end. There was a tinny bubbling of canned laughter and a woman's voice, high-pitched and strident. The TV was on. Keller advanced down the hallway, the pistol held in a two-handed grip in front of him. He reached the end of the hallway and the gun fell to his side.

Crystal Puryear lay on the couch, dressed in a flimsy silk bathrobe that had fallen open to reveal her nude body. Her limbs were splayed in a parody of invitation made grotesque by her utter limpness. Her head lolled against the back of the couch, her mouth open. A thin line of drool ran down her chin.

Keller holstered the gun and strode over to her. He took in the objects on the coffee table: A silver cellular phone. A black pager. An empty plastic envelope. A burned-out candle. A soot-covered spoon. He looked around for the syringe. Finally he located it. It was still lodged in her arm.

"Holy shit," Marie said. She sprang to the couch and placed her right index and middle fingers against Crystal's throat. "I've got a pulse, but it's weak," she said briskly. "Call 911."

Keller moved toward the phone, then stopped. Calling 911 would bring paramedics, but it would most likely also bring police. He turned back to Marie. She had belted Crystal's robe shut and was gently removing the syringe from the girl's arm. A bright red bead of blood formed, turned to a rivulet that inched its way down the pale flesh.

"We don't have time to wait for them," he said. "We'll take her in your car." He scooped the pager and cell phone off the table. Each had a plastic clip for fastening to a belt.

"Damn it, Keller," Marie said, "she needs a doctor."

Keller clipped the devices onto his belt and bent down to lift the girl. Her body was a sodden deadweight in his arms. He grunted as he lifted her.

"She needs a doctor now," he said, his voice taut with the strain. "By the time the ambulance makes it here, it might be too late." He set off down the hall.

"This is crazy," Marie protested, but she followed him. He burst into the sunlight. Marie jogged ahead, pulling her keys from the pocket of her jeans. She threw the back door of her Honda open. Keller tried to lay the girl gently into the back, but lost his grip and she tumbled onto the back seat. A grunt escaped her as she landed and her robe fell open again.

"You know CPR, right?" he asked Marie.

"Yeah, but—"

"Hop in the back with her, then," he said. "In case she goes into cardiac arrest. I'll drive."

"You are out of your mind," she said as she got in the back. "I can't give CPR in the back seat of a—whoa!" Keller had started the car and begun pulling away. Marie barely had time to pull the door shut.

They drove in silence, broken only by the screech of tires and the angry blare of horns as Keller ignored stoplights and yield signs. He stole a glance at Marie in the rearview mirror. She had her eyes on the girl whose shallow breathing seemed about to cease at any moment. Keller heard a slight chirring noise and felt a vibration against his right hip. He reached down and plucked the pager off his belt. He looked at the number displayed on the pager's LED screen. He memorized the number and put the pager down on the seat.

"What was that?" Marie said.

"Her pager. Someone's trying to reach her. Maybe someone who can give us a lead."

"It's probably her pimp," Marie said. "Or her dealer. What would they know about her cousin?"

"I don't know," Keller said, "but I'm out of other ideas."

They had reached the emergency entrance of the hospital. Keller slammed to a stop at the front door and leaped out. Marie opened the back door and Keller reached in for the girl. Marie stopped him with a hand on his chest. "Don't try to move her again," she said. "They've got gurneys. And doctors." Keller stepped back as Marie stood up and ran to the entrance. The heavy automatic sliding door was barely open before she bolted inside. She was back in moments with a white-coated man and a pair of nurses wheeling a gurney between them. They elbowed Keller out of the way and descended on the back seat of the Honda. They briskly loaded her onto the gurney and sped back through the front door. Marie followed, spitting out the statistics of

Crystal's condition in abrupt, precise sentences. It was left to Keller to close the car doors and move the vehicle away from the front entrance. He found the ER visitors' parking lot and parked the car. He was headed back toward the entrance when he saw Marie walking out. He stopped to wait for her. She was shaking her head and putting her sunglasses on as she reached him.

"Get in the car, Jack," she said. "And I'll drive, if you don't mind. It *is* my car." He handed her the keys. They walked back to the car and got in.

"Keller," she said as she started the car. "That was a really stupid stunt." He said nothing. She put her hand across the back of the seat and looked back as she backed out. "I mean, I know you're not real crazy about cops right now." She put the car in gear and drove off. "And let's face it, they're not all that fond of you, either. But that girl could have died while you were trying to do it all yourself."

"I figured you could handle it," he said.

She made a face. "Thanks," she said. "But next time, let's get together on the decision. Or better yet, leave this kind of thing to the pros, all right?"

Keller shrugged and said nothing. Marie sighed. "I'd like to find that girl who sang about 'where have all the cowboys gone' and slap her in her silly face," she muttered. That made Keller laugh. "Okay," he said. "You win."

The cell phone chirred again on the seat between

them. Keller looked at Marie. "Maybe you should get that," he said.

Marie looked at him in amazement. "Why me?"

"Because a man's voice might cause them to hang up." He handed her the phone. She shook her head, but flipped it open and put it to her ear. "Hello?" There was a sudden burst of words from whoever was on the other end. Keller couldn't make out the words or the voice, but he could sense the anger and the threat in the voice even from across the car.

"Whoa, Whoa," Marie said. "Amber's not here. She's, ah sick."

Another blast of sound from the phone. Marie's face reddened. "Listen, you," she snarled, "this is—" Keller reached out and plucked the phone from her hand. He put it to his ear.

The voice was so deep and raspy that Keller at first didn't realize it was a woman. ". . . tell that little cunt if she doesn't get her lazy ass back to work, I'll fuck her face up so bad her own mama won't want to kiss her. You got that, bitch?"

"I got it," Keller said. "But I doubt she'll be much good for work for a few days."

Silence, then, "Who the hell are you?"

"A friend of the family," Keller replied. "Crys—I mean Amber's in the hospital. She's at Fayetteville General if you want to . . ." There was a click and the line went dead. Keller put the phone down.

"You told her where to find the girl," Marie said. She didn't sound happy.

"Yeah," Keller said. "Drop me off at my car. I'll double back to the hospital and see who shows up."

"I don't think I like you using that girl as bait," Marie said.

"It's possible that DeWayne might hear about it, Marie. The guy who killed your partner. He might show up there. Then he's all ours."

"All yours, you mean."

"Hell, you can have the collar," Keller said. "It might get you back in good with the department."

She shook her head. "I feel like I'm making a deal with the devil."

"Welcome to my world, Marie."

8

They had moved him out of intensive care
into a private room. Raymond had overheard an argument over that. Detective Barnes clearly didn't
want to commit the city to paying for a private
room. He faced off outside Raymond's ICU cubicle
with some guy from the hospital who refused to put
another patient in with a "dangerous criminal."
From this, Raymond surmised that they had
matched up the slugs from Leonard Puryear with
the ones from the gun found with Raymond. In the
end, fear of citizen lawsuits had prevailed and Raymond was left pretty much to himself. He suspected
that the doctors were keeping him in the hospital
longer than they normally would because they knew

he was headed straight to jail to await trial once they turned him loose.

The city may have been forced to spring for a private room, but they weren't going to give him a TV. Raymond spent much of his time staring out the window at a narrow blue strip of sky between two other buildings. The only breaks in the monotony of his days were when they got him up and made him walk up and down the halls for exercise. Raymond was stashing his pain medication rather than taking it. It hurt his gut like fire to walk up and down the halls, but he bore up.

He was always escorted on these walks by a uniformed cop who looked bored when he wasn't flirting with the nurses. The pair of them sometimes drew odd looks from visitors, but the rest of the staff by now hardly gave them a second glance.

It was on one of these morning constitutionals that he noticed a familiar figure sitting in one of the visitor's lounges. The lounges were glass-windowed enclosures to which family members and friends of patients were banished whenever it came time for the nurses to perform some uncomfortable and humiliating ritual on the patient. This morning, the lounge was empty except for a big man in a checked flannel shirt sitting in one of the chairs. The man held a magazine up before him, but the ice-blue eyes that could be seen between the top of the magazine and the baseball cap pulled down low on his forehead were fixed on the hall. As Raymond passed by, the magazine lowered to reveal Billy Ray's face. Raymond gave no sign other than a slight nod. The nod was returned, barely. The cop, who was busy talking about movies with a chubby blonde nurse, never noticed. Raymond turned around and started the slow trek back to his room. The cop followed, looking disgruntled at his interrupted conversation. When Raymond reached the door of his room, he stopped and leaned on the doorjamb as if to catch his breath. He saw Billy Ray pass. His eyes flicked to the number beside the door, then swung back to look straight ahead down the hall. He walked around the corner, out of Raymond's sight.

Raymond shuffled back to the bed and got in slowly, grunting with the pain as the motion flexed his ripped and torn muscles. The cop stood by, waiting with the cuffs to secure him back to the bed.

"I don't know why you got to use those," Raymond complained. "I'm so busted up, I ain't going nowhere."

"Yeah, right," the cop said. "You got these doctors fooled, Raymond, but not us." Raymond sighed with theatrical resignation, then lay back on the bed and lifted his arm. The cop snapped one cuff on Raymond's right wrist and locked the other to the bed rail. Then he walked out to take up his position in the chair outside Raymond's door. Raymond turned his head and looked out the window, waiting.

• • •

Keller entered the hospital through the front entrance. He walked to the front desk, where a middle-aged woman in a blue-and-white-striped uniform was talking on the phone. She had dark hair shot with streaks of white, cemented in place with enough hair spray to give it a shellacked appearance. Keller started to speak, but she silenced him with an upraised hand. "Fayetteville General," she said in a singsong voice. "I'll connect you." He waited while she answered and routed several calls. Eventually, there was a lull in the traffic and she looked up at him. "May I help you?" she chirped.

"I'm trying to locate a Crystal Lee Puryear?" he said.

The woman turned and began tapping the keys of a computer terminal in front of her. "Are you a family member?" She asked. "It says here she's to receive no visitors except—"

"I'm her brother," he lied. "Leonard."

"Room 433," she said after a moment. "Follow the green line on the floor to the elevators, go up to the fourth floor, and follow the yellow lines to the patient rooms."

"Thanks," he said, but she was already on another call.

He found the room with only slight trouble. The door stood slightly ajar. He pushed it open gently.

It was a double room. Crystal Puryear lay in the bed closest to the door, her face nearly as pale as the sheets. She was asleep or unconscious, and there was a thin clear oxygen tube crossing her face under her nose. There was a girl seated in the chair next to the bed, her hand resting lightly on Crystal's. The girl stood up quickly as Keller entered.

The girl was tall and painfully thin. Her narrow face was pale and nearly green in the glare of the harsh fluorescent light over the bed. Her light brown hair was plaited in cornrows that hung in braids to beneath her shoulders. The braids were woven in with colored beads that rattled and clacked when she moved. She was dressed in a ragged midriff top that did what it could to emphasize almost nonexistent breasts. A pair of frayed jeans was slung low on her slim, boyish hips.

"Who are you?" she said. Her voice sounded slurred and Keller wondered if she was drunk. Then he noticed a flash of light reflecting off the metal stud through the girl's tongue.

"My name's Keller," he said. "I'm the one that brought her in."

"I'm Rita," the girl said. She gave him a professional smile with no actual warmth.

"She going to be okay?" Keller asked.

The girl looked back at the pale figure on the bed, chewed her lower lip. "She's going to live," she said, "but she ain't nowhere near okay."

"She been shooting up long?"

The girl sat down and shook her head. "She never did anything like that before. Said she was scared of needles. She just did a little reefer, a little blow, nothing serious. But after her brother and her parents got killed, Jesus, in the same week and all—I guess she just decided what the fuck, y'know?"

"What about that cousin of hers," Keller said. "You know, DeWayne? Anybody contact him?"

Another shake of the head. "Nobody knows where he is. They say he shot a cop. He's on the run."

Keller shrugged, trying to appear casual. "I just thought, he's the only family she has left. He ought to be here."

The girl laughed bitterly. "Right," she said. "They hardly ever saw each other. Me and Mara, we're the closest thing she has to family."

"Mara?"

"We work together. I mean, not together, you know, although Mara and I used to do a show together sometimes. But the three of us worked at the same place."

"The club?"

Rita looked puzzled, but quickly nodded. "Yeah. Right. The club."

She obviously didn't know what Keller was talking about. The girl was another hooker, he realized.

"Still," he persisted. "Somebody ought to let him know. She ever tell you how to reach him?"

"No," she said. She looked up, suddenly suspicious. "How come you're so interested in DeWayne, anyway?"

"I know the family," Keller said. "Maybe she told your boss something."

Rita's face became hard. "What boss? Who the hell are—"

"I talked to your boss on the phone," Keller said. "She tried to call Crystal while I was driving her to the hospital."

Rita stood up. "What are you, a cop? Son of a—"

Keller shook his head. "No. Not a cop."

"Her dealer then? Did you give that shit to her?" The girl advanced on him, her hands clutching at him like claws. Keller noticed her nails. They were at least two inches long. He didn't feel like going up against them, so he backed up. "No," he said firmly. "How many dealers you know would drive someone to the hospital when they OD'd?"

The girl's hands fell to her sides. "You trying to get Amber to work for you, maybe? Trying to steal her away? Let me tell you buddy, you don't want to tangle with my boss. You may think she's a pushover 'cause she's a woman. There's people who've made that mistake. But she's got people that'll fuck you up, but good."

"Yeah, she likes to point that out. But I'm not a pimp, either," Keller said. "So you can tell your boss that."

"What, you think she sent me down here?"

"It's a pretty good bet. I doubt you'd stir your ass out of bed otherwise." The girl swung a clawed hand at his face. He caught her wrist and held it in a painful grip. She gritted her teeth, but didn't cry out.

"Tell your boss," he said evenly, "that I'm not after her or Crystal. I'm after DeWayne."

"Hah," Rita hissed. "I knew it. You *are* a cop."

Keller shook his head. "Nope. I work for DeWayne's bondsman. I came to talk to Crystal—Amber—because she might know where he'd go if he was on the run."

The girl nearly spat into Keller's face. "Fuck you. She isn't going to tell you shit."

"Even if I knew," a small voice said.

They turned to look at the bed. Crystal's eyes were open. Her face sagged with fatigue and sickness, and Keller saw what she would look like when she got old.

Rita gave a scream of theatrical joy and threw herself on the bed beside Crystal, who winced with the jouncing. "Baby, sweetie," Rita crooned, running her fingers through Crystal's disheveled hair. "We were so worried about you." She looked at Keller with an expression of spite on her face. "Don't tell this guy anything, baby. He's trying to arrest DeWayne." She turned to him. "She isn't going to tell, so you can just get the fuck out of here."

"She better," Keller said. He looked at Crystal. "I

want to bring DeWayne in, Crystal. And I actually have an interest in seeing him brought in alive. It's the only way I get paid. But how many cops you think feel the same way, after he gunned one of them down? Somebody's going to catch him. Nobody can run forever. How do you rate his chances if it's a cop who finds him first?"

Crystal closed her eyes. A tear ran down her cheek. She shook her head. "I'm sorry," she whispered. "I don't want to lose him, too. But I just don't know anything."

"You see what you've done?" Rita snapped. "You got her all upset." She turned back to Crystal. "Don't you worry, sweetie, Mara went to get you some clothes and makeup. We're going to get you out of here."

"Yeah," Keller said. "She and your boss. They'll have you flat on your back again in no time."

Rita turned to him. "Fuck you," she snarled.

"Sorry," Keller said, "but I'm a few bucks light right now."

He took a business card out of his wallet. He took a pen off the bedside table and wrote another number on the back. "Call me if you hear from DeWayne," he said. "Or have him get in touch with me, I don't care. But you know it's his only chance." He handed the card to Crystal.

"Even if you don't call me," he said, "call the other number I wrote on there. It's a rehab center. A friend of mine runs it." He walked to the door and leaned on the jamb. "You need to get out of the life, Crystal. It isn't just Leonard and your parents' death that's pushing you over the edge."

"Don't listen to him, baby," Rita said, a note of pleading in her voice. "What does he know? He doesn't care about you, he just wants to catch DeWayne." Rita stretched out her hand to take the card away, but Crystal closed her hand over it. As Keller turned to go, she spoke up.

"Thank you," she said softly. "I'd probly've died if you hadn't brought me in."

Keller stopped in the doorway. "It's likely," he said. "So I guess you owe me one. Call the number."

She stared at Keller, not speaking, as he walked out.

Keller left the hospital and drove back to Marie's house. When he got there, she was in the front yard. A blond-haired boy about three years old was riding the Big Wheel down the driveway as Keller was pulling up, so he parked on the street. Marie came out of the garage as Keller was coming up the drive. She was dressed in a pair of white shorts and a man's denim shirt tied beneath her breasts. Her hair was bound up in a pale blue and white scarf and there was a smudge of grime on her cheek. Keller stopped and watched her come toward him. "Trying to get the garage organized," she explained.

"There's so much crap in there, I can't even get the door closed."

"Looks like a big job," Keller said.

She looked away. "Yeah. Well. Just trying to stay busy. Keeps my mind off things. You know?"

"I know," Keller said. He felt strange and awkward. He wanted to kiss her, but was stayed by the solemn gaze of the boy with the Big Wheel, who had stopped to regard him gravely. Keller and the boy stared at each other for a long moment, then the boy unhorsed himself from the Big Wheel, ran to Marie, and attached himself to her leg, where he watched Keller warily.

"Ben," Marie said, a laugh bubbling just under the surface of her voice, "this is Mister Keller. Can you say hello?"

The boy's answer was to bury his face in Marie's thigh. She gave him a reassuring pat on the head. "How'd it go?" she said.

Keller shrugged. It seemed somehow grotesque to discuss what he had seen in the hospital room in the middle of this domestic scene. "She doesn't know anything."

She wiped the sweat from her brow. Keller wanted to gently wipe the smudge from her face, could imagine himself doing it, but the boy was staring at him again. "I got a Big Wheel," the boy announced suddenly.

"I can see that," Keller said. "It looks like fun."

The boy pondered for a moment. "You want to ride?"

"Thanks," Keller said. "But it's been a while. I might fall off and hurt myself."

"Okay," the boy said. He detached himself from his mother's leg and went back to the Big Wheel. He saddled up again and began industriously pedaling his way up the driveway, his tongue sticking out of the corner of his mouth with concentration. Keller and Marie watched him, standing a few feet apart.

"You going to keep an eye on her in the hospital?" Marie asked finally.

Keller shook his head. "She won't be there long. She's got no insurance, most likely, so they'll show her the front door as soon as they can without risking a lawsuit. If she gets lucky, somebody will refer her to rehab. If not—well, I gave her the number of a friend of mine."

Marie turned in surprise to look at him. "You did?"

"Yeah," Keller said. "A guy—a doctor I knew in the army runs a rehab center. Does good work. If he knows I sent her, he might not be so sticky about insurance questions. Why, are you surprised?"

She shook her head, a slight smile on her face. "You're a hard guy to figure out, Keller," she said. "One minute, I feel like you're staking the girl out like a goat set as tiger bait. The next, you're sending her to rehab." She slid her arm around his waist and kissed him on the cheek.

He shrugged. "Maybe she goes, maybe she doesn't. It's not like it costs me anything. Besides, I finally decided that with as many people as he has chasing him, DeWayne Puryear would be an idiot to try to contact her at that hospital."

"C'mon, Crystal," DeWayne muttered, "answer the damn phone." He hunched over a little more, trying to make his face inconspicuous. The pay phone was stuck on a metal pole in the corner of a convenience store parking lot, and DeWayne felt as exposed as a bug on a sidewalk. He had considered calling from Debbie's apartment, but he suddenly got paranoid about the possibility of phone taps and traces. That was the problem with that rock cocaine, he thought. It felt good going down, almost better than sex, but afterwards, when the blast wore off, you felt all jittery and sick and your mind kept running into all these dark places. All the colors looked too bright and sharp and the sound of the phone ringing was boring into his ear like a needle. He was about ready to slam the receiver down when he heard somebody pick up on the other end. A female voice said "Hello?"

"Crystal?" DeWayne began. "It's DeWayne."

There was a short pause. "Crystal's not here. This is a friend of hers."

DeWayne took a deep breath. "Do you know when she'll be back?"

A longer pause. "She's in the hospital."

Keller, DeWayne thought. The son of a bitch got to Crystal. "What happened? Who is this?"

"I'm Mara," the voice said. "I'm a friend of hers. We work together at the—we work together."

"What are you doing in Crystal's house?"

"Hey man," the voice held an edge of irritation. "Ease up, all right? I came by to get some things for her. Clothes and shit. Don't be gettin' all in my—"

"Is she hurt?" DeWayne asked. "What happened?"

"Who did you say this was?" the voice demanded suspiciously.

"It's DeWayne, her cousin. I need to ask her about our folks. I need to find out what she knows."

"Oh. Yeah. She mentioned you." The voice softened somewhat. "Sorry about your folks."

DeWayne resisted the urge to slam the phone against the side of the booth. "What happened to my cousin, damn it?"

"Look, you don't have to get all hostile, all right? I mean, I know you're upset and all, but I got feelings, too."

DeWayne was trying not to scream. "Look, I'm

sorry. I just found out last night about my aunt and uncle. I'm upset. They raised me, y'know?"

"Yeah, whatever," the voice still sounded offended. "Anyway, Amber, I mean Crystal, didn't take the news too well, you might say. She decided to check out for a while."

"What are you saying, she tried to kill herself?" DeWayne thought of feisty little Crystal, who would stand toe-to-toe with either him or Leonard and face them down when they were kids. He had trouble imagining her trying to do herself in.

"Not, like directly. But she started in on the hard stuff. She always told me she'd never do nothin' like that. She tol' me she was afraid of needles. But I guess, you know, after what happened, she just wanted to get away for a while, y'know what I'm sayin'?"

DeWayne thought of the rock he had smoked at Debbie's. He remembered the desperate need he had felt for numbness. "Yeah," he said. "I know what you're saying. Where's she at?"

"Fayetteville General," Mara said. "Room four thirty-three."

"Thanks," DeWayne said.

"No problem," Mara said. "And sorry again, about everything. Hell of a thing to happen."

"Yeah," DeWayne said. "Hell of a thing. Thanks." He hung up. He took a deep breath and straightened his shoulders as he walked back to

Debbie's car. She was seated in the driver's seat, staring blankly out the window.

"Crystal's in the hospital," he said as he slid into the passenger seat.

"Hmm," Debbie said. She sounded utterly disinterested.

"I gotta go see her," DeWayne said.

Debbie turned back to him. "You said we was gonna get some more rocks," she said.

The whine in her voice set his teeth on edge. "I got more important things to do right now than get you high, bitch," he said.

She looked sulky. "Maybe you can just get out of my damn car, then."

DeWayne reached between the seats and pulled out the gun. He jammed it up under her chin. "And maybe you can just shut the fuck up," he snarled.

"Okay," she said. "I'm sorry. Just don't hurt me." Her eyes were wide with fear, but there was something else there, too, something very much like excitement. He heard her breathing quicken. "I'll do anything you want."

The blood pounded in DeWayne's temples and the sickness came back in a wave. Suddenly, he wanted another hit of the thick white smoke worse than anything else in the world. "Jesus," he said. "You are one twisted bitch." He lowered the gun. "Just drive," he said wearily. "We'll get some more. Then we'll go find Crystal."

She smiled brightly, like a child promised a trip to the candy store. She dropped her hand from the steering wheel to squeeze his thigh. "Now you're talkin', baby," she said. She put the car in drive and returned her hand to his leg. "Now you're talkin'."

Raymond looked up as the door opened. He saw the heavy silver cart from which the meals for the entire floor were distributed by a cheerful young black guy dressed in the light blue coveralls that were the uniform of the hospital's service staff. But it was a different guy this time. The last time Raymond had seen him, the man pushing the cart had been dressed in a flannel shirt and a baseball cap.

"'Bout damn time," Raymond said.

"Took some time to figure out how to get in here," Billy Ray said. "We lucked out, though. Fella that works the kitchen's a customer of ours. He let me, ah—borrow this here cart for a little bit."

Raymond smiled. "Never thought I'd see you delivin' meals to shut-ins, Billy Ray," he said.

The man grunted. He reached beneath the cart and pulled out a pair of Tec-9s, stubby semiautomatics that looked like oversized pistols. Long magazines stuck out from in front of the trigger guards. "Fifty-round mags," he said, "and these are converted to full auto." He pulled out a silencer and screwed it onto the perforated barrel. He handed the

pistol to Raymond, who took it with his free hand.
"What about the cuffs?" Raymond demanded. "A
fifty-round mag ain't gonna do me much good if
I'm still tied to the bed."

Billy Ray reached under the cart and pulled out a
pair of long-handled bolt-cutters. "Watch the door,"
he said as he began working on the handcuffs with
the cutters. Raymond held the Tec-9 awkwardly in
his left hand, tilting it slightly sideways facing the
door. Billy Ray grunted as he chewed on the handcuff chain with the cutters. Suddenly, with an audi-
ble snap, the chain parted, leaving Raymond with a
single cuff and chain dangling from his wrist. He
transferred the gun to his right hand. "Alright," he
said. "Now where do we go?"

"Delmer is downstairs in the car," Billy Ray said.
He took a cell phone out of the pocket of the blue
coverall. "I better call and make sure he ain't gone
to sleep. There's some clothes for you in the cart."
Raymond located a pair of blue jeans and a shirt on
a shelf inside the cart as Billy Ray dialed. As Billy
Ray spoke urgently into the phone, Raymond
searched the closets. "Hey," he complained. "The
sonsabitches took my shoes."

"It's a warm night," Billy Ray said. "An' we
gotta go."

At that moment, the door swung open. The
blonde nurse Raymond had seen earlier chatting
with the cop entered, holding a silver clipboard.

Her blue eyes widened in shock as she saw Raymond out of bed and the guns in his hand. She dropped the clipboard, which rattled noisily on the floor. Billy Ray strode quickly to the woman and yanked her toward him. He spun her around and wrapped one arm around her from behind. As the cop came into the room, he raised the pistol in his other hand and stuck it against the nurse's ear. Raymond raised his own gun and pointed it at the cop. "Don't do nothin' stupid," he said, "or he'll scatter this bitch's brains all over the room." The nurse moaned in fear.

The cop raised his hands, as if placating them. "Easy, there, fellas," he said softly. "Let's don't do something that everybody's going to regret."

"Good idea," Raymond said. "Whyn't you start by takin' your gun outta the holster. With your left hand, two fingers. Or I'll do somethin' *you* sure as hell will regret."

The cop hesitated a moment, every instinct warning him against giving up his weapon. Billy Ray yanked the nurse against him again, hard. She squeaked in fear, too frightened to scream. The cop shook his head. Slowly, he reached over with his left hand and unbuttoned the holster. He awkwardly removed the pistol, holding it between thumb and forefinger.

"Now put it on the floor. Slow." Raymond said. "Then slide it over here with your foot."

The cop bent over, his eyes never leaving Raymond's face. He placed the gun on the worn linoleum. He slowly straightened up. "Okay," he said. "Now what?"

"For you?" Raymond said. "Nothin'." He pulled the trigger. The silenced pistol chattered. A line of red holes appeared across the cop's chest. This time the nurse did scream.

"Damn," Billy Ray grimaced. He shoved the sobbing nurse toward the door, holding onto her collar with one hand and holding the gun into the small of her back with the other.

"He still had a radio," Raymond shrugged. "He'd be on it as soon as we got outta the room. An' I ain't takin' no cop along with us." He followed Billy Ray out the door and into the hallway. A male nurse coming out of the room across the hall gaped at them as they came out. "Get back in there," Raymond ordered. "And stay there." The man obeyed, leaving the long hallway empty for the moment. Raymond knew that wouldn't last; the hospital was a hive of activity at all hours of the day and night.

He looked at the ceiling. A row of widely spaced sprinklers ran down the center of the hallway, interspersed with heat and smoke sensors. "You got a lighter?" Raymond said. Billy Ray released the nurse long enough to fish a cigarette lighter out of the breast pocket of the coverall. Raymond flicked it on and held it up, directly under one of the sensors.

After a few seconds, a loud Klaxon horn blared, its ear-splitting honking repeating over and over. The sprinklers began spewing a soaking mist of water into the hallway. The nurse screamed again as the drenching downpour immediately soaked them to the skin, plastering their clothing to them. People began spilling into the hallway, nurses pushing patients in hospital beds and wheelchairs.

"No more water," Raymond whispered, "but the fire next time."

"Let her go," Raymond said, motioning to the nurse. "She'll only slow us down." Billy Ray obeyed, shoving her into the crowd.

"He's got a gun!" she screamed, and the crowd became a mob, pushing and shoving to get away from the water and the armed men. It was a scene of utter chaos, with people stumbling into one another and gurneys and wheelchairs colliding.

"Where's the stairway?" Raymond shouted.

"Back this way," Billy Ray said, backing up. He fired a quick burst into the ceiling above the crowd, increasing their panic before the two men turned and bolted around the corner. They located the stairway marked AUTHORIZED PERSONNEL ONLY and plunged down it, four steps at a time, past three floors and the lobby floor to the basement level. They burst out into a dimly lit hallway.

"Which way?" Raymond panted. The sutures across his side blazed like flames.

"I dunno," Billy Ray said. "This wasn't how I planned to get out."

"Fuck," Raymond said. He jogged down the hallway past a line of battered vending machines. He had to stop and catch his breath. It was then that he noticed the sticky wetness along his side. He looked down to see a slow seepage of blood coming through his shirt. Billy Ray pulled up alongside of him. He noticed the blood and grimaced.

"Man," he said, "We get out of here, we better find you a doctor. I know a guy—"

"Later," Raymond grunted. He saw a heavy pair of metal doors at the end of the hallway. He walked over and pushed them open. The doors led to a small grass courtyard with a rusty metal picnic table. The lights of the parking lots glimmered beyond. "C'mon," Raymond said. "We gotta get out of here."

9

Keller sat on the couch, drinking a beer as Marie cleaned up in the kitchen. She had asked him to stay for dinner. The meal had been a hectic affair, with Marie spending half her time trying to talk to Keller and the other half trying to ensure that more food got into her son than ended up on him. Now, with dinner over, Marie had banished them both to the living room. Keller took a sip of his beer and stared at a baseball game on TV without actually watching it as he listened to Marie clattering around in the kitchen. Ben seemed absorbed with a set of brightly colored wooden blocks a few feet away on the living room floor. It was such a normal scene that Keller felt out of place, like a visitor from another planet.

Keller looked up to see the boy standing in front of

him, a thin book in his chubby hands. "Read," the boy said simply. Feeling a little foolish, Keller took the book. It was a dog-eared and jelly-stained retelling of the story of the Little Engine That Could. The boy clambered up on the couch beside him and pointed to the book. "Read," he said again, a little impatiently. Keller sighed, opened the book and began to read. He had gotten to the point where the Little Engine was puffing up the hill and he was reading the Engine's mantra of "I *think* I can, I *think* I can," trying to pitch his voice with a suitably strained inflection, when he looked up and saw Marie. She was standing in the kitchen door. She had covered her mouth with her hand to stifle her laughter but her eyes were dancing.

"You're enjoying this," he said.

"You better believe it," she said. "Tough guy."

"Read," the boy ordered, then added, "tough guy."

Keller sighed and went on. When the book was finished, Marie applauded. "C'mon, little man," she said, sweeping Ben off the couch. She gave Keller a quick peck on the cheek. "It's time for a bath and then to bed."

"I wannanother book," the boy complained, but allowed himself to be led toward the bathroom. Keller got up and stretched. "Stick around," Marie said, waving him back toward the couch. "After that, you probably could use a little grownup conversation."

Keller got another beer and sat down. He tried to sort out what he was feeling. What was going on between him and Marie seemed like a betrayal of Angela. But he knew there was no commitment with Angela, no relationship to betray. He thought again of Angela's word that he was always looking for a damsel in distress. If so, he seemed to have no luck whatsoever in finding them.

After the boy was bathed and safely tucked in bed, Marie came back in and sat on the couch. Keller put his arm around her and she snuggled into the hollow of his shoulder. "It was sweet of you to read to Ben," she whispered, and kissed him lightly on the cheek.

"He didn't give me much choice," Keller said.

She laughed. "He's not shy about letting you know what he wants," she said. "Just like . . ." She trailed off.

"Like his father?" Keller said.

She bit her lower lip, then shook her head. "I don't want to talk about him," she said.

"Okay."

Something in his tone made her look at him. She put a hand on his chest. "Jack," she said. "I'm not trying to shut you out. Really. It's just that—hell, I don't know." She paused for a long moment. "Talking about him makes me feel bad," she said. "And I want to feel good right now, okay? I haven't felt this good in a long time."

"Thanks," Keller said.

She laughed and kissed him again, harder.

"You're welcome," she said. "Besides, I want to find out more about you."

Keller willed himself not to tense up. "What do you want to know?"

"Oh, hell, I don't know," she said lightly. "Where're you from? What're your folks like? Stuff like that."

Keller took a deep breath. "I'm from Charleston. My grandmother raised me. Next question." He cursed himself inwardly for the anger he couldn't keep out of his voice.

She was silent for a moment. "I'm sorry," she said. "If it's something that makes you feel bad, it's not fair to ask you to talk about it. I guess."

Keller shook his head. "No," he said, "don't be sorry. You didn't know. I shouldn't have snapped at you like that."

"No," she agreed. "But it's okay." she moved closer to him and began rubbing his neck. Keller closed his eyes, letting her strong fingers relax the tension in him. Finally, he opened his eyes.

"I never met my father," he said. "Mom said he was a sailor from the naval base. She said he was killed in Vietnam. I don't know if that was true. Truth was—kind of a flexible thing with my mom."

"She left you?" Marie whispered. Keller nodded, unable to speak further. She pulled him close and kissed him deeply. His hand came up to caress her hair and she moaned softly.

"You can't stay the night," she whispered as they

broke the kiss, "it wouldn't be right for Ben to see you—well, you know." She kissed him again. "But you can stay a while longer."

"What about . . . ?" He gestured toward the boy's bedroom.

"Already asleep," she said. "And when he's down, you could stampede a herd of buffalo through his room and he wouldn't wake up. But we'll lock the door," she said, "just in case." She stood up and took his hand, leading him to the bedroom.

They began more gently this time, the need for quiet holding them to soft caresses and whispers at first. But as they moved together, they gained urgency until she stuffed the corner of a pillow into her mouth and bit down hard to stifle her cries. He buried his face in her shoulder to muffle his own sounds of pleasure as he joined her in climax. Afterwards, they lay entwined as their breathing returned to normal. After a few moments, she raised her head and kissed him on the ear. He rolled over on his back and drew her to him. In moments they were both asleep.

He awoke a few hours later. Marie was in his arms, her head cradled against his chest. He watched her sleep for a few moments, marveling at how good it felt to simply hold her. She stirred slightly, then opened her eyes and looked at him.

Her eyes had no iris or pupil, just dark red embers that quickly brightened to bright yellow, then white-hot flames. Her skin began charring and peeling away from the bone beneath, revealing a core of raging fire where her face had been. The blackened remnants of a skull grinned sardonically up at him, framed by cooked gobbets of flesh still clinging to the bone. Keller screamed and shoved the apparition away from him. She fell to the floor, then, impossibly, stood up, reaching out to him with fingers burned down to the bone. Her mouth opened and a long hissing shriek came out like steam escaping from a locomotive. A reeking cloud of smoke blew into his face, the stinking breath of a crematorium. He screamed again and struck out blindly at her.

He was screaming, she was screaming, but it was Ben's cries that pulled him from the pit of the dream. Keller realized that he was on top of Marie, straddling her body, his hands around her throat. She was clawing at his wrists, her nails leaving bloody scratches as she tried to break his grip. Ben was pounding on the locked door and wailing in terrified incomprehension. Keller leaped up off the bed. He backed away from her so quickly that he slammed hard into the wall. She rolled off onto the floor, gasping for breath. Ben's cries were rising to the point of hysteria. Marie stood up and grabbed her robe. "Get in the bathroom until I can get him calmed down," she hissed at Keller. "He can't see you here." Keller obeyed numbly, his mind still reeling with shock.

He retreated to the bathroom until he heard her close the bedroom door behind her. He could hear her voice in the hallway, the words muffled by the door, but the tone reassuring. The boy had stopped wailing, but he was demanding to know what was happening in a loud tearful voice. After a moment, Keller heard the door of the boy's bedroom close and the voices were cut off.

Keller exited the bathroom and quickly gathered up his clothes. He dressed himself and stumbled to the door. As he passed by the doorway to the boy's bedroom, he could hear the soft sounds of Marie singing a lullaby. He paused for a moment to listen. He rested his head against the door and reached up to touch it lightly with the fingers of one hand. Then he straightened up and walked down the hallway to the front door.

Once outside, he paused a moment to take a deep breath of the soggy air. He realized he was trembling. He sat down on the front stoop to gather himself. He ran his hands over his face as if trying to scrape something away.

He heard the front door open behind him. He knew it was Marie, but he couldn't bring himself to look at her. He was afraid of what he might see in her eyes: disgust, fear, or worst of all, pity. He felt her sit on the step above him. There was a brief pause, then she leaned against him from behind. Her arms went around his chest and hugged him tightly.

"It's okay," she whispered. "It was just a nightmare."

Keller shook his head angrily. "I tried to—I mean I could have—and I scared the kid. I'm sorry."

Another pressure of her arms around him. "He's already asleep again," she said. "It'll be fine." Keller said nothing, made no response to her embrace. After a moment, she released him and straightened up. "Come on back to bed," she said. "It's late."

"No," he said. "You're right. I can't stay the night. It's not right with the kid—with Ben there."

"Yeah," she said. Her voice was puzzled and hurt. "Okay. I wasn't talking about the whole night, but—okay." He didn't hear her move away. There was another long pause. Finally, she said, "I can't help you if you won't talk to me, Jack." He didn't respond. He heard the door close. He turned around as if to say something but stopped as he heard the solid snick of the deadbolt. It was as loud as the slam of a cell door. He stood up and walked down the driveway to his car. When he got there, he picked up the cell phone and looked at it. He dialed a number he hadn't dialed in years, but it was a number he knew as well as his own.

After a few rings, a deep voice, furred with sleep, answered. "H'lo?"

"It's Jack Keller," Keller said.

"Jack?" the voice said. "Jesus Christ, man, it's three-thirty in the goddamn morning."

"I know," Keller said. "I'm sorry to wake you up. I need to talk to you again."

"Then call my office and make a goddamn appointment—okay, sorry. Tell me what's wrong."

"The dreams are back. And they're worse."

"How bad?" the voice said gently.

Keller took a deep breath. "I almost hurt somebody."

The voice sharpened. "Did you actually hurt anybody? Is anybody in any danger right now?"

Keller looked at the closed door and shook his head. "No," he said. "I'm gone."

"How about you?" the voice said. "You feel like hurting yourself?"

Keller thought about that. "No," he said finally. "So I guess it can wait."

"But not long," the voice said. "Call my office first thing. I'll be in by eight thirty. Someone else can take my group therapy session."

"Thanks, Major," Keller said. "I owe you one."

"All you owe me, Sergeant," the voice said, "is to let me finish the job this time."

"Okay," Keller said.

"Get some sleep, troop," the voice said. "And no dreams. That's an order."

Keller smiled slightly at that. "Yes, sir," he said.

Raymond had finally broken down and taken one of the pain pills, since Delmer was driving. Delmer wasn't good for much; Raymond sometimes wondered if the kid was a retard. But he sure could drive, and Raymond had employed him in that capacity for several years at the request of Billy Ray, Delmer's cousin, who was leaning over the back of the front seat, talking to Raymond.

"Buddy," he said. "That don't look good. We better get you to that doctor and get you stitched back up."

Raymond shook his head. "A doctor'll call the cops," he said. "It'll quit in a little while." Billy Ray shook his head.

"He ain't bleedin' all over my seats, is he?" Delmer asked.

"Shut up, Delmer," Billy Ray said. He turned back to Raymond. "We got a call from our friends down south. They was worried when I told them you was in the hospital."

"You tell 'em I was under arrest?"

"Yeah, but I told 'em it didn't have anything to do with the business. I told 'em it was personal."

"Shit," Raymond said. The last thing he needed was the Colombians getting nervous about him. Paco Suarez was fully capable of having Raymond killed just to make sure he didn't say anything incriminating while under sedation. It was the kind of paranoia that had kept Suarez alive and out of jail through twenty years of drug wars and government task forces aimed at him. It made dealing with Suarez a tricky proposition, however, especially since all communications were filtered through several layers of equally paranoid and trigger-happy lieutenants.

Billy Ray went on. "They was asking when we would be able to move some more product for 'em."

"Right away," Raymond said automatically. "Who'd you talk to?"

Billy Ray's eyes flickered toward Delmer, but the younger man was intent on the road. "Geronimo," he whispered.

An idea began to form in Raymond's mind. Geronimo was their nickname for one of Suarez's chief muscle boys. His real name was Guillermo, but Raymond had misheard it as Geronimo at their first meeting, and he thought the crazy Colombian had actually liked it. He apparently thought it was some sort of Native American honorary title, and Raymond had never bothered to set him straight. Geronimo had access to firepower and people who weren't afraid to use it. That was exactly the kind of people Raymond needed right then.

"Good," Raymond said. "Pull over at this phone booth. Geronimo's just the boy I want to talk to."

DeWayne was out of rocks, out of money, and running out of patience with Debbie's whining. "Stay in the car," he ordered. He got out and slammed the door. "I'll be back in a little bit."

"I ain't gonna stay in no car," the girl said. "I ain't a dog. I'm comin' in with you."

"Damn it." DeWayne said. His nerves were jangling like a multiline phone with all lines ringing. His eyeballs felt sandy and irritated by the morning sun. He felt as if he hadn't slept in a month. His skin felt scoured and raw. If he concentrated he imagined he could identify each and every nerve ending, and they were all screaming. "There ain't nothin' for you to do in there," he said. "I'm just goin' in to visit my cousin."

"What, I'm not good enough to meet your family?" Debbie said in that whiny voice that bored into Dwayne's ear like a dentist's drill set on high. For one brief moment, he contemplated pulling his pistol out and shooting her right there. The number of other people in the hospital parking lot saved her. Instead, he stood up and slammed the door on her, turned around and walked toward the glassed-in entrance. He ignored her squawks of muffled outrage.

The woman behind the reception desk was a fortyish blonde with an ample bosom barely contained by her blue-and-white uniform. She eyed DeWayne suspiciously as he came in. "May I help you?" she said.

"I'm here to visit Crystal Lee Puryear," he said with as much confidence as he could muster.

"Are you a family member?" the woman said as

she turned to her computer. Her fingers began clicking busily on the keys.

"Yeah," DeWayne said, "I'm her brother."

The woman's fingers stopped for a brief second. She kept her eyes straight ahead and her voice neutral. "And your name is . . . ?" she asked.

The too-casual tone in her voice made a chill of paranoia run down DeWayne's spine. "Uhhhh . . . ," he said. "Leonard," he blurted out.

The woman turned and looked at him. "Well, the computer says you were here yesterday. Don't you remember the room?"

The shiver down his backbone shot back up and set alarm bells clanging in his head. "Ahhh—yeah," he said. "I ahhh—I forgot the number."

"Your sister has been released to a—to another facility," the woman said, still eyeing DeWayne up and down. "She didn't tell you?"

DeWayne smacked himself on the head with the palm of his hand. "Boy," he laughed nervously, "I'd fergit my head if it weren't screwed on. Where'd she go again?"

The woman stiffened and reached for the phone. "I'm not allowed to give out that information," she snapped. "Wait here, and I'll call somebody."

"No, no," DeWayne said, "That's okay, don't bother. I remember now." He turned and bolted out the glass doors, pursued by the woman's shout.

DeWayne slowed to a brisk walk as he headed for

the parking lot. Someone had been to see Crystal, pretending to be him. Or Leonard. He could only think of one person who would do something like that.

"Keller," he muttered under his breath. The guy was always there, following him. He needed to do something about Keller. He walked to the place where he had left the parked car.

It was gone.

"You fucking *bitch!*" DeWayne screamed. An elderly couple walking slowly by looked up in horror. DeWayne didn't care. He ran at the nearest car, kicking the rear bumper in a frenzy. He slammed his fists down on the trunk lid, screaming in rage, then kicked the bumper again. The old couple scurried faster to get away from the madman. DeWayne nearly pulled the gun and shot them, but then he heard the beeping of a car horn. He turned. Debbie was sitting in her car, fifty feet away. She had moved to the end of the row and had been watching him. He could see her laughing.

DeWayne snarled deep in his throat and ran toward the car. He yanked the gun out of his waistband and pulled the slide back to chamber a round. She started the car, but didn't pull away. She was still laughing. When he got to the door, he saw that the windows were rolled up and the doors locked. He stood beside the driver's side window and pointed the gun. "Open the goddamn door!" he screamed.

"I coulda left you!" she shouted, still laughing, but

with an edge of hysteria, so that it sounded more like crying. "But I didn't! Now you see! Now you see!"

"See what!?" he yelled. "God damn it, you crazy bitch, open the door!" He looked up and saw a pair of uniformed men standing in the doorway. Hospital security. Rent-a-cops, but still trouble.

"You need me!" Debbie yelled. By now she really was crying. "You need me! Say it!"

The rent-a-cops had located the source of the yelling and were moving purposefully toward him. Debbie was still screaming at him. "You need me!" she repeated.

"Fuck it," DeWayne muttered. "Right now, it's true." He bent down, close to the car window. "Okay, baby," he said, trying to sound placating through his near-panic. "I do. I need you. Now please, sugar, open the *fucking door!*"

A smile burst across her face. "I knew it," she sniffled. She leaned across and unlocked the passenger side door. "Get in," she smiled at him. "I'll drive." DeWayne bit back another snarl. He ran around to the passenger side and slid in. He was barely in the car when she stomped the gas and peeled out of the parking space; the door slammed shut from the forward momentum of the car before he had a chance to pull it closed. They blasted past the startled rent-a-cops, one of whom had to leap out of the way to avoid being run down. DeWayne looked back and saw them standing there, their mouths half open in shock.

"So," Debbie said. "How was she?" her tone was conversational, as if the previous altercation had never happened.

"She's gone. They moved her somewhere. They wouldn't tell me where."

Debbie plucked a cigarette out of the pack wedged under the sun visor. "Drug rehab," she said positively as she popped the cigarette lighter in.

"How do you know that?" DeWayne said.

She lit the cigarette, then shifted it to one corner of her mouth. "'Cause they wouldn't tell you," she said through the cloud of smoke. "It's a law. They can't even say if a person's had drug treatment. So when they get all secretlike—then you know."

"Well, I got no way of finding out where," DeWayne said.

She smirked. "I bet I can," she said.

"How?"

She reached over, put a hand on his thigh, and squeezed. "Tell me you need me again."

She really does have a screw loose, DeWayne thought. "I need you, baby," he said. The patent insincerity of his voice seemed to make no difference to her. She gave his thigh another playful squeeze. "Wait'll we get back to my place. Then I'll show you. I'll show you why you need me."

10

"You know, Keller," Berry said, "life is kind of funny. I don't hear from you for five years, and then I hear your name twice within twenty-four hours."

They were walking on a grassy lawn in front of a large, white Victorian house. The home was the main building of Rescue House, the drug and alcohol rehabilitation facility where Dr. Lucas Berry, Major, U.S. Army Medical Corps (Retired) was director.

Berry was a huge man, almost six-seven. His close-cropped hair was streaked with gray. Combined with his broad, square, brown face, the gray hair gave him a distinguished appearance. The feeling of mass that Berry gave was complemented by his deep, resonant voice.

Keller thought for a moment before realizing Berry's meaning. "Crystal Puryear called you."

Berry nodded. "Yes. Or at least her doctor at the hospital did. But he was careful to mention your name. Fortunately we had a bed coming available. Otherwise I would have had to bump someone off the waiting list."

"You'd do that just because someone used my name?"

"You don't hit the panic button easily, Jack. If you thought enough to call for help for someone, they're in bad shape."

Suddenly, incongruously, Berry grinned, which robbed his chiseled brown face of some of its sternness and made him look almost impish. "Maybe I should put you to work recruiting for me."

"Thanks," Keller said. "I like the job I have."

"Hmm." The sound was neutral, but the meaning unmistakable.

"You don't approve of what I do."

"It's not up to me to approve or disapprove, Jack. I just wonder why you keep putting yourself in dangerous situations."

Keller shrugged. "It's what I do."

Berry grunted. "Obviously. But that's not an answer. Why do you do it?"

Keller stopped and looked away across the lawn at the neatly kept white guest cottages that served as the center's dormitories. "Why does anybody do what they do?" he said. "Why'd you go from treating shell-shocked grunts to drug and alcohol rehab?"

"It's a growth industry," Berry said. "But you're still ducking the question."

"Maybe because I don't know the answer. The job needs nerves, adrenaline. If I stop to think too much about what I'm doing and why, it could get me killed."

"Not thinking about it is just killing you more slowly."

Keller didn't answer. Berry sighed and started walking again. Keller followed. They walked in silence to the porch of the main building and sat down in a pair of rocking chairs on the front porch.

"Nice place you got here," Keller said. "The money must be good."

"The house was donated," Berry said. "The place was a wreck when we got it. No one had lived here for ten years." He ran a hand along the immaculately varnished rail of the porch. There was obvious pride in his voice. "We worked our asses off to get the place in shape."

"I can tell."

Berry turned to him. "So, Jack, you ever thought about killing yourself?"

"Why?" Keller said. "Are you suggesting it? Wow, treatments really have changed in five years."

"Damn it, stop avoiding my questions. I wouldn't keep asking if it wasn't important."

"No," Keller said. "Nothing like that."

"You said you almost hurt somebody. Tell me about it."

Keller took a deep breath. "I've been seeing a woman."

Berry leaned back and folded his big hands across his chest. "Someone you met on the job?"

"Yeah. She's a cop."

"Okay. Go on."

Keller looked at the lawn. "We were asleep. Together. I had one of the dreams. She was on fire."

"Ah."

Keller looked back at him. "What do you mean, 'ah'?"

Berry waved him off. "Just ah. Keep talking."

"I think she tried to wake me up. I woke up with my hands around her throat."

"What happened then?"

"She has a kid. A son. I woke him up. He was crying. I scared him." As he spoke, Keller involuntarily leaned forward, his hands wrapped across his stomach. When he had finished, he was curled over like a man shot in the gut.

Berry's voice was steady. "Then what happened?"

Keller straightened up. "I left."

"She say anything to you?"

"Yeah," Keller said. "She asked me what was wrong."

"Did you tell her?"

Keller shook his head. "I just left."

"You ran." Berry said it without anger or accusation; his voice was flat and matter-of-fact. Keller started to protest, then just nodded. "Yeah."

"She mean anything to you? This woman?" Berry asked.

Keller thought for a minute, then nodded. "Yeah."

"What had been going on between you? Before the dream?"

Keller looked at him. "We were making love."

"Before that, then."

"We were—she had asked me about my family."

Berry raised an eyebrow. "And you told her?"

"A little, yeah. Just the basics."

Berry whistled. "That's serious progress, Jack," he said.

"Yeah, but—"

Berry cut him off. "You're starting to open up to someone. That's good. It's a damn sight better than the way you were when you last saw me five years ago. Then, you were . . ." He trailed off.

"What?" Keller said. "I was what?"

Berry looked straight at him. "You were the walking dead, Jack. You'd cut yourself off from everything. I was kind of amazed when you called. I was amazed that you were still alive."

"Yeah," Keller said. "Well, I guess I'm better now."

"A little," Berry agreed. "But some of the stuff

you've been cramming down into the back of your head for years is coming out. Believe it or not, that's good too. It was going to come out anyway, Jack. So does she care about you?"

"I think so. Probably. Yeah, she does."

"Congratulations," Berry said. "Love and work, Jack. That's what Freud said everyone needs."

"I thought you said Freud was a quack."

"Mostly," Berry said. "But sometimes he hit it right on the nose." He stood up. "You still against the idea of prescription meds? They've got some new stuff on the market that doesn't have as many side effects."

Keller shook his head. "No. I'm still working. I can't take anything that might slow me down."

Berry sighed. "It's hard to treat someone for anxiety who gets shot at for a living." He shrugged. "Well, you're not suicidal, at least not any more than your job requires. Come on with me to the front desk and we'll make you another appointment."

Keller stood up. "Okay. How much do I owe you?"

"I don't know," Berry said. "I haven't done outpatient psychotherapy like this in a few years. I'll send you a bill when I figure out what to charge."

"Thanks, Doc," Keller said. "I mean, for taking all this trouble."

Berry clapped him on the shoulder. "You were always my greatest challenge, Jack." They went inside to the front parlor that had been converted into an

office and reception area. As the receptionist pen-
cilled in Keller's appointment, he heard a voice behind him. "Mr. Keller?"

Keller and Berry turned. Crystal Puryear was
standing in the doorway. She was dressed in a pair
of ragged jeans and a T-shirt. Behind her, a group
of people were slowly filing out of a room across
the hall.

"Crystal," the receptionist said, "you know the
rules. After group, you have to get back to your
room for meditation."

"Fuck off, lady," Crystal said.

"That's enough, Crystal," Berry said in a voice
that sounded like it should have been coming from a
burning bush on Mount Sinai. Crystal looked chas-
tened. "Doctor," she said in a small voice, "I just
wanted to talk to Mister Keller for a minute. I wanted
to thank him."

"We don't allow visitors the first two weeks—"
the receptionist started, but Berry silenced her with
an upraised hand. "Five minutes," he told Keller.
"On the porch. I'll see you tomorrow."

Keller walked out onto the porch with Crystal in
tow, both ignoring the murderous look from the
frustrated receptionist. They sat down in the rockers.

"You were right," she said. "I owe you one. So
here I am."

"So we're square then," Keller said.

"Don't bullshit me, Mister Keller," she said.

"Everything has a price, and it's always more than you thought you'd pay. No one knows that better than a whore." She sighed and looked away. "I ain't heard from DeWayne. If I do, I'll let you know. But you have to promise you won't hurt him. He's a fuckup, and he's half crazy most the time, but he's all I got left."

"I don't want to hurt him, Crystal," Keller said. "But I'm not going to let him kill me." The sentence hung in the air between them. Finally, Crystal nodded.

"Okay," she said. "That's fair, I guess." She put her head in her hands. "I can't believe he would kill nobody," she said. "He was always wild, but he weren't never mean." She sat in silence for a few minutes. "And Leonard," she said finally. A tear ran down her cheek. "He was always so gentle. I really can't believe Leonard hurt somebody."

Keller shrugged. "From what I hear, they tried to hold somebody up. Armed robbery's a killing waiting to happen. They should've stuck with the small stuff." He stood up. "You better get back inside," he said. "I don't want you to get in trouble."

She nodded and stood up. "Thanks," she said. "For getting me in here, I mean. I been all messed up for a long time. I need to get my mind right."

That makes two of us, Keller thought. "Good luck," was what he said.

She started back into the house. She stopped for a

moment and looked back. "You think I got a chance?" she asked.

Keller nodded. "Yeah," he said. "You checked yourself in. Most people aren't here by choice. They get sent here by the courts. So you're ahead of the odds already."

She thought about that for a moment. Then she smiled. "First time that's ever happened," she said. She went back inside.

"You know Crystal's Social Security number?" Debbie asked. She was standing in the kitchen of her tiny apartment. She had the phone wedged between her shoulder and her ear. DeWayne started to answer, but she held up a hand to stop him as someone came on the line. "Good afternoon," she said, "this is Mrs. Gunderson from Consolidated Insurance. Can you connect me with patient accounts?" In the brief pause, DeWayne shook his head no. Debbie nodded understanding.

"Hello," she said after a moment. "This is Mrs. Gunderson from Consolidated Insurance. We're trying to follow up on some paperwork for one of your patients. The name is Puryear. Crystal Puryear. Yes, I can hold."

"You sure they'll tell you anything? Ain't it supposed to be, you know, confidential?"

She covered the mouthpiece with one hand. "Oh,

yeah. Medical Records won't tell you squat. You want to know what's going on, talk to the billing people. I know, I used to work in a hospital. Confidential goes right out the window when they're tryin' to get paid. Watch. Yes, I'm still here," she said into the phone. "We're having some trouble processing this claim form. No, I don't have her Social Security number, that's part of the problem, I can't read how it's written here. Is that a five or a three? Maybe you just better read the whole thing off for me." She grabbed a pencil from the counter and jotted the number on a pad. "Thanks *so* much," she said in a bubbly voice. "Now, what was the name of the place where she was moved—good, got it. No, I'm not sure when the claim will be paid, I have to send it upstairs. Have a nice day." She hung up.

"She's at a place called Rescue House." She picked up the phone directory and rifled through it. "Here's an address."

DeWayne nodded. "Pretty slick."

She got that weird light in her eyes again. "Tell me how much you need me."

DeWayne tried not to shudder. "Oh, I need you, baby, you know that."

Marie had considered keeping Ben home with her. With no job to go to, she would have enjoyed the extra time. But he actually seemed to like the day care where she had him, and he had fussed at the interruption in routine the first day she kept him out. She was also afraid that if Ben missed too many days in a row, she might lose the space. Good day care was hard to come by. When she unlocked the front door and stepped into the silence of her house, however, she began to wonder if she had made a mistake. She shook her head. *All the time I keep bitching to myself about never having some time alone,* she thought. *And now that I have it, I don't know what to do with myself.* She walked into the kitchen. She glanced over toward the kitchen cabinet where the liquor was stored. Briefly, she thought of pouring the sweet burning liquid in until it drowned all the places where she hurt inside. Something in her recoiled.

No, she said, *Jack was right. It doesn't help.* At the thought of Keller, she felt another sudden twist in her stomach. She had clung to him like a drowning woman, and he had pulled her out. Then she had reached out to him when he had seemed in pain—and he had slammed shut. She felt a brief flash of anger. *Damn him anyway,* she thought. It was then that she noticed the message light blinking on her answering machine, an insistently pulsing number two. She walked over and pushed the message button.

"It's your dad," a gruff voice said. "Call me." That was all. The second was from a detective named

Stacy. He had been a friend of Eddie's, but she had always managed to make herself scarce when Stacy came around. He was big and mean-looking and the way he looked at her made her flesh crawl. The choice of who to call first was an easy one.

"Yeah?" the voice on the other end said.

"Hi, Dad."

The voice softened. "Hi, kiddo," her father said. "How you holding up?"

Not so great, Dad, she wanted to say. "I'm fine," she said.

"Bullshit," the reply came back immediately. "We went through this yesterday, kid. We going through it every time I call? You lost your partner. You almost got killed. You seeing anybody?"

For a brief panicked moment, she thought he meant romantically. She didn't want to discuss Keller with her father. Then she realized what he meant. "Uh—no. I've been meaning to call the doctor the department recommended."

"Screw that," her father said. "Get your own."

It sounded so much as if he was correcting an erring rookie that Marie laughed out loud. After a brief pause, he laughed too, a little ruefully. Then he said. "I mean it, kid. The worst thing that could happen to a cop just happened to you."

"I thought getting yourself killed was the worst thing that could happen," she said.

"Hah. You still feel that way?" he said.

She thought a moment. "No."

"So get some help. And not from some pet shrink who'll go running back to the department with a bad evaluation."

"Okay."

"You heard from Internal Affairs yet?"

"They took a statement from me at the hospital. And I've got a message from a detective named Stacy."

"Fuck those assholes," her father spat. The vehemence shocked her. "Listen, kid. We can't do anything about the statement you gave at the hospital. But from now on you do not, repeat do not, talk to any IAD puke without a lawyer. I'm talking cop to cop here, not as your dad."

"You sure there's not just a little dad in there?" Marie said.

He laughed and his voice relaxed slightly. "Okay, a little dad," he said. "But I mean it."

"Okay," she said. "I'll find my own shrink. And call a lawyer."

"Better yet," he said gently. "Why don't you and Ben come home? We'll take him hunting, like we used to go. He's old enough to go with us."

She closed her eyes. "I'll think about it," she said.

"Do that," he said, in a voice that said he knew she wouldn't. "One last thing, kiddo. You got drunk yet?"

"Umm . . ."

"Don't answer. Just listen. It's okay if you have.

Once. Maybe twice. Have a few for Eddie. But then stop. Don't crawl into the bottle. I seen too many cops do that and never make it back out."

"That's sort of what Jack—that's what a friend of mine said."

"That's a good friend, then," her father said. He paused. "I love you, Marie."

It was hard to breathe past the lump in her throat. "I love you too, Dad." They said their good-byes and hung up.

Marie looked at the flashing light on the message machine. She thought about her father's words. Was Stacy working IAD? She decided not to take the chance. She had to get out of the house. Suddenly, she knew where she wanted to go.

When Keller walked into the office, he could hear Angela's voice from the back room. "Wait a minute," she was saying, "that may be him now." She appeared at the door with a portable phone in her hand. She looked drawn and haggard, as if she hadn't slept. She held the phone out to him. "It's Scott McCaskill," she said.

He walked over and took the phone. "Hello?"

"Where've you been, son?" there was an edge of tension underlying the joviality in McCaskill's voice. "There's a lot of people who'd like to have a talk with you."

"I'm sure," Keller said. "I had some personal business to take care of."

"The police have upped the stakes, Jack," McCaskill said. "They don't just want you for questioning now. There's a warrant out for you. Murder Two on John Lee Oxendine."

Keller's hand tightened on the receiver. "That's bullshit."

"I know, son, but it's bullshit we're going to have to deal with. They matched the blood on your clothes with blood from the scene. You're known to carry a shotgun, and that's what killed Oxendine."

"It was self-defense."

"I know that. But no one found a gun anywhere near Oxendine's body. And there were no witnesses."

Keller remembered the touch of a gun barrel on the back of his neck, remembered a softly accented voice. "There was a Latino guy there. He took the gun."

"The Phantom Latino theory may convince a jury, especially if I sell it right. But right now, I don't think the cops want to hear it. No one else knows anything about this guy."

"What about the brother? Raymond Oxendine?"

There was a brief silence. "Raymond Oxendine and an accomplice shot their way out of Fayetteville General last night," McCaskill said finally. "They killed a cop." His voice became brisk and businesslike. "I need to arrange for you to come in to the station for booking," he said. "It'll look better than if they pick you up."

"When?"

"Now would be good."

"Bail?"

McCaskill paused. "I can't promise it, Jack. Not for this. And you're already bonded out on another charge."

"Not now, then," Keller said. "I have some things I need to do first."

"What have you got to do that's more important than this?"

"It's personal. Give me till noon tomorrow."

McCaskill sounded exasperated. "Jack, they won't hold off that long."

"Noon tomorrow. And I give myself up to Barnes. Not Stacy."

"You're not in a real good position to be negotiating, son. If you could give me some reason why you can't come in today, I might be able to hold them off, but—"

"Tell them I have a doctor's appointment." Keller hung up. He looked over at Angela. She was sitting behind the desk. She shook her head wearily. "You're making a big mistake."

"Probably." They looked at each other in silence for a few moments. Then she said softly, "When I called earlier, you were with a woman. I heard her voice."

"Yeah," he said.

"Do you love her, Jack?"

He wanted to turn away and stare out the window, but he forced himself to look into her eyes. "I don't know," he said. "Maybe. I think I could."

She was the one who looked away. Her eyes closed for a moment and she took a deep breath. "That's good," she said finally.

He walked over and stood beside her. He put his hand on her shoulder. "What's this about?" he said. "I thought you said . . ."

She took his hand in hers, kissed the back of it. "I know I did," she said. "And I meant it. I still do. It would never work with us, Jack. It's just that— this is hard, is all." She looked up at him and smiled. She pressed the back of his hand against her cheek before releasing it. "Does she make you happy?"

This time, Keller did look away. "I'm not sure I'm capable of it," he said.

She stood up, put her arm around him. "I hope you're wrong," she said. "You deserve to be happy."

He shook his head. "I think I may have screwed it up."

She released him and sat on the edge of the desk. "What happened?"

He took a deep breath. He told her about the night before, about the dream and how he had left. At one point, Angela stopped him. "Wait a minute," she said. "This is the Jones woman we're talking about? The cop?"

"Yeah," Keller said. "Marie Jones."

"Keller, are you crazy?" Angela said. "You're wanted for murder and you're dating a cop?"

"She's suspended from the force. She's got no reason to help them out."

"Uh-huh."

"Besides, she has to know I wouldn't kill anyone in cold blood."

"Trying to strangle her in her sleep would really set her mind at ease on that point."

Keller thought about that for a moment. Then he picked up the phone. "I need to talk to her."

Angela slid off the desk and put her arms around him. "For God's sake, be careful, Jack," she whispered against his chest. She turned him loose and stepped away. "There's so many ways this could go wrong for you."

"I know," Keller said. "But I've been going through my life so far taking stupid risks. This time, I'm taking a risk on something important."

She nodded. She reached up and took his cheeks in her hands. She pulled his face down and kissed him on the forehead. "Make the call, Jack," she whispered. She turned and left the room.

Keller dialed the phone. After four rings, the phone clicked. There was a crackle of static and a whirring sound on the line.

"Hi," Marie's recorded voice said. "Ben and I can't come to the phone right now. Leave a message."

"Marie?" Keller said. "It's Jack Keller. If you're there, pick up." Silence. "Okay," he said. "I need to talk to you. About everything. Call me at the office or on my cell." He gave both numbers and hung up. He stared at the wall for a moment before standing up and walking back out to the front desk. Angela was seated behind it. She looked up. "She wasn't home," he said. "I left a message."

"You could drive to her house," Angela suggested. "You can keep using my car. I've got the truck."

He shook his head. "It's an hour and a half from here to Fayetteville," he said. "And it's getting late. I'll try to call again tonight. I've got an appointment with Major Berry tomorrow morning. I'll see her after."

Angela's face brightened. "You're seeing Lucas again?" she said. "I thought he was doing drug rehab now."

"He is. But he said he'd pick up where we left off."

"He's a good man. Looks like your luck may be changing, Keller."

11

The 9mm Glock spoke rapidly, twice in succession. The slide came back as Marie expended the last two shots into the man-shaped target at the far end of the indoor range. She ejected the spent magazine and set the gun on the waist-high shelf in front of her, pressing the button to bring the target to her on its steel cable. She grimaced as she looked at the target. There was a group of holes in the center of the target's silhouetted torso, where the center mass would be. There was another, smaller group in the center of the target's "head."

Better, she thought, *but not great. At least I didn't miss any this time. I really need to practice more.*

She had shot through two boxes of ammo before

the gun felt natural in her hand again, and her shot grouping had been awful. But as she relaxed, the old rhythm and flow returned. Draw, *tap-tap*. Draw, *tap-tap*. As always, the focus on the simple tasks involved in hitting the target cleared her head. There was something clean, uncomplicated about it. *Only two ways for it to come out,* she thought. *Hit or miss, and it's in your hands.* She looked at the watch lying on the shelf in front of her. *Whoa,* she thought. *Got to go pick up Ben. Lost track of time for a bit.* She took a deep breath of the cordite-laced air, the gunpowder stench creating a mild but pleasantly familiar burn in her nostrils, and smiled.

She packed the gun away in its case and hung the ear protectors on the wall. She walked up a set of creaky wooden stairs and opened the heavy door at the top. She stepped into the bright fluorescent lights of the gun shop. Shiny glass display cases showed off a variety of handguns laid on dark green felt, while a forest of barrels sprouted from the brown and black stocks of rifles and shotguns racked side by side behind the counter. A large man half sat, half leaned on a stool behind the counter, his arms crossed over a considerable paunch. His arms were a riot of dark ink, winding and swirling up his massive forearms and biceps and under the sleeves of his dark green T-shirt. His windburned face scowled at the world over a bristling hedge of black beard that reached down almost to the crossed arms.

Marie waved at him. "Thanks, Stoney," she said.

Stoney nodded almost imperceptibly. He didn't look at her and the scowl didn't change. "Some dude called looking for you," he said. "Said his name was Stacy. Sounded like a cop."

Marie felt a chill in her belly. "Oh," she said lightly. "He's a friend of mine."

"Uh-huh," Stoney said. "He didn't sound too friendly. In fact, he sounded like an asshole." He looked at her for the first time. "I told him you weren't here."

She sighed. "Thanks, Stoney," she said. "It's nothing, really."

"Uh-huh," he said again. "That why you're working out here instead of the police range?"

She tried to smile at him. "I like it here," she said. "Not as crowded."

He grunted and went back to scowling at the front door. Marie walked out to her car. She took the cell phone from beneath the seat. She dialed her home number and punched in the code for her messages when the answering machine picked up. There was another message from Stacy. She fumbled in the glove box for a stub of pencil and wrote the number down on the back of a store receipt she found on the floorboard. She looked at it for a moment, then took a deep breath. She dialed.

The person on the other end picked up on the second ring. "Stacy."

She was surprised at how steady her voice was. "This is Marie Jones. You left a message for me?"

"Jones," Stacy growled, "Where the hell have you been?"

"I've been out," she said.

"With Jackson Keller?" Stacy asked.

Until that moment, she had been prepared to tell Stacy that she wouldn't meet him without a lawyer present. But the use of Keller's name threw her off her guard. "What about him?" she said.

"Well, for one thing," he shot back, "Jack Keller's got a murder warrant out for him. And for another, you were seen leaving Eddie Wesson's funeral with him."

Marie's breath caught in her throat. The knuckles on the hand wrapped around the cell phone went bone-white. "What?" she said, the word coming out in a strangled croak. Then she rallied herself. "Maybe I should talk to a lawyer first," she said.

"Yeah," Stacy said, "maybe you should. You can call one from jail when we pick you up. 'Bye, Jones."

"Wait!" Marie hated the pleading note in her voice. There was silence on the other end. Then, "I'm here."

"I—I have to get my son from day care."

"Oh, don't worry. I'll call Social Services to come get your kid."

"Please," Marie's voice was shaking. "I can talk. Just not right now. Tomorrow. First thing. I promise."

Another long pause. "Okay," Stacy said finally. "Tomorrow. Nine A.M. sharp. Your house. And Jones?"

"Yes?"

"No lawyers. I even see a Gucci loafer, I'm taking you in right then and there, and your kid goes into foster care."

"I'll be there," she said. There was a click as Stacy hung up. Marie shut off the cell phone. Then she put her head on the steering wheel and wept.

Raymond's house was a one-story brick ranch, large and roomy, but not ostentatious. In many ways, he was a cautious man, and he knew the dangers in calling too much attention to himself. The house wasn't even in his name, and very few people even knew where he stayed. It stood in the middle of a hundred-acre tract of farmland, screened from the main road by a stand of trees. The rich earth around the house hadn't seen a crop in years; Raymond paid a local kid to keep it mowed flat so he could see anything coming. He stood behind the huge picture window in his living room and clearly marked the progress of the large black Chevy Suburban coming up the quarter mile of driveway. Raymond fumbled in his pocket for the plastic bottle of pain pills. He took one out and washed it down with a swallow from the glass of iced tea on the coffee table.

"You might wanna go easy on them things," Billy Ray said. He was sprawled in an oversized recliner across the room. "They's supposed to be addictive."

Raymond didn't answer. He ran his fingers across his side, feeling the expanse of bandages wrapped around his torso beneath his shirt. The bleeding had stopped, but the wound still felt like someone holding a red-hot poker into his flesh. He was afraid it might be getting infected. Soon, though, it wouldn't matter.

The Chevy pulled up in the gravel parking lot before the front door. Raymond went to the door and opened it. He was shocked to see that the person getting out on the passenger side was Paco Suarez. Geronimo got out of the driver's side. Two goons he didn't know exited the rear passenger doors. Raymond relaxed slightly with the knowledge that if Suarez himself was here, it was unlikely that they had come to kill him. Suarez was also careful. He always arranged to be miles away from any bloodshed.

Raymond and Suarez embraced as Suarez reached the front door. The Latin custom had always made Raymond slightly uncomfortable, but there was no actual warmth in the gesture. It was a formality, nothing more. Suarez stepped back and looked at Raymond. He was a small man, with a narrow, bony face and the merciless eyes of a bird of prey.

"You don't look well, my friend," Suarez said. "You look like you need a doctor." His accent was barely noticeable. Suarez had received most of his education in the United States, first in the schools and universities, and then courtesy of the U.S. Army in the days when they weren't picky about who received advanced "antiinsurgency" training.

"I'm fine," Raymond said. "Healing, anyway." He stepped back and motioned Suarez through the door. Suarez stepped back and let Geronimo and the other two goons precede him. Raymond followed.

Suarez sat on the couch in the living room, Geronimo on his left. The two other men stood flanking the door. Billy Ray got up and gave Raymond the recliner.

"I have your assurance that this place is safe?" Suarez said. "You have attracted a great deal of attention to yourself."

"It's safe," Raymond said. "Ain't many people that know about it."

Suarez nodded his approval of this. "And the local police, I know, are still firmly in your hip pocket." He leaned forward. "Or are they? You are now a hunted man. Can you still do business?"

Raymond nodded. "My network's still together. You deliver a shipment to the usual place, and we'll move it. Guaranteed."

Suarez looked doubtful. "What of your other, ah, legal problems?"

Raymond leaned forward. "There was only a couple witnesses to what happened at that house. The main one I'm worried about is DeWayne Puryear. He's one of the men who shot my Daddy."

Suarez bowed his head and raised a hand in sympathy. "A senseless tragedy. Please accept my condolences," he said. His face hardened. "Had you let us know about this," he said, "we could have taken steps ourselves."

"He was my daddy," Raymond said. "The job was mine to do."

Geronimo spoke up for the first time. "But now you ask for our help."

Raymond turned to him. Geronimo was taller than Suarez, and broader, with a fleshy frame and a round baby-face. People who looked at him tended to think him soft or foolish. He was neither. Next to Suarez, Geronimo was the most dangerous man Raymond had ever met.

"Yeah," Raymond said. "Like you said, things have got out of hand. I need to get out of the country for a while."

"That is putting it mildly," Suarez said. "And what will become of your business?"

"It's yours," Raymond said.

Suarez's normally impassive face registered shock for the first time. "All of it?"

"All of it," Raymond said. "The club, the labs, the warehouses—even the trucks. All yours." He pulled a small notebook from his back pocket. "It's all in the lists right here. Nothin's in my name, but my lawyer can draw up papers to have it put in any name you want."

Suarez leaned back and steepled his fingers beneath his chin. "Just for a way out of the country."

"No," Raymond said. "That's not all."

"Ah," Suarez said. "And what else?"

"I want Puryear. I want the other guy that was there, the one who shot my brother. He's a bondsman out of Wilmington, name of Keller. And there's one other."

Suarez sighed. "This will be the last condition, I hope?"

"Yeah," Raymond said. "There was a Latino guy that was helping us. Said his name was Oscar Sanchez."

"Probably not his real name," Geronimo offered.

"Probably. But he ran out on me. He took my truck."

Suarez looked amused. "You want to kill a man over a truck?"

"No," Raymond said. "But I want him taught a lesson."

Suarez nodded. "Is that all?"

"That's it."

Suarez thought for a moment. Then he stood up. "Allow me a few minutes to confer with my associates." Geronimo stood as well. The two men headed to the door.

Raymond stood up and went to let them out. He almost stumbled from the lightheadedness of the pain pills, but caught himself.

"We'll let ourselves out," Suarez said.

Outside of the house, the Colombians gathered on the far side of the truck. "Guillermo," Suarez said to the man Raymond called Geronimo, "Your thoughts."

"The man is a fool," Guillermo said in Spanish. "He's throwing everything away for the sake of killing some two-bit punk."

"He's dying," Suarez said. "Or so he has convinced himself. The last thing he wants before he goes into the ground is his revenge. And when he goes, what will become of his network? He has the facilities, the people, police contacts—and he is willing to turn them all over for the sake of his vengeance. So," he said, "we give it to him. Guillermo, take care of this. Use some of your trusted men, good shooters. And do it quickly."

"What about this way out of the country he says he wants?"

Suarez shrugged. "He may survive this," he said.

"When everything is done and all the assets have been turned over, get him on one of our planes. Tell him we're taking him someplace safe. When you get over the water . . ." Suarez smiled and pantomimed throwing something, his arms held low so as not to be seen from behind the truck.

Guillermo responded with an ugly grin. "Before I do, I'll make him say my name right."

Suarez clapped him on the shoulder. "Let's go in and tell him we have a deal."

Angela looked up from behind the counter as the bells on the front door jingled. Angela immediately pegged the two men who walked in as cops. The first one was short and balding. He was wearing a pair of wraparound sunglasses that hid his eyes. The one who followed was tall, broad-shouldered, red-faced. His shades were mirrored. The outside heat had them sweating slightly in their cheap sport coats.

The balding man took off his shades. He tucked them in an inside jacket pocket. His hand came out of the pocket with a slim brown wallet. "Ms. Hager?" he said. Without waiting for an answer, he flipped the wallet open, showing a flash of gold badge that swiftly disappeared as he tucked the wallet back in his pocket. "I'm Detective Barnes, Fayetteville P.D. This is my partner, Detective Stacy." Stacy crossed his arms over his chest. He didn't show a badge or take off his sunglasses.

"I'm Angela Hager," she said, standing up. "What can I do for you?"

"We're attempting to locate a Jackson Keller," Barnes said. "I understand that he's employed here."

"Mr. Keller is an employee of mine," Angela said guardedly. "May I ask what—"

"What does Mr. Keller do here, Mrs. Hager?" Barnes interrupted.

"He does fugitive recovery," Angela said.

Stacy spoke for the first time. "A bounty hunter," he said.

Angela stiffened. "I'd like to see *your* credentials, Detective Stacy," she said. The big man bristled, but at a look from Barnes he reached into his jacket pocket and produced his badge. He flicked the case open, then closed, managing to make the gesture look insulting. Angela sat back, trying to look calm, but her mind was racing. "What is it you want to see Mr. Keller for?" she asked.

"First things first," Barnes said. "Do you know where he is?"

"It's his day off," Angela said.

"That wasn't what we asked, lady," Stacy said.

"He's not at his apartment," Barnes said.

Angela shuffled some papers behind the counter. "You seem to know an awful lot about him already," she said.

Barnes and Stacy ignored the observation. "Does he have a cell phone number?" Barnes said.

"First, I think you need to tell me what this is about," Angela said.

"You know damn well what this is about, lady," Stacy grated. "A cop, a friend of mine, is dead. We got a house looks like a fucking war zone and we think your boy Keller is responsible." He grinned nastily. "By the way, you might want to keep a closer eye on him. He's screwing someone else."

Angela ignored him. She turned to Barnes. "I don't have any idea where he is." Barnes started to say something, but Stacy cut him off. "Bullshit," he said. "You need to think real hard about just who you're fucking with here, lady. We can make your life pretty goddamn hard if you don't play ball with us."

Angela looked at Barnes. He shrugged. "He's got a point," he said mildly. "Interfering in a police investigation is a serious matter. You could lose your bondsman's license."

Angela looked at him for a long moment. Then she began rolling up her sleeve. "Six years ago," she said, "I tried to leave my husband. He responded by breaking both my legs with a baseball bat and setting me on fire." She started on the other sleeve. "I was in a burn ward for eight months. I was wrapped in bandages from my neck to just above my knees. The blood and fluid from the burns caused the bandages to stick to me. Every time they changed the bandages, it was like being skinned alive. They changed the bandages twice a day. Every time they did it, I screamed until my voice was gone." She held up her arms. Stacy's eyes widened at the web-work of puckered scars on the backs of her hands and forearms. She looked back and forth between the two men's faces. "When I got out, it took me a year to learn to walk again."

Barnes remained expressionless. "Ms. Hager . . . ," he said.

Angela looked directly at Stacy. Her voice was a whisper. "You think there's anything—*anything*—you two can do to scare me, Detective Stacy?" There was a long silence. Angela continued to stare into Stacy's eyes. He held her gaze for a moment, then looked away.

"Get out," Angela said. "You want to talk to either me or Mr. Keller again, you do it through my lawyer, Scott McCaskill in Fayetteville."

Barnes took a card out of his coat pocket. "If Mr. Keller gets in touch with you," he said, "tell him to call me at this number." He held out the card. Angela didn't take it. Finally, Barnes laid the card gently on the counter. He turned and walked out behind Stacy.

DeWayne sat in the passenger seat, squint-ing against the late morning sun. "Are you sure this is the place?" he said.

"Oh, yeah," Debbie said. "They tried to lock me up in this loony bin one time. I told them to fuck off. I ain't got no fuckin' drug problem."

They were parked at the head of a long paved driveway that led through the open gate of a massive iron fence. The drive crossed a broad lawn as flat and green as a golf fairway. At its end, the drive flared out to a small parking lot, in front of a huge Victorian house with a broad front porch. The lawn was empty. The house was flanked by lush gardens and shrubbery that seemed to cradle it in a green embrace. A small wooden sign by the gate identified the place as Rescue House.

"It looks like a mansion," DeWayne said.

"It was a dump. Some old guy willed it to some foundation. Some fancy nigger doctor runs the place. Thinks he can tell everybody what to do." Debbie took a drag on her cigarette. "No one tells me what to do."

DeWayne made no reply. Debbie had been wild-eyed and giddy last night, practically dragging him into the bedroom. This morning, however, she was depressed and vicious. Nothing DeWayne could say seemed to placate her, so he said as little as possible, even when she had insisted on coming with him. He still thought her presence was a bad idea, but he was too tired and burnt out from all the rocks they had smoked the night before to argue about it. He considered just shooting her, but he had thought that so many times that it had become one of those ideas you thought about but never did, like quitting a lousy job.

Debbie started the car and turned down the driveway. "They won't let you see her," she said with a sort of grim satisfaction. "They try to keep you away from your family and friends. It's easier for 'em to brainwash you that way."

"I ain't goin' in the front door," DeWayne said. "I'm gonna sneak around them gardens and stuff in the side yard and see if I can spot her. Maybe I can get her to come to a window." Debbie shrugged and pulled the car into one of the parking spaces. "Yeah. Sure. Whatever," she said. DeWayne got out. He tucked a pistol into the waistband of his jeans and strolled toward the gardens to the right side of the house, trying to look nonchalant.

12

Keller checked his watch as he pulled into the driveway. He grimaced. He was running late. It was going to be hard enough to explain to the Major why he wasn't going to be coming back for a while. He pulled into a parking space next to a blue Trans Am. As he got out, he thought he could see the outline of a blonde girl slumped in the seat of the car. The windows were tinted dark enough so that it was hard to make out her features, but she appeared to be asleep. *Visitor or client?* he wondered idly as he walked up the front steps. He put it out of his mind as he opened the door.

. . .

The garden to the right of the house was a grassy area shaped like a long U, with the open end of the U against the side of the house. An iron gate between the hedge and the house offered access. The garden was surrounded by hedges higher than a man's head, which provided a feeling of isolation from the world. A greenish statue of a robed woman rose from the center of a pool. Red and yellow flowers surrounded the pool and further rows of flowers nestled under the hedges. Wrought iron chairs and benches were spaced at regular intervals around the garden.

DeWayne paused for a moment and looked around. He longed to sit down in one of the chairs and rest, just for a moment. Everything had been so fucked up since they shot that old man. Ever since then, fear had been what defined his life. He was tired of running. But he knew to stop running would be his death.

DeWayne looked around at the flowers. He wished his cousin was there. Leonard's favorite job had been working in a greenhouse. He had liked growing things. DeWayne had never cared for it; it was too much like farmwork. He hated farmwork with a passion. He sighed and turned away. He looked at the windows on the side of the house, wondering which one Crystal might be behind. The windows were set high off the ground, higher than

DeWayne could see. He grabbed the nearest of the wrought iron chairs and dragged it beneath the window. Then he clambered up to peek through.

The same receptionist was there, seated behind the desk in the front-parlor-turned-waiting room. She looked up as Keller walked in.

"I'm here to see Major—ah, Doctor Berry," Keller said.

She smiled. "He'll be out in a minute. Please have a seat."

Keller sat uncomfortably in one of the antique armchairs in front of the desk. He looked over at the pile of magazines on the side table. Mostly women's magazines promising instruction on how to have cleaner homes, thinner thighs, and better orgasms. He passed on those and looked out the window. As he did, a face appeared outside the window, peering carefully over the sill.

It was DeWayne Puryear.

For a moment, Keller sat there in shock. His first thought was that he was hallucinating, that he had finally gone off the deep end. But the look of shock on Puryear's face convinced him that he wasn't imagining it. Puryear dropped out of sight as Keller sprang to his feet. The receptionist looked alarmed. "Mr. Keller?" she said. Then she screamed as

Keller sprang to the window. He looked out to see a figure on its hands and knees, scuttling toward the garden gate.

Even with the heavy chair beneath him, DeWayne had to stand on his toes to look in the window. There was a woman sitting at a desk, talking on the telephone. DeWayne looked beyond her to the waiting room. A man sat in one of the waiting room chairs, hunched slightly forward with his elbows on his knees. The man looked up. Their eyes locked.

"Holy shit!" DeWayne whispered and threw himself backwards in a reflexive attempt to get away. He attempted to turn in the air like a cat, but he lacked a cat's instinctive grace. He landed on his side with a painful grunt. Immediately he scrambled to his hands and knees and propelled himself toward the gate. He stumbled to his feet just as he reached it, ripped the gate open, and sprinted for the parking lot. He bellowed at Debbie to start the car.

Keller bolted out of the parlor room and toward the front door. He yanked it open in time to see DeWayne sprinting toward the car he had seen earlier in the parking lot. He was halfway across the porch in one stride, down the steps in another, then halfway to the parking lot. He saw DeWayne turn slightly and pull something from his jeans. Something small and black.

Gun, Keller's mind registered. If he slowed down, DeWayne would probably still shoot him. He put his head down and charged. He hit DeWayne around the midsection, running full speed like a linebacker. He knocked the air out of DeWayne with a huge grunt. The gun went flying. It landed a few feet away at the edge of the parking area, where gravel and grass were separated by a thin wooden border. The two men collapsed to the gravel of the parking lot, Keller on top of DeWayne. DeWayne made the mistake of trying to turn and crawl toward the gun. Keller took the opportunity to straddle Dewayne's back. He grabbed a handful of the smaller man's long hair. He yanked DeWayne's head back, then viciously slammed his face into the gravel. DeWayne screamed. Keller did it again. He remembered the sight of DeWayne by the side of the road, his grin in the flashing lights of the patrol car. "Son of a *bitch,*" Keller grunted. There was a red haze over his vision. "Kick me in the fucking *head . . .*" He pulled DeWayne's head back for another blow.

Something slammed into him and knocked him off DeWayne's back. He found himself on his back, face-to-face with a skinny blonde girl he had never seen before. She was screaming, her face contorted in incoherent rage. He raised a hand to ward her off. She bit it savagely, worrying it with her teeth like a dog, her screams muffled by the blood that welled out of Keller's torn flesh. Keller screamed along with her. He slugged her on the side of the head as hard as he could. She only bit harder. Her eyes were wide and staring, her nostrils flared. She looked insane. Keller could feel a hard object under his back. *The gun,* he thought. Using all his strength he rolled over and got her beneath him. He reached down with his free left hand, felt it close around the solid cold hardness of DeWayne's gun. He didn't even know if it was cocked or a round was chambered, and it wasn't his shooting hand. He settled for clouting the girl as hard as he could in the temple with the butt of the pistol. Her eyes went foggy. She released her bite enough for him to rip his hand from her mouth. He staggered to his feet. DeWayne was climbing into the driver's seat of the Trans Am. He was blubbering in fear, tears running down his face. Keller made it to the car before DeWayne could close the door. He grabbed a handful of DeWayne's shirt and yanked him up out of the seat. DeWayne's face was covered with scratches and cuts from the gravel. The sight of the blood made Keller's ears buzz with the rush of adrenaline. He slammed DeWayne against the car and rammed the barrel of the pistol up under his chin. His hand was slick with his own blood; the gun almost slipped out of his hand.

He gripped it tighter. He took a deep breath to clear his head, caught the slight tang of blood in the air. "You were going to shoot me with this gun, weren't you, DeWayne?" he said. His voice was a low growl, almost a purr.

"Please, man," DeWayne sobbed. "Don't hurt me."

"Weren't you!?" Keller screamed into his face so loud that DeWayne flinched. "No, man, no, I swear it."

"You're a fucking *liar!*" Keller emphasized the last word by lifting DeWayne up and slamming his body against the car again. "Tell the *truth,*" another slam, "You little *fuck!*" a third. Keller felt like he was standing on a high-voltage line. His blood was singing in his veins.

"Okay, okay!" Snot ran from DeWayne's nose as he cried. "Whatever, man. Yeah. I was gonna shoot you, but I didn't mean it, please, man, I'm sorry. I'm sorry. Please, please don't kill me."

The words brought clarity to Keller's mind, focusing the high, wild feeling that was consuming him. There was only one thing that would be better, one thing that would make this feeling complete. Keller laughed. It came out as a high, mad chuckle that made DeWayne moan in terror. Keller's finger tightened on the trigger. *A little more,* he thought, *just a little, not even a half inch, so easy . . .*

"Keller!" A voice roared. Keller looked up, over the top of the car.

Berry was standing there a few feet away. He was slightly crouched, his arms out in warning or supplication. His dark brown eyes held Keller's. "Don't do it, son," Berry said evenly. "Don't do it. It's murder."

Keller looked back at DeWayne. The man's face seemed to be coming apart with fear. "He's gonna kill me, mister!" he sobbed to Berry. "Oh, God, please stop him, he's gonna kill me like he killed my folks."

Keller felt the rush back off just a little bit. He looked down at DeWayne, baffled. "What the hell are you talking about?" he said.

DeWayne sniffled. "You killed 'em. You killed my folks to try to make 'em tell where I was. It was on TV."

At those words, Keller felt the rage flow out of him as if someone had pulled a stopper from a drain. He released DeWayne's jacket and stepped back, still holding the gun on him. He saw DeWayne Puryear as what he was: a sad, scared, stupid man who was in way over his head. Keller felt shaky and ashamed. He shook his head. "I never met your folks, DeWayne." he said. "Jesus, how dumb are you? Don't you think it might have been that other guy? The one that killed your cousin Leonard?"

"But—the TV said . . ."

"Oh, for Christ's sake," Keller said. "Turn

around, DeWayne." DeWayne hesitated. Keller sighed. "I'm not going to shoot you. Now turn around. Put your hands on the car and spread your legs." Reluctantly, DeWayne complied. Keller performed a quick one-handed frisk, still holding the gun on his captive with the other hand. When he was satisfied that he had the only armament, he stepped back and looked at Berry.

"Major," he said, "this is the guy I've been looking for."

"Well, I had hoped you hadn't started attacking random strangers," Berry replied.

"Funny," Keller said. "You think you can find me something to secure him with?"

Berry looked doubtful. "We're a rehab center, Keller, not a prison. We don't have any cuffs. I don't know—"

"Some rope. Even some duct tape," Keller said. Berry nodded and turned back toward the house. A crowd had gathered on the porch. Crystal Puryear was among them. Her face was white and she had her hand over her mouth.

"It's okay," Keller shouted to her. "I didn't hurt him."

"Like hell he didn't!" DeWayne yelled.

"Shut up," Keller said. Crystal turned and fled back into the house.

Keller heard a low moaning sound, like an animal in pain. He looked over. The skinny blonde had recovered somewhat. She sat at the edge of the parking lot, in the gravel, her knees drawn up to her chest. She had her arms wrapped around her legs. She rocked back and forth, keening like a banshee. Tears spilled down her face, mingling with the blood that oozed from the scratches on her face and flowed from the laceration in her temple. A stocky red-haired woman in a white nurse's uniform ran to the blonde and knelt by her side. After taking a moment to examine the wound, she put her arm around the girl's shoulder and helped her to her feet, shooting a glare of pure disgust at Keller.

"You can't take him from me," the girl sobbed brokenly. "He needs me." The nurse led her off toward the house.

Keller felt another quick flash of shame until he looked down at the gnawed webbing between his right thumb and forefinger. He pulled a handkerchief out of his pocket and dabbed at his own wound, wincing with pain.

"Who's that?" Berry said. He had arrived with a roll of thick nylon rope and a clasp knife.

"Damned if I know," said Keller. He handed the gun to Berry. "Hold this," he said. "If this guy moves . . . ," he almost said "shoot him," until he saw the stony look cross Berry's face, ". . . just give it back to me, quick." He deftly bound DeWayne's hands behind his back and hobbled his feet by tying a short length of rope between them. He gave a last tug on the rope to check it. "Back to the trunk, De-Wayne," he said. "Don't worry, it won't be far." All of the fight seemed to have gone out of DeWayne. He meekly allowed himself to be led to the back of Keller's borrowed car and bundled in. As Keller slammed the trunk shut, Berry said "You better let me look at that before it gets infected, son."

"Later," Keller said. "I've got to make a delivery."

"Jack," Berry said. "We need to talk about what just happened."

"I'm kind of busy now, Lucas," Keller said.

"You almost lost it there, son," he said. "You came close to killing this boy. And you liked it. I could see it in your eyes. I'm, ah, I'm kind of worried about that."

"I'll come right back," Keller said. "I promise." He pulled his cell phone off his belt and dialed Marie's number. "C'mon," he muttered as the phone rang. "Be there."

She picked up on the fourth ring. "Hello?"

"Marie," he said. "It's Jack Keller." There was a brief silence. "Hey," she said finally. Her voice sounded strained.

"I know, we need to talk," he said. "But first, I've got DeWayne Puryear. He's in my trunk right now. I'm going to bring him to you."

Another brief pause. "Gee, Keller, most guys would just bring flowers to say they were sorry." Her laugh sounded tinny, artificial.

"I'm serious. You can have the collar. That may get you back in with the department."

"What about you?"

"I'll come with you. I—have some business of my own to take care of." He debated telling her about the warrant out for him, decided against it. He'd tell her when they got there. He needed her thinking about taking in Puryear.

"Okay."

"I'm bringing him to your house. Get ready. All I've got is rope. You'll need cuffs."

"Okay." More silence. Keller thought of asking her what was wrong, but he thought he knew. He'd straighten everything out when this job was done. He hung up.

Traffic was light; it took Keller twenty minutes to drive to her house. On the way there, he listened carefully for sounds from the trunk to see if De-Wayne was going to try anything. There was nothing. The man seemed to have accepted defeat, but Keller knew better than to rely on that.

The door opened immediately to his knock, but only as far as the security chain. Marie peeked through the crack for a moment, then closed the door. There was the brief rattle of the chain being drawn aside, then the door swung open.

She was dressed in full uniform. Her cuffs hung at her belt with her baton and service pistol. "Hey," she said. She didn't meet his eyes.

"Hey," Keller said. "Puryear's in the trunk. I've got him tied and hobbled, but knowing him, he's been gnawing on the ropes like a rat."

She didn't answer, but turned on her heel abruptly and walked into the house. Keller followed. "Look," he said. I'm sorry for running out . . ." He stopped as he reached the living room.

Detective Barnes was standing by the bookshelf. His face had its accustomed weary, resigned look. His partner Stacy lounged on the couch, his legs crossed. He was grinning at Keller.

Keller looked at Marie. "What . . ." He stopped when he saw the look on her face. Her jaw was set and her eyes were like cold iron. "You called them," he said.

Barnes stopped forward. "Jackson Keller?"

Keller made no answer. He continued to look at Marie. "You called them," he said again.

She raised her chin slightly. Her voice was steady as she said, "No. They called me. They told me about the warrant. You should have told me, Keller."

"Jackson Keller, you're under arrest for the murder of John Lee Oxendine." He turned to Marie. "Your collar, officer Jones. You brought him in. Cuff him."

They know I won't fight her, Keller thought bitterly. Marie unsnapped the cuffs from her belt and advanced on him. "Turn around, Keller. Hands behind your back." He just looked at her. "Jack," she said. "Don't make this any harder than it already is."

"Isn't that his line?" Stacy chortled.

Barnes sighed. "Shut up, Stace."

Stacy went on as Keller turned his back and placed his hands behind him. "We never knew you had such a talent for the undercover work, Jones."

Keller felt the cold steel circlet fasten around his wrist. "Hurry up and get the cuffs locked," Keller said, "before I break that asshole's jaw."

Stacy's face reddened. He jumped to his feet, his fists clenched. "Stace," Barnes said. "Check on Puryear in the car Keller was driving. If he's still tied up, you drive that car. Jones and I will take Keller to the station in mine."

Stacy walked toward the door. As he passed Marie, he gave her a little pat on the buttocks, his hand lingering for just a second. Marie whirled on him. "Don't you ever do that again, you son of a bitch," she hissed.

The grin never left his face. "C'mon, Marie," he said. "You might get used to it. And if you do, I might not ask too many questions about your, ah, relationship with this suspect." He turned and smirked at Keller.

Keller felt his muscles tighten. The blood throbbed in his temples, but he stared straight ahead.

"Detective Stacy," Barnes said. "If you don't get a move on and do what I said, I'll write you up myself." Stacy's control slipped for just a moment. He glanced uncertainly at Barnes before plastering the smirk back on his face. He sauntered past Keller, still leering at Marie. "We'll see if you're still a tough guy when we get your ass to the station, Keller," he whispered.

As he left, Barnes turned to Marie. "Read him his rights, Jones," he said. "I'll go start the car." He left behind Stacy.

"You have the right to remain silent," Marie said. "Anything you say—"

"Marie." Keller said.

"Anything you say" her voice rode over his, "can and will be used against you in a court of law. . . ." He let her finish the litany. When she was finished, she asked, "Do you understand these rights that I've just explained to you?"

"Yeah," he said. They stood looking at one another. "Marie," Keller finally said. "I'm sorry."

For the first time, her mask of control cracked. Tears glistened in her eyes and her voice shook. "Damn it, Keller," she said. "Did you think I wouldn't find out there was a warrant out for you?"

"I wasn't thinking about any of that," he said. "I was only thinking about being with you."

She wiped a tear away with the back of her hand. "The worst part is that I'm going to be back on the force. Barnes says I might even get a promotion. But there'll always be these whispers. I'll be lucky if I don't turn into a laughingstock. And that animal

Stacy, grinning at me, thinking he can put his hands on me—*damn* you, Keller!"

"I'm sorry," he said again.

She shook her head savagely, wiped the last tear away, and squared her shoulders. She looked him in the eye. "I wouldn't have run out on you, Jack," she said. "I swear it. I would have gone to bat for you. If you'd have just trusted me." She shook her head again. "Let's go," she said. Her voice was steady again.

They rode to the station in silence, Keller slumped in the back seat of the unmarked car, Barnes and Marie in the front. Stacy followed with DeWayne Puryear still in the trunk of Keller's borrowed car. As they pulled into the parking lot, Barnes muttered, "Oh, shit." Keller straightened up.

A white van was parked in front of the station. A long metal pole stuck up from the roof of the van, with a dish resembling a radar antenna atop the pole. The words ACTION NEWS LIVE were blazoned across the side of the van. Keller could see the camera crew and the brunette news reporter from Eddie Wesson's funeral poised and waiting.

"Stacy, you asshole," Barnes snarled. "Only you would think to call the newsies in at a time like this."

The next few minutes were a chaotic whirl. Barnes stepped to the back and pulled Keller from the car. Marie ran interference, placing herself between Barnes and Keller and the news team. It was a mistake. She was the one they had come to interview.

"Officer Jones," the brunette reporter yelped, "can you tell us how you lured the suspects into custody?" The implication was unmistakable. Marie didn't answer, just gritted her teeth and bulled straight past them, with only a "no comment" escaping between her gritted teeth. Behind them, Keller caught a glimpse of Stacy with his hand on the back of DeWayne's shirt. Puryear's head was bowed as if he was trying to avoid the view of the camera, but with his hands bound, there was no way to shield his face from its blank, pitiless glass eye. Keller didn't even try; he looked straight ahead, refusing to acknowledge the presence of the camera or the reporter. The frustrated reporter tried to shove past Marie to point her microphone into Keller's face. Marie straight-armed her, almost knocking her back into the cameraman who was directly behind her left shoulder. Then they were through the heavy metal doors and into the building.

"Hey, Raymond," Billy Ray said. "Take a look at this."

There were five men in the room: Raymond, Billy Ray, Geronimo, and the two soldiers that had come with Suarez. Geronimo had left with Suarez and returned without him, but with the back cargo area of the Suburban filled with long wooden crates. They had unloaded the crates, stacked them in the living room, and pried them open with a crowbar from the garage. Now the two gunmen were removing several short, ugly submachine guns from the crates and cleaning them of packing grease. Billy Ray had been watching the operation, his attention wandering between the efficient, assembly-line operation before him and the big-screen TV.

Raymond came into the room followed by Geronimo. Billy Ray picked up the remote and turned the sound up. A male anchorman with the high cheekbones and perfect hair of a male model was speaking.

"*News at Noon* Reporter Carmen Reyes is on the scene," he said. "Carmen?"

The face of a strikingly attractive brunette replaced that of the male anchor. "John," she said in a deeply concerned voice, "I'm at the Cumberland County Detention Center, where at this moment detectives are bringing in Jackson Keller and DeWayne Puryear, the two men implicated in last week's gun battle in a Fayetteville neighborhood that left three men dead, including a Fayetteville police officer. *News at Noon* has learned that a Fayetteville policewoman, who was the partner of the murdered officer, conducted her own investigation into the killing and brought the two men into custody."

As she spoke, the camera pulled back to reveal the two cars pulling into view. The cars stopped and there was a confusing flurry of activity, made even more incomprehensible by the shaking and jiggling of the camera as the reporter and cameraman moved to the curb. Raymond recognized the older cop who had interrogated him in the hospital, the one who had called him Chief. He was followed by a female cop Raymond didn't recognize. Between them was the handcuffed figure of Jackson Keller. A hot ball of rage formed in Raymond's gut, contending with the line of pulsing fire around his surgical scar. He couldn't make out the words being said by the cops for the sound of the blood pounding in his ears. Keller looked straight ahead, as if the cameras weren't there. "I have you, you sumbitch," he whispered. "I know where you are." He raised his voice slightly. "That's him," he said. "That's the man who shot my brother." The camera focused on the duo coming behind Keller. The small man with his hands behind his back was bent over practically double to try to hide his face. "And I'll bet that guy is one of the ones who shot my Daddy."

"Well, shit, *vato,*" Geronimo said in disgust. "How th' fuck we supposed to whack 'em while they're in jail?"

"We'll think of something," Raymond said.

The live feed was replaced with a videotaped shot of a storefront. The words H & H BAIL BONDS were stenciled across the front windows and repeated in a smaller format on the door.

"Keller reportedly worked as a bounty hunter for this bail-bonding business in Wilmington. Calls to that business were not returned." The camera was back on the face of the brunette reporter. One of the men on the couch said something to his partner and laughed sharply. He stood up and grabbed his crotch with an obscene humping motion toward the big screen. The two men laughed again. Geronimo spoke sharply to them in rapid Spanish. The smiles left their faces. They sat down and got back to work.

"Keller and Puryear will be arraigned tomorrow in Cumberland County Superior Court. Carmen Reyes, *News at Noon*." The picture switched back to the male model. Raymond took the remote from Billy Ray and turned the sound back down.

"That's it," Raymond said. "That's when we take them. When the cops move them to the courthouse."

"Man," Geronimo said. "You crazy. They're gonna have cops all over the damn place."

"No," Raymond said. "Usually only two. One deputy driving and another with a shotgun in the back of the van."

"I don't like it," Geronimo declared.

Raymond looked at him. "We had a deal. We do this my way or your boss doesn't get my business. *Comprende?*"

Geronimo muttered something under his breath in Spanish and walked out.

13

The Cumberland County Jail is a massive
brick structure that sprawls across two city blocks.
The face that the building turns toward the down-
town area is a pleasant if somewhat sterile metal
and glass facade that would not look out of place on
a museum or corporate headquarters. Behind it, the
vast bulk attached to the public space is forbidding,
blank, and featureless from the outside. The inside,
however, is like any other place where men hold
their fellow men in captivity—a place of harsh
lighting, sudden sharp sounds, and loud voices. The
man who said that the mass of men lead lives of
quiet desperation has never spent time in a modern
jail. The desperation in such places is deafening.

Keller sat at a gunmetal gray table in one of the in-

terrogation rooms. He was dressed in a shapeless orange coverall, badly worn at the elbows and seat. His
shoes had been replaced by cheap, ill-fitting plastic
sandals. The official reason for the footwear was security; there were no laces that could be used as a gar-
rote or a noose, no hard edges to use as a bludgeon.
Keller suspected that the real reason was the gait the
wearer was forced to adopt, a weary shuffle that was
the only way to keep the flimsy things on the feet.

Keller stared at the mirror on one wall, keeping
his face expressionless. This was another part of the
game, he knew. The waiting was meant to make a
subject nervous by giving him time to think, letting
his imagination run over the possibilities. In this
place, the possibilities were mostly bad. The result
was that, while he waited, the prisoner's own fear began the corrosive breakdown of his resistance. Waiting didn't bother Keller. He was good at waiting.

He knew someone was on the other side of the
mirror, but he didn't know who. Barnes, almost certainly. Probably Stacy. He hoped Marie wasn't there.
He didn't like to think of what thoughts might be going through her mind if she was looking at him.
Would she be feeling anger? Satisfaction at having
caught him? Pity? He shook his head angrily. This
was getting him nowhere. He was thinking too much.
He was playing the game they wanted him to play.
He took a deep breath and tried to clear his mind. He
hunkered down inside his head and waited.

As if the headshake had been a signal, the door banged open. Barnes came in holding two packs of bright orange peanut butter crackers in one hand and two plastic bottles of spring water in the other. He put a pack of crackers and a bottle of water down in front of Keller. He sat down across the table and opened his.

Keller looked at the crackers and the water. He debated not taking them, feeling somehow that it would put him in the detective's debt, giving Barnes some sort of advantage. *Thinking again,* he said to himself. *Trying to puzzle out the hidden meaning. It's just a pack of crackers. And I am hungry.* He picked them up.

"You're welcome," Barnes said sourly.

Keller opened the pack. "Thanks," he said. He took a bite, washed it down with a sip of water. "My lawyer get here yet?"

Barnes sighed. "He's on his way. You know, Keller, if you'd just tell us what happened, we might be able to put in a good word for you. Once you get all lawyered up, though . . ." He spread his palms apart in an it's-out-of-my-hands gesture.

"Skip it," Keller said flatly. "I'm not exactly new at this."

Barnes took another cracker. "Guess not." He let the silence stretch, chewing the cracker while gazing at Keller thoughtfully. "This was a pretty big collar for Jones," he said.

Keller felt his facial muscles tighten involuntarily. Barnes noticed the sudden tension and his eyes glinted. "Yep," he said with elaborate casualness, "they may even fast-track her to detective. Showed a lot of initiative bringing you in." Keller raised another cracker to his lips. He bit back a curse as he saw that his hand was shaking with rage. Barnes smiled in satisfaction and stood up. "See you around, Keller," he said softly and left.

Keller sat in silence for a few minutes. He tried to restore his detachment. He knew what was coming next. Sure enough, after a few minutes, the door opened and Marie walked in. She was in uniform. She sat down across from Keller.

"I'm still not talking until I see my lawyer," he said.

"Jack—" she began.

"Why are you here, Marie?" he said. "Is this off the record? Just you and me?"

She sighed. "You know better."

"Yeah," he said. "I do. You're here as a cop, not as . . ." He trailed off, raised one hand in a helpless gesture, and let it fall.

"I am a cop, Jack," she said. "It's who I am."

"And that's your answer."

She looked puzzled. "What was the question?"

"Why I didn't tell you that I was in trouble."

She shook her head. "No," she said. "That isn't the question. It never was."

"What was it, then?"

"Why you came to me in the first place," she said.

"Why you . . ." She glanced at the mirror as if she had forgotten it was there. She bit her lip. Then she straightened her back and took a deep breath. "So," she said. "Are you going to tell me what happened?"

He spoke slowly, biting off each word as if speaking to a frustratingly stupid child. "Not—without—my—lawyer," he said.

She stood up abruptly, so fast that the chair almost tipped over. "Okay," she said. "That's it, then. There's nothing more I can do for you."

"No," he said. "I guess not."

She didn't look at him as she left. He sat there alone for a few moments, then looked at the mirror. "Nice try, Barnes," he snarled. The mirror made no reply.

He waited for another endless time before the door opened again. A uniformed jailer stood in the doorway. The guy was slack-jawed and slack-bellied. His eyes were small and mean. A toothpick dangled from one corner of his mouth. "Time to go back," he said.

"What about my lawyer?" Keller asked.

"Don't know nothin' about that," the jailer said. "My orders is to take you back to lockup. Hold out your hands." When Keller hesitated a second too long, the deputy's hand dropped to the sap on his belt with the ease of long practice. Keller gritted his teeth and held out his hands. The jailer snapped the shackles on. Keller shuffled behind the jailer down

the long, brightly lit concrete hallway lined with
heavy metal doors.

"If these guys get caught at this," Raymond
said, "we're all fucked."

Geronimo looked at him and smiled thinly. "You
would rather use your own vehicles, perhaps? With
license plates that could be traced back to you?"

They were sitting in the black Suburban, parked
on a darkened residential street. He didn't know
what town they were in, but it was at least an hour's
drive from Fayetteville.

"Relax," Geronimo said. "Antonio and Jesus have
done this sort of thing before." He smiled again, this
time with a hint of nostalgia. "Compared to taking
out a government minister, this will be nothing."

A car started at the end of the street and advanced
toward them with the headlights off. It was a large,
black Ford pickup with a crew cab. *"Bueno,"*
Geronimo said. "That will be the blocking vehicle.
When it is reported stolen tomorrow, the police will
first look in the immediate area. By the time the
search expands to Fayetteville, we'll have finished
and ditched the car."

"Whatever," Raymond said. As the truck passed
by, Raymond caught a glance of one of Suarez's
gunmen behind the wheel. *Antonio or Jesus?* he
wondered. He had never bothered to learn which

was which. He reached into his jacket pocket and took out the bottle of pills.

"You taking an awful lot of those, my man," Geronimo observed. "Will you be able to do your work tomorrow?"

"Don't worry," Raymond said. "And don't forget. Your boys take out the cops. But Keller and Puryear are mine. I want to look in their eyes when they die."

"Si, si," Geronimo said. "They're all yours. And after that, we will conclude our business. You will like Bogotá."

"Yeah," Raymond said. "Bogotá."

"You can't put him in here with me!" De-Wayne screamed. He propelled himself backwards against the wall with his feet on the bunk. It was as if he was trying to drive himself through the concrete block wall of the tiny cell. "That guy's crazy," DeWayne insisted to the guard. "He's done tried to kill me once."

There was a malicious twinkle in the jailer's small dark eyes. "Looks like you two lovebirds have a lot of catching up to do," he said. "Pleasant dreams."

"You stay the fuck away from me, man!" De-Wayne said. His voice was trembling in fear.

"Oh, put a sock in it, DeWayne," Keller said. "That's over. And you know damn well I didn't try to kill you. If I recall, it was you who tried to kick my head in. Besides, it's not like I can turn you in to anyone now."

A look of suspicion crossed DeWayne's face. "So what are you doin' here, man?" he demanded. "This ain't some sort of trick, is it? What are you in here for?"

"Murder," Keller said. "Second degree. One of the guys that came to kill you and your cousin drew down on me with a pistol." Keller sat down on the floor. "I shot him."

"But if he had a gun—"

"Nobody found the gun. There was a third man there. He took the guns and the money."

DeWayne shook his head. "The money," he said. "The damn money. I can't believe all this shit went down over some damn money." He shook his head. "Seemed like a good idea at the time."

"Yeah," Keller said. "They all do."

It was past midnight, and the single light in the office was the gooseneck lamp that illuminated the desk. Angela sat behind the desk, office phone in hand.

"They're giving me the runaround," Scott Mc-Caskill was saying. "I won't be able to see him until tomorrow."

Angela's hand clenched more tightly on the receiver. Only the calming effect of McCaskill's voice, a voice that had captivated a thousand juries, was keeping her from screaming. She was afraid that it was only going to have a short-term effect on her roiled emotions.

"Why are they doing this?" she said, amazed at how calm her voice sounded. "What are they doing to him?"

"Easy, Angela," McCaskill said. "Don't let your imagination run away with you. Too many people know he's there for them to try any monkey business. This is that prick Stacy's way of trying to show us who's boss. He wouldn't be trying this sort of chickenshit mind game if he wasn't worried about his case."

"What about you?" she said. "Are you worried?"

McCaskill paused just a second too long. "You are worried," Angela said.

He sighed. "Yes, I am, a little. We've got a dead man killed by a weapon that Jack is known to favor. They can put him at the scene because of the blood on his clothes. He claims self-defense, but no one found a gun near the body. And, of course, there aren't any witnesses to back him up."

"You're saying they won't believe him."

"I'm saying that if we put him on the stand, a good prosecutor will be able to bring up what he does for a living much more effectively. They'll be able to paint him as a violent and unstable individual. In that situation—who knows." His voice softened. "There's nothing we can do about it tonight, Angela," he said. "Get some sleep. I'll be at the arraignment tomorrow."

"So will I," she said.

"Of course. See you there." There was a click and the line went dead.

She heard a knock at the front door.

She tensed. Her hand went automatically into the desk drawer where she kept a Glock 9. She stood up, gun in hand. She walked to the office door and looked across the reception area toward the front of the office. Through the glass door, she saw a figure silhouetted against the light from the street. "We're closed," she called out. "Try Speedy Bail Bonds. It's down the street."

"Are you Señora Hager?" a voice said.

She approached the door, the hand holding the pistol held behind her back. "Yes," she said. "Who are you?"

"I have some information about Mr. Keller. Something that might help him."

Angela's heart pounded. She ran the rest of the way to the door. She hesitated with her hand on the knob. "What information?" she said through the door. "What can you tell me?"

"I was there when those men were killed," the voice said. "My name is Oscar Sanchez."

The next morning, a different guard came for
them, an older deputy with gray hair. He took them
out of the cell one at a time, DeWayne first. Each
man's hands were cuffed behind him, then fastened by
cuffs to a heavy chain that went around their waists.
The guard took took them though a maze of halls and
metal doors until they reached the garage. It was a
large echoing chamber that looked far too big for the
single patrol car parked just inside the closed door.

"Shit," the older deputy said, "where's the van?"

"Already run," the driver, a dark-haired man with
a sour, lined face replied. "Full up."

"Well, I can't put 'em in a regular car like this," he
said, gesturing at Keller's hands cuffed in back.
"Can't belt 'em in right. All I need is for one of 'em to
hit his head and file a lawsuit." He continued grum-
bling as he uncuffed Keller's hands and fastened
them in front. He did the same with DeWayne's. He
guided each of them into the car with a hand on their
head, then belted them in securely. He then slammed
the door before climbing into the front seat with the
driver. He motioned to a young deputy standing by
the doorway. The garage door of the prisoner bay rattled upwards in its tracks and the car pulled out.

The driver wheeled the car out using one hand to
steer as he plucked the radio mike off the dash-

board. "Unit forty-five is ten seventeen to the courthouse," he said. "Two ten eighty-twos."

"That might be them," Raymond said as the car emerged from behind the metal fence that surrounded the jail. He and Geronimo were sitting in the cab of the stolen black truck. They were parked across the wide four-lane street from the jail. They were in a parking lot beside a long, narrow building that looked as if it had been abandoned and boarded up for years. Down the street, the other two gunmen waited in a stolen white Lexus obtained earlier that morning in another nearby town.

Raymond raised a pair of binoculars and peered through them. The pain pills he had taken seemed to drop a sort of haze across his vision, but he could make out Keller's blonde hair. His identification was confirmed when he caught a glance of Puryear's face peering out of the glass.

"That's them," he said. "Let's move." He pulled back the hammer on the huge revolver across his lap as Geronimo started the engine. Down the street, he could see the Lexus's headlights flash twice as it pulled away from the curb.

"So I told him," the older deputy was say-ing, "if he thought he was gonna get me to pay five thousand for that piece-of-shit car, he had another think comin'." The sheriff's car turned right onto the wide four-lane boulevard that led to the county courthouse. The street was divided by a disused stretch of rusting railway track that ran between the two sets of travel lanes. As they approached a stoplight, the older deputy went on: "And you know what that sumbitch told me? He says *watch out, you* . . ." As he talked, a large black pickup roared up beside them, then accelerated ahead and swerved drunkenly into their path. Keller saw the red glow of the brake lights growing larger in the front windshield as the truck abruptly slowed. The tires of the sheriff's car squealed as the driver slammed on the brakes. Keller's head snapped to the left at the sound of another powerful engine beside them. A white Lexus had roared up and slid to a stop next to them. Keller saw a gun barrel extended from the open window.

"Get down!" he screamed. His head almost collided with DeWayne's as he ducked below the level of the front seat. The seat belt held him in place, keeping him from going any lower. There was a series of quick, sharp bangs, like someone pounding on the car with a stick. Keller heard the sound of shattering glass from up front. Something warm and wet sprayed over his back. The guard up front was screaming. Keller heard the front door open, then there was another quick burst of fire and a scream of pain.

"What the fuck?" DeWayne was screaming.

"Keep your head down!" Keller yelled back.

Suddenly, the door was yanked open. Keller looked up to see Raymond Oxendine standing there, pointing a gun at him. The man's dark face had an unhealthy grayish tinge, and his green eyes looked slightly unfocused, but the hand that held the gun was steady. He reached over and unfastened the seat belt.

"Git out the car," he said in his flat voice.

"Mr. Sanchez," Scott McCaskill said, "I understand not wanting to draw police attention. But you will need to tell the court yourself. I can't tell you how important—"

"I told you what I saw," Sanchez said. He gestured at the gym bag on the floor of the courthouse's tiny conference room. "There are the guns that were used that day. Can't you just tell the court what I told you?"

"No sir," Angela said. She had stayed up most of the night talking to Sanchez and her face was drawn and wan-looking. "It's called hearsay. No one can testify to what someone else said."

"I was with them," Sanchez said. "If they cannot find this Oxendine, the police will blame me because I am the one they have."

"You told me that a yard full of people saw Raymond Oxendine point a gun at you and demand you come along." McCaskill said. "We can show you were under duress." Sanchez just looked at the table.

"Mister Sanchez," Angela finally said, "it's not just the police you're thinking of, is it? Do you blame yourself for what happened?"

Sanchez looked up. "*Si*," he said. "It is true they held a gun on me. But I helped them. I led them to those two old people that Raymond killed. I could have stayed dumb, like they thought I was. But I thought that what those men were doing was honorable. They were trying to right the wrong of their father's death, and I wanted to help. But in the end . . . ," he shrugged helplessly, "they were just men with guns. Just killing and more killing. And I helped make it happen." He gave a bitter laugh. After a moment he spoke again. "You know what I did in Colombia?" he said. "I was a schoolteacher. I came here because I thought I could make a better life for me and my sons. A safer life. Away from the men with the guns and the bags of money. And look what happened. I became a man with a gun and a bag of money. Another *pistolero*." He spat out the word like a curse.

"There's a difference between you and the Oxendines, Mr. Sanchez," Angela said. "You didn't kill anyone. And you can keep Jackson Keller from going to jail for something he didn't do. Maybe that will make some of this right. That's why you came to me, isn't it?"

Sanchez's smile was bitter. "And is this Keller so

innocent?" he asked. "After all, he was there. With a gun."

"No one would ever call Jack Keller innocent," Angela said, "but I know him. He would never kill a man in cold blood."

Sanchez looked at her appraisingly. "You care for him. I can tell."

She looked him steadily in the eye. "He's my best friend."

They looked at each other like that for a moment. Finally Sanchez smiled. "He is lucky to have such a friend." He turned to McCaskill. "All right," he said. "Who do I talk to?"

"Thank you, Mr. Sanchez," Angela said.

"Call me Oscar," he replied.

"You're doing the right thing, sir," McCaskill told him.

Sanchez hadn't taken his eyes off of Angela. "I don't have a choice," he said, still smiling. "I would be ashamed to act the coward in front of one so brave."

Angela's face flushed slightly. "Ummm—" she said. "Thank you."

McCaskill cleared his throat. "Of course," he said, "once we have a little talk with the district attorney's office, it's entirely possible that there won't even be a hearing. They don't have a whole lot of interest in trying a losing case." He stood up. "Okay, people," he said. "Let's go introduce Mister Sanchez to the district attorney."

14

Raymond led them behind the patrol car, hands still cuffed in front of them. The patrol car's engine was still running, but the body of the driver was slumped over the wheel. The front seat of the car was a swamp of blood spattered by the impact of the machine gun slugs. The two shooters in the Lexus had roared away once they had emptied their clips into the driver. Keller had to step over the body of the older guard. The dead man lay where the impact of the heavy machine gun bullets had driven him back. His left eye stared blankly up at the sky. His other eye was lost in the shattered ruin of the right side of his head. His gun was on the concrete a few feet away.

"You ain't gonna be able to make much use of

that gun, trussed up like you are," Raymond said. He was standing a few yards away, next to the curb. The gun in his hand was trained on Keller.

"Don't worry, man," DeWayne said through chattering teeth. "I wasn't—"

"Shut up, asshole," Raymond said. "I wasn't talking to you."

"At least your brother had a chance, Raymond," Keller said. "At least I didn't shoot an unarmed man."

"He didn't know what he was doin'," Raymond said. "He's never done nothin' like that before."

"Then you shouldn't have put him there with a gun in his hand," Keller said. "If he hadn't pointed it at me, I wouldn't have shot him."

"Come on, man," someone yelled from inside the pickup. "Do 'em and let's get outta here."

"I had to do it, Raymond," Keller said. "It was self-defense."

"I don't care," Raymond said. He raised the pistol.

"Police officer!" a voice shouted. "Put the gun on the ground!"

Keller turned his head. Marie Jones's Honda had pulled up across the street in the far opposite travel lane. She was standing just outside the passenger side, the body of the car between her and the bloody tableau in the middle of the street. She had her service automatic out, extended in a two-handed grip over the roof of the car.

Keller turned back. Raymond had turned slightly

to bring his gun to bear on the new threat. Keller took a step forward with his left leg. He brought his right knee up almost to his chest, pivoted on his left leg, and drove his right foot out in a vicious kick to Raymond's side. Raymond screamed in agony and rage and fell backwards, the gun dropping from his nerveless fingers. He screamed again hoarsely as he landed on his back, where he lay unmoving.

Bam-bam-bam. Bam-bam-bam.

Keller saw a Hispanic man in dark slacks and a black silk shirt emerging from the passenger side of the pickup. He was holding a submachine gun. As Keller watched, he raised the gun and squeezed off another burst. The man obviously knew what he was doing with the weapon; he squeezed off perfect three-round bursts, rather than wasting ammunition with full automatic fire. He fired another burst over the bed of the pickup at Marie's car. Huge rents appeared in the metal and the glass exploded from the side windows. Marie went down behind the car. When the man turned back toward Keller, however, she popped back up and squeezed off a shot. The man screamed something in Spanish and fired again.

"Come on, come on goddamnit, where is it?" The voice seemed to come from near Keller's feet. He looked down. DeWayne was on his knees beside the body of the slain guard. His bound hands were busy at the man's belt. He was looking for the keys,

Keller realized. He saw DeWayne locate the keyring snapped to the dead man's belt. He gave a hysterical giggle of triumph and yanked the ring free.

Keller dropped to his knees beside DeWayne. He heard another shot from Marie's side of the street, followed by an answering rattle of machine-gun fire.

"Unlock my cuffs, DeWayne," Keller said.

"No way, man," DeWayne said. He fumbled through the keys with his bound hands, searching for the right-sized key. Finally he found it. He held it up triumphantly, clasped between his thumb and forefinger. "If anyone gets outta here, it's gonna be me."

"DeWayne," Keller said. "You can't reach the lock on your own cuffs. Unlock mine first and I'll unlock yours."

DeWayne actually tried it for a second, but could not bring his wrists holding the key around far enough to reach the lock. There was a wail of far-off sirens, coming nearer.

"We haven't got time for this," Keller said through clenched teeth. He held out his hands. "Come on. Do it."

"Okay, man," DeWayne said, fumbling the key into the lock. "But you'd better—" he didn't have time to finish. As the cuff came off Keller's right hand, he grabbed DeWayne by the throat. He used the momentum to drive the smaller man backwards into the side of the patrol car, slamming his head into the metal hard enough to leave a dent. De-

Wayne's eyes unfocused and his body relaxed. Keller rose to a crouch and grabbed DeWayne's belt with his free hand, and tossed him into the back seat of the patrol car. He ran around to the driver's side and yanked it open. The ripped and torn body of the driver lolled halfway out of the door. Keller gave a yank on the man's shirt and the body fell into the roadway, shattered pieces of safety glass spilling around him like diamonds. Keller slid behind the wheel. The glass of the windshield was a spiderweb of cracks, but still mostly intact. Keller could see the man with the machine gun. He was still fixated on Marie, who kept up her intermittent fire from her side of the street.

The sirens were getting closer. Marie checked her dwindling supply of ammo and hoped they would make it in time. She wiped the sweat from her eyes with the sleeve of her suit jacket. The silk sleeve came away stained. She was surprised to see a light streak of blood mixed with the sweat. *Must have caught some flying glass,* she thought. *Fuck it, I hate this court suit anyway.*

She had been on her way to the courthouse to testify at Keller's arraignment. She came to the intersection and glanced off to her left. For a moment, her eyes had not registered the bizarre scene in the street—the sheriff's patrol car stopped with its windows blown out, the big black pickup parked in front. Then she had looked closer and her blood went cold. There was blood all over the patrol car. Keller and Puryear were standing behind and slightly to one side of it, their hands shackled. A curly-haired man with a gun was standing in front of them. Marie's hand went instinctively to where the radio would be if she was in her patrol car. She cursed when she realized that there was no way to call for backup. At first she thought that someone was trying to break Keller and Puryear out. When the man began to raise the gun, however, she realized that this wasn't an escape attempt. It was an execution. She whipped her little car through a screaming left turn over the sunken railway tracks that ran through the middle of the intersection. She slammed to a stop in the far opposite facing lane from the sheriff's car and reached for her weapon on the passenger seat.

Now she was wondering if she had done the right thing. The man with the machine gun had caught her totally by surprise. She was lucky he hadn't killed her with the initial burst. She just had to keep him interested long enough for the cavalry to arrive. She straightened up to try to pop off another couple of rounds. The pistol fired once, then jammed. She swore again as she slid down to the ground behind the car. She worked the action frantically, cursing under her breath as she tried to clear the jam.

Keller could see the machine-gunner gri-
macing in frustration. He paused to slam another
long clip into his weapon, then began firing longer
bursts, as long as he dared without melting the gun
barrel into slag. Marie was pinned down by the
steadier rate of fire. The man grinned like a death's
head and began advancing toward the Honda. He
had his quarry pinned down and he was coming to
kill her. His path took him between the back of the
pickup and the front of the patrol car. Keller gripped
the blood-slicked wheel in both hands and floored
the gas pedal.

The roar of the big police engine was still not
enough to drown out the sickening crunch of flesh
and bone or the man's scream as he was caught between the rear bumper of the pickup and the front
grille of the patrol car. He seemed to fold sideways
across the hood of the car. The machine gun clat-
tered onto the hood, then slid forward as Keller
jammed the car into reverse gear. Man and gun disappeared between the vehicles.

"Come on," Marie muttered, frantically try-
ing to work the slide on the pistol. She heard the rate
of fire pick up, heard the zip-zip-zip of bullets over

her head. She resisted the urge to curl into a ball and
whimper. She realized that the sound of the machine
gun was coming closer.

Suddenly the sound of the ruined patrol car's motor rose from a rumble to a full-throated bellow. The
sound was followed by an inhuman shriek of raw
agony and a horrific snapping like branches cracking under the weight of ice. It sounded as if some
enormous predator was dismembering its quarry
alive. She peeped over the hood of her car.

The man with the machine gun was falling to the
ground like a broken doll. He came to rest with his
torso turned at almost a ninety-degree angle to his
hips. Incredibly, he was still screaming. The car
roared again and shot backwards. Marie saw Keller
behind the wheel. He turned toward her for a moment. She expected to see rage, elation, even fear;
but his face and eyes were totally calm, the eyes of a
hunter.

Keller stomped the pedal again and
whipped the car around in reverse one hundred
eighty degrees until he was beside the pickup. He
automatically scanned the scene for more threats.
He spotted Marie crouched behind her car. He
yanked the gearshift into drive. She looked panicky
for a second, as if she thought he was about to run
over her. He punched the gas and ran the car over

the tracks, across two lanes and up onto the side-walk beside her.

"Get in," he yelled over the engine.

"You're out of your mind!" she yelled back.

Keller didn't answer. He pointed over Marie's head. She looked back.

Raymond Oxendine was slowly getting to his feet. There was blood staining the right side of his shirt. He staggered slightly as he walked over to where the dark-skinned man was still thrashing and screaming. He walked past the man as if he wasn't there and bent down to pick up the machine gun.

Marie leaped for the door of the patrol car and yanked it open. She landed almost on top of the prone body of DeWayne Puryear. She sorted out the tangle as the car began moving. The door flopped crazily for a moment against her feet as they thud-ded off the curb. She struggled upright and yanked it closed just as they slammed over the railroad tracks again, hard enough that she bit her tongue. The first police cars were screaming up, lights flashing.

Marie leaned forward, banging her hands futilely against the metal grate. "Keller!" she shouted. "Get on the radio! You've got to warn them!"

"I'm kind of busy right now," Keller muttered, but he picked up the handset and keyed the mike. "All units," he barked, "Heads up, you've got a man behind that black pickup with an automatic weapon, repeat, an automatic weapon. Two officers and an accomplice are down." He released the mike button.

The reply came back immediately. "Who is this? Who's on this channel? Get off immediate—" the voice was cut off in a scream as Raymond opened fire. The windshield of the lead car blew in and it slewed crazily across the street into their lane. Keller spun the wheel to avoid the out-of-control police car as he jammed the accelerator to the floorboard. The patrol car rocketed away.

The pain in Raymond's side cut through the fog of the pills like a laser. When he closed his eyes, he could almost see it, pulsing bright red and clear. He could feel the lower part of his shirt stuck to his skin with blood. The foul smell of the wound let him know that there were other, less wholesome fluids leaking from him as well. The pain filled his awareness, taking over his mind until he had all the rational thought of a wounded bull in a ring. The howl of the sirens as the first patrol car pulled up pricked at him like the *picador*'s spear. He raised the machine gun to his shoulder and fired. The recoil of the gun jarred him and he almost screamed with the renewed pain. But the agony was replaced with a feeling of exultation filling him as the siren abruptly cut off and the police cruiser slammed into the curb. The following cars also slammed on brakes and went sideways. Raymond dimly registered the sound of Geronimo screaming in agony. He walked over behind the pickup and looked down.

Geronimo's shattered body lay in the street. One leg was bent at a bizarre angle. The other showed a splintered stub of bone protruding through the blood-soaked pants leg. Geronimo stopped screaming long enough to look at Raymond. His breath came in long, bubbling moans.

"Get me up, man," he rasped. "Get me outta here."

"I cain't carry you," Raymond said. "An' you know where I live. I cain't let the cops ask you questions." Geronimo's eyes widened as Raymond raised the gun. Then those eyes disappeared in a red cloud beneath the hammer of bullets.

He stepped over the body. "It don't matter anyway," he said to the still figure. "It all ends today." He waded through the blood and shattered glass in the street and got into the truck. He saw the sheriff's car getting away and gritted his teeth in frustration. He punched the gas and took off after them.

"Man," DeWayne whined as he sat up awkwardly in the back seat. "What the fuck'd you hit me for?"

"Shut up, DeWayne," Keller and Marie said at the same time. DeWayne muttered something and slipped down lower in the seat. The radio crackled with shouted questions and orders.

"Sounds like a real cluster-fuck back there," Keller observed.

"Where are you going?" Marie asked him.

"Damned if I know," he said. "Any ideas?"

They were approaching an intersection. The traffic was growing heavier. "Yeah," Marie said. "Back to the police station."

"That didn't work out too well for me last time, Marie," he said.

"You saved my life back there, Keller," she said. "I'll tell them. That ought to count for something."

He wheeled around a VW putt-putting along in the right lane. The driver of the Bug gaped at the spectacle of the shot-up car as they passed. "Yeah, maybe I'll only get ten years for trying to escape instead of twenty."

"I saw what was going on, Keller. It's why I stopped."

"Then you probably saved my life, too." Horns blared and brakes squealed as he made a right turn on a red light without looking. "Guess we're even."

"JACKSON KELLER," a voice boomed over the radio. It sounded as if the person broadcasting had cranked on all the power in the world. "COME IN. I KNOW YOU'RE LISTENING."

"Damn it," Keller said. He made no move to pick up the mike.

"KELLER. THIS IS DETECTIVE BARNES. DON'T DO ANYTHING STUPID."

Keller picked up the mike and keyed it. "Little late for that, Barnes."

"WE FOUND JONES'S CAR SHOT UP. IS SHE WITH YOU?"

Keller put the mike up to the metal grating and pressed the key.

"I'm fine, Detective," Marie said. "Mister Keller got me out of there. You get the shooter?"

"NEGATIVE. HE LEFT THE SCENE IN THE BLACK PICKUP. OFFICERS ARE IN PURSUIT."

"He's behind us," Keller said into the mike.

Marie whirled around. The black pickup was looming in the back window. She could see Raymond Oxendine behind the wheel.

"Oh, shit," she heard DeWayne say. She turned back.

There was a stoplight ahead, cars filling both travel lanes. Their way was totally blocked. Keller muscled the patrol car up on the grass median that ran down the center of the boulevard. Dirt flew from beneath the wheels as the car bucked and shuddered on the uneven ground. Again, horns blared and brakes screeched as Keller accelerated into the center of the intersection. An SUV turning left across their path slid to a stop. A terrified child pressed her white face to the glass of the passenger side. Keller yanked the wheel to the right. They cleared the front bumper of the vehicle by inches.

"God *damn!*" DeWayne whooped. "That was fuckin' *intense!*"

"Is he still back there?" Keller demanded.

Marie turned. The black pickup followed doggedly in their path into the grass median and through the intersection. The driver of the SUV was still attempting to get through the intersection. The pickup struck it in the right front side and spun the vehicle around. It came to rest sideways, blocking the median.

"He's still back there," she said. "And I think we've lost our backup." She could see the flashing of the patrol cars' lights behind the snarl of traffic in the intersection.

"This day just gets better and better," Keller muttered. He picked up the mike. "Barnes," he said, "we're headed south on 301 toward I-95. Raymond Oxendine is still following us, and your pursuit just got tied up in an accident in the intersection."

"KELLER," Barnes said. "TURN THE CAR AROUND AND COME BACK THIS WAY."

"Forget it," Keller replied. "You people are just as likely to shoot me as Oxendine."

"THAT'S NOT GOING TO HAPPEN, KELLER. YOUR GIRLFRIEND TURNED UP A WITNESS."

"Girlfriend?" Marie said.

Keller grimaced. "Not exactly."

"THE WITNESS BACKS UP YOUR STORY," Barnes went on. "HE EVEN TURNED OVER THE GUN THAT WAS POINTED AT YOU."

"Did you hear that, Jack?" Marie said. "You're cleared. Now turn around. If that guy follows us—"

"Barnes could be lying," Keller said. He keyed the mike. "How do I know you're telling the truth, Barnes?"

There was a long pause. Then Barnes's voice crackled back. "THE WITNESS IS A HISPANIC MALE, WITH A HEAVY ACCENT. THAT RING ANY BELLS?"

Keller remembered the touch of the gun on the back of his neck and a soft Spanish voice: *"I am a man with a bag of money and a gun. Soon I will have a big truck. Is that not the American dream?"*

"Hang on," Keller told DeWayne and Marie. He took his foot off the gas pedal and placed it over the emergency brake while reaching beneath the dash with one hand for the brake release. He yanked the wheel a quarter turn to the left while stomping down as hard as he could on the emergency brake. The tires screamed in protest as the car went into a slide. When the car had skidded a full one hundred eighty degrees, Keller yanked the brake release and stepped hard on the gas. The car shot forward, across the grass median and into the northbound two lanes of traffic.

. . .

Raymond saw the sheriff's car slow down
slightly, then execute a perfect bootlegger turn. He
picked up the submachine gun in one hand and laid
it across the window frame, hoping to get off a shot
as the car went past. He couldn't get a decent angle,
however, and he cursed as the car vanished behind
him. He knew that to follow it was to head right
back into a wall of police guns. He had resigned
himself to the idea of dying, but he wasn't going to
throw his life away. He needed to get rid of this
pickup truck. He was nearing the area where he and
Geronimo were supposed to have met Antonio and
Jesus, ditched the stolen cars, and switched vehicles. He hoped the other two gunmen were still
there.

They were. Raymond found them leaning against
the black Suburban behind an abandoned warehouse
near the Black & Decker plant. Their eyes widened
as Raymond slid drunkenly from the driver's side of
the pickup.

"Donde está Guillermo?" one of them asked.
Raymond thought it was Antonio, but he wasn't sure.

"Muerte," Raymond said, hoping he had gotten
the word right.

The two men looked at each other uneasily.
"What happen?" Antonio asked.

Raymond looked at him. "I thought you didn't speak no English," he said.

The man shrugged. "A little. When I need. What happen to Guillermo?"

"Keller," Raymond said. "Keller ran into him with a car." He brought his hands together in a sharp clap to demonstrate. "Pow. *Muerte.*"

Antonio's face darkened. "Don Paco, he not like this."

"I reckon not. We got a score to even with this Keller."

Antonio nodded. He said something in rapid-fire Spanish to the other man. They both nodded. Antonio turned back to Raymond. "What you want us to do?"

"First we get out of here," Raymond said. "I'll tell you what to do in the car." He staggered a bit as he approached the car. Raymond saw the looks on their faces as they noticed the blood on his shirt and the smell of the infected wound. "You need a doctor, man," Antonio said.

"It don't matter," Raymond said.

15

"**Do I understand this correctly?**" Judge Tharrington said. "The district attorney's office is dismissing all charges against Mr. Keller?"

"That's correct, Your Honor," the assistant DA said. She was young, just out of law school, and clearly had been designated to catch the flak on this one. She stood alone at the prosecutor's table nervously brushing a strand of blonde hair away from her forehead. Detectives Barnes and Stacy sat behind her in the spectators' seats. Barnes was looking away as if this case was of no concern to him. Stacy had his arms crossed over his chest. He was staring at the floor.

The ADA went on. "Evidence has come to light

that substantiates Mr. Keller's claim of self-defense in the shooting of John Lee Oxendine."

Tharrington looked at Keller, standing beside McCaskill at the defendant's table. Marie Jones sat with them. Angela and Sanchez sat behind.

Keller had come straight from the roadblock where he had given himself up to the police. There were still spots of blood amid the grime on his face and clothing. A few pieces of broken glass still glittered in his hair. *At least this time I'm not in cuffs,* he thought.

"There is also the matter of the assault on Officer Wesson," Tharrington said, "There's the matter of his flight to avoid prosecution. And, if I understand correctly, Mister Keller was just involved in the theft of a sheriff's patrol car."

Marie Jones stepped forward. She had been able to stick a Band-Aid on her forehead where she had been cut by flying glass. She looked almost as disheveled as Keller. She smelled of sweat and cordite. Tharrington looked at her with an expression of distaste. He clearly did not approve of these apparitions disturbing the decorum of his courtroom. She looked back, clearly not giving a damn.

"Your Honor," she said. "Mister Keller was attacked while being transported over here. There was an obvious attempt on his life by the same subjects responsible for the earlier incident. When I attempted to intervene, the subjects opened fire on me.

If Mr. Keller had not acted, I'd probably be dead. As for the prior charges involving Officer Wesson," she paused and glanced back at Barnes and Stacy. They wouldn't meet her eyes. She looked back at the judge and straightened her shoulders. "I was Officer Wesson's partner. I was there. Mister Keller didn't assault Officer Wesson. It was the other way around."

"Bitch." Stacy's voice cut through the quiet of the courtroom. He was staring at Marie with an expression of pure hatred on his face.

"Detective Stacy!" the judge snapped, his face reddening with anger. "If you can't control your outbursts—" Stacy didn't give him a chance to finish. He stood up and walked out.

Tharrington shuffled through the papers on the bench in front of him. Finally he sighed. "Very well," he said. "If the district attorney's office declines to prosecute, I suppose I have to accept that they know what they're doing, even though," he looked severely at the blonde ADA, "I have severe concerns about this case. The charges are dismissed. You're free to go, Mr. Keller."

"And," McCaskill said, "he may have his vehicle and the tools of his trade returned to him?"

The judge looked as if he were about to choke. "Yes," he said. "Of course."

"Thank you, Your Honor," McCaskill said smoothly. He turned and shook Keller's hand.

"Thanks, Scott," Keller said.

"Thank your friends," McCaskill said. "They came through for you."

Keller turned. Angela was standing there. She came into his arms and embraced him, squeezing tightly. He put his own arms around her more gently. She broke away and stepped back.

"Thanks," Keller said. He looked up at Sanchez who was standing a few feet away, looking uncomfortable. "And thank you, Mr. Sanchez."

Sanchez inclined his head in a slight bow. "Sorry about the gun," he said. "It was a mistake for me to go with those men." He sighed. "This revenge business. Once you start, it never ends."

"You got that right," Keller said. "Sometimes it takes a while to figure things out." He extended his hand and Sanchez took it.

Keller turned to Angela. "You need a ride back to the office?"

"No," she said, and actually blushed. "Mister Sanchez and I are going out for coffee."

Keller looked back at Sanchez. "Oh?" he said. Sanchez was looking ill at ease again. Then Keller grinned. "Well, if you're taking a day off," he said to Angela, "I suppose I might as well, too."

Angela smiled back. "I think we've both got some vacation time coming," she said.

Keller looked around for Marie. He saw her going out the door. "Excuse me," he said to Angela and Sanchez.

He caught up with her in the hallway. "Thanks again," he said. "It took guts to say what you did about Wesson."

"Yeah. Well," she said. Her shoulders slumped. "I just blackened the name of a dead hero. I guess this means my career in this department is pretty well fucked."

"Probably," he said.

She looked at him sourly. "You're not much for being comforting, are you?"

He shrugged. "I've been learning that it's best to play straight with people," he said. "At least I hope I'm learning that."

She smiled. "I hope so, too." They looked at each other for a long moment. Finally, Keller broke the silence. "You need a ride home."

"No, I've got my—" she remembered. "Shit. My car."

"That's what I mean. You need a ride home. It wasn't a question."

"Okay," she said. She looked ruefully down at her ruined clothes. "I could really use a shower."

"Yeah," he said, "me too."

"You want to use mine?"

"Sure," he said.

It was almost ten PM when they got back to Wilmington. Coffee had turned into a long afternoon of conversation, which had turned into dinner. Sanchez had been embarrassed when Angela had offered to pay, but had eventually acquiesced after promising to pay her back when he found work.

They pulled up in front of the H & H office, behind the big brown pickup that Sanchez had taken from Raymond Oxendine. "I suppose I should turn it in to the police," Sanchez said, "but I need transportation to find a job."

"I understand that," she said, "but if you get stopped by the police—"

"*Si*, I know," he said. He looked at her. "Thank you for the dinner," he said. "And the company."

"Thank you, Oscar," she said. "It was nice. It's nice to find a man who doesn't . . . "

"What?"

She straightened her shoulders. "Who doesn't treat me like I'm some sort of breakable porcelain doll."

"That man, your husband," Sanchez said. "He tried to break you. If what he did did not do it, then no, you are not breakable by anything I could do." He looked at her for a moment, then looked away.

"What?" she said.

He smiled. "It is nothing," he said. There was a brief silence between them before he spoke up again. "I would like to see you again."

"Oscar," she said, "I—" she hesitated. "I'm not sure that—that would be a good idea."

He turned to her. "Why?" he said.

The simplicity of the question stopped her in her tracks. He held her gaze, his dark brown eyes calm. Finally, she laughed softly.

"Okay," she said. "I can't really answer that, except to warn you. I'm not the easiest person in the world to deal with."

He shrugged. "That may be," he said. "It is a chance I will take."

She thought back to Keller's words to her. *I've been going through my life so far taking stupid risks,* he had said. *This time, I'm taking a risk on something important.*

"Okay," she said. She reached out and squeezed his shoulder. "Well, you can't say you haven't been warned." He turned and put his hand on hers.

"Well, ain't this nice," a voice said. The passenger door was yanked open. Raymond Oxendine was standing there, a pistol pointed at Sanchez. The other door was yanked open to reveal a dark-haired man. He held a stubby machine gun pointed at Angela. She looked around in panic as the man grabbed her by the shoulder and hauled her out of her car. There was a Chevy Suburban parked behind her with another Hispanic man at the wheel.

"Get in," Raymond said. "We're goin' for a drive."

They lay together on the bed, with Marie's head resting on Keller's shoulder. It had taken over five hours to get the paperwork straightened out for the return of Keller's vehicle. By the time they had gotten it back to Marie's house, the postadrenaline letdown, followed by the mind-numbing boredom of dealing with the bureaucracy, had left them both stupid with fatigue.

Keller had showered after Marie, and when he came out, she was curled into a ball on the bed, dressed in her robe, sound asleep. He found a bedspread in a nearby closet and pulled it over them both. He wrapped his arms around her from behind and kissed the back of her neck.

"Mmmh," she murmured and squirmed back to fit her body more tightly against his.

"Where's Ben?" he whispered. "Do you have to pick him up?"

"Unh-unh," she muttered. "'S grandparents have him. They saw about what happened 'n' called. He's stayin' with 'm."

"Nice folks."

"Mmm-hmmm," she said, then relaxed back into a slumber in his arms. They stayed like that for a long time, until fatigue overtook Keller as well and he slid into a deep and dreamless sleep.

When he awoke he was ravenously hungry. He kissed Marie lightly on the forehead and gently slid his arm out from under her head. She made a small murmur of protest, then clutched the pillow to her and rolled over. Keller tiptoed out of the bedroom as quietly as he could. He rummaged around in the kitchen until he found a box of Raisin Bran in the pantry. He was searching in the cabinet for a bowl when he heard Marie cry out. He dropped the cereal box and bolted to the bedroom.

Marie was sitting up in bed, the bedspread pulled up to her neck. Her eyes were wide and unseeing, blank with terror. Small whimpers escaped her throat. Keller leaped onto the bed and threw his arms around her. "It's okay," he soothed. "It's okay. It's okay."

Slowly, her eyes focused on him. "I had a bad dream," she whispered.

"I know," he said. "I have them, too. But it's okay. I'm here."

She reached out and ran a hand down his face. "Yeah," she said, "you are." He drew her to him and kissed her. His hands caressed her back outside the robe, then parted it and slid inside to caress her naked flesh. She moaned.

Keller's cell phone chirred on the bedside table.

Marie broke the kiss and put her head on his shoulder. "You better get that," she said.

Keller sighed and picked up the phone. *This had better be damned important,* he thought. "Hello?"

"Guess who this is," a flat, nasal voice said.

Raymond sat in the recliner in his living room. The lights in the house were off; the only illumination was provided by the big-screen TV. Raymond had a submachine gun cradled across his chest. Oscar Sanchez sat on the couch, flanked by Antonio and Jesus. Angela was across the room, bound to one of the dining room chairs with her hands tied behind her.

"I got your lady friend here, Keller," he said. "Looks like she was runnin' around on you with that little greaseball Sanchez."

"What do you want, Raymond?" Keller's voice was tight with rage.

"You got away from me once, Keller," Raymond said. His voice was slurred with fever and painkillers. "You ain't doin' that again. You comin' to me this time. Alone."

There was a pause. "Where are you?"

"I'll tell you in a minute. First I want you to hear somethin'." He put the phone on the floor motioned to Antonio and Jesus. "Get him up." The men yanked Sanchez to his feet. He tried to resist, only to earn a clout in the back of the head with Jesus' pistol. The two gunmen dragged him over to where Raymond sat. "Turn him around," Raymond ordered. As they complied, he drew a small .22 caliber pistol from a pocket in the side of the recliner. He placed it against the back of Sanchez' left knee. Sanchez was trembling, whispering something in Spanish. There was a note of pleading in his voice.

"Hold still," Raymond said. "If you move it'll only make it worse." He pulled the trigger.

The report of the gun was slightly muffled by the flesh of the back of Sanchez's leg. What noise did escape was drowned out by his howl of agony. Blood and bits of bone sprayed out the front of his knee as the bullet tore through his kneecap. The two men holding him let him go, laughing as he collapsed and rolled on the ground, screaming and clawing at his wounded knee. Raymond picked the phone back up. "That was to let you know I'm serious," he said. "Also to teach the little fucker not to mess with my property." He gestured to the two gunmen. "Bandage his leg up before he bleeds to death." Sanchez had stopped screaming. He had passed out from the pain. The two gunmen picked up his limp body and dragged him into the kitchen.

"Now," Raymond said, "I figger you can be here by sunup. I don't see you by then, I do his other knee. Then we start in on your girlfriend here. You call the cops, I'll know. You show up with anybody else, I'll gut shoot both of 'em right here. They'll bleed to death before you can do shit."

"God damn you, Raymond, just give me the fucking directions!" Keller was practically screaming now. Raymond smiled. He gave Keller the address, then broke the connection.

"You bastard," Angela whispered from across the room. "I hope he kills you. I hope he sends you straight to Hell." Her pale face and hair seemed to shimmer with an unearthly light in the glow of the TV. That and her words gave her an eerie, eldritch appearance, like the "haints" Raymond's granny used to tell stories about, spirits that came out of the swamps on moonless nights and took misbehaving children out of their beds. Raymond was beyond caring. He dry-swallowed a painkiller. "It don't matter," he whispered.

Angela looked up. It had been almost two hours since the phone call to Keller. She was amazed that she had been able to fall asleep, but exhaustion had finally taken over. Now she saw Raymond standing at his picture window. Sanchez, his leg wrapped in an improvised bandage, lay at her feet. One of the gunmen who had taken them, the one she had heard called Antonio, was lying on the couch, snoring gently. His machine gun was propped up by him. She didn't know where the other man was.

Something on the big-screen TV seemed to catch Raymond's eye. He turned to look. Then he smiled. He picked up the remote and turned up the sound.

The picture showed a low cinderblock structure, painted in dark colors. The building was illuminated by flashing white and yellow emergency lights and searchlights trained on it. The brightest

illumination, however, was provided by the red and
yellow gouts of flame that wreathed the building.
"Authorities are investigating an early-morning fire
at a Robeson County nightclub that was only the
first of what appear to be a string of suspicious
fires last night." The camera zoomed in for a close-
up. Angela could make out the words 95 LOUNGE
crudely painted on the building.

Antonio was sitting up, awakened by the sudden
volume. His mouth was hanging open as he stared at
the conflagration before him. He looked at Raymond.

"You lie to us!" he shouted. "It was supposed to
be ours now! You betray us!" he reached for the machine gun. Raymond's big revolver, however, was
already in his hand. It barked twice and Antonio was
flung back against the couch by the impact of the
heavy-caliber bullets. Angela screamed in terror. Jesus came charging out of the bedroom, shoeless, but
holding his own machine gun at the ready. Raymond
fired once and knocked him backwards. Jesus' gun
chattered, the muzzle flash blinding in the darkened
room, but the impact of Raymond's shot had
knocked him backwards. The bullets went into the
ceiling. Bits of plaster fell like snow in the cold,
blue light of the TV. Raymond stepped over to Jesus
who was thrashing on the floor. Raymond's first bullet had severed his spine. Raymond fired again. This
bullet took off most of the top of Jesus' skull.

Raymond turned back to Angela. She had stopped

screaming and was staring at him, her eyes wide. "Looks like I won't be the only one in Hell today," he said. He left the room. A few minutes later he came back. He held a metal can in each hand. He put them down and unscrewed the caps. She moaned in fear as the raw stench of gasoline filled the air. Raymond began slopping the gas out of the cans onto the carpet and furniture.

Keller stopped at the treeline as Raymond had told him to do. He could see the house at the end of the long driveway. His shotgun was nestled in its rack and his pistol was lying on the passenger seat. His cell phone rang. He picked it up.

"Okay, you bastard," he said. "I'm here."

"You alone in the car?" Raymond's voice rasped.

"Just like you said," Keller answered.

"Prove it."

"You going to come down here and see?"

"Not hardly. Put the car sideways in the road and open the doors. So I can see you don't have nobody hiding in the back seat." Keller complied, getting out of the car to open the back doors, like a magician displaying a piece of apparatus.

"Okay," Raymond said. "Come up the driveway. Slow. No weapons."

It was possible that Raymond intended to shoot him down at the edge of the property, but Keller thought it more likely that Raymond wanted to look him in the eye as he killed him. It was more his style. The first rays of the sun were drawing streaks in the sky. Keller took a deep breath of the thick, humid air. He put his hands in the air and began walking up the driveway.

Raymond stood in the window and watched Keller advance. The fumes from the gasoline and the fever from his own infection made feel woozy and lightheaded. But he was in the homestretch now. Soon it would all be over. He hadn't been able to kill the other man responsible for his father's death and he felt bad about it. But a man did what he could. He wondered if the angels would let him talk to his Daddy one time before they fed him to the flames. He wanted the old man to know he'd tried.

Keller was approaching the front door. Raymond went to open it.

Even from ten feet away, the stench that rolled out of the door when Raymond pulled it open was sickening, a miasma of gasoline, gunpowder, and a sharp coppery smell that could only be fresh blood. Keller felt his fists clenching. "We had a deal, you bastard," he called. "You said—"

"I didn't say nothin'," Raymond called back.

"But your girlfriend's still alive." He coughed. "So is Sanchez, but he's a little worse for wear."

Raymond held the door open and backed up, inviting Keller into the darkness beyond. As he passed through the doorway, Keller could detect another smell, a sickly sweet odor of decay that seemed to hang around Raymond. He stopped through the front door into the living room.

The place was a slaughterhouse. The body of a man lay on a blood-soaked couch. Another corpse lay in a puddle of blood a few feet away. Angela was sitting tied to a chair in the flickering glow of the television. Keller glanced at the TV. Elmer Fudd was stalking across the screen. "A-hunting we will go, a-hunting we will go. . . ." Sanchez was sitting up on the floor next to Angela. His leg was wrapped in a homemade bandage stained with his blood. His face was drawn with pain.

"Sit over there," Raymond said, indicating the couch. His face split in an ugly grin. "You can move Antonio. He won't mind."

"I was listening to the radio on the way over here," Keller said. "Sounds like somebody's trying to burn the whole county down."

Raymond grinned again. "I reckon I showed a few people what's what," he said.

"And what would that be?"

"That nobody *fucks* with me!" Raymond exploded. "*Or* my family! Couple of damn ignorant crackers think they can kill some old Indian never hurt nobody a day in his life, and walk away with the money he sweated his ass off to get? *Fuck* that! The only person who'd do anything about it was *me*!" He grinned then, the drawn rictus of a walking corpse. "We're Lumbee," he said. "We take care of our own."

"You've killed more people than the ones who killed your father," Keller said. "People who never did anything to you. That how you carry on the tradition?"

"I got my own tradition," he said. "Two eyes for a fuckin' eye." He came over and stood over Keller on the couch. He fished something out of his pocket and held it over his head.

It was a disposable cigarette lighter.

The gray dawn light from the window fell on Raymond's face as he raised the lighter over his head. His thumb was on the striker. He began laughing in hysterical triumph, the sound eventually mutating into a high-pitched ululation, a Hollywood version of an Indian war whoop. *"Woo-woo-woo-wooo—"* The chant was cut off suddenly as a bright red splash appeared in the center of his chest. Keller felt fragments of glass shower on him as the big picture window blew inwards. He leapt forward as he heard the report of the rifle. He grabbed the arm holding the lighter and bore it down, his body crashing into Raymond's. The two of them fell together to the floor. Keller raised up and drew his fist back to smash it into Raymond's face. He stopped. The face was slack and relaxed, the head lolling limply. A trickle of blood ran from the corner of Raymond's mouth. Keller gasped with relief. He stood up, tottering on his feet. He staggered over to where Angela and Sanchez were. He dropped to his knees by Angela's chair, his fingers plucking at the knots of the ropes. It was futile, they were too tight. "I need a knife," he muttered. He got up and staggered to the kitchen. He rummaged through the drawers until he located a butcher knife and returned to the living room. He stepped over Raymond's body and cut Angela loose from her bonds, then Sanchez. Angela staggered to her feet, leaning on Keller's shoulder. Sanchez tried to rise, but cried out in pain as his knee refused to take his weight. Keller hauled him up and the three of them stumbled toward the door. He yanked the door open and the light of dawn streamed in. Marie Jones was coming up the front steps, holding a deer rifle in one hand.

"Nice shooting," Keller croaked, his throat raw and burning from the gasoline fumes.

"Some skills never leave you," she said, slipping an arm around Angela to support her. They started down the steps. Keller heard a noise behind him. He turned.

Raymond Oxendine was in the doorway. He had dragged himself to his knees. He held the cigarette lighter in his hand.

Keller turned to Marie and Angela. *"Run!"* he yelled. There was an enormous sound, like God himself sighing in pain as all the air in the immediate area was sucked into the vortex of igniting gasoline fumes. The light of the rising sun was momentarily reduced to insignificance by the flash of the explosion. The pressure wave knocked Keller and Sanchez forward onto their faces. The air was filled with flying debris, the wood and brick of the house transformed into deadly shrapnel as the house disintegrated. Keller didn't look back for fear of catching a fragment in his face, but he could hear the crackling roar of the flames behind them.

"Come on," Keller grunted. "We've got to get away."

"I can't run," Sanchez groaned. "Leave me."

"No, goddamnit," Keller grunted. "Not this time. This time, everybody gets out." He hoisted Sanchez onto his shoulder. He stumbled down the steep driveway, falling several times but always rising up with Sanchez beside him. Suddenly his burden felt lightened. Marie was on the other side, supporting Sanchez on her shoulder. Together, the three of them reached the car. They looked back at the house. The flames had already almost consumed the structure. There was another huge explosion from inside the house and a chunk of roofing blew off, arcing through the sky like a magic carpet. They could hear sirens in the distance.

"I don't know how safe it is here, even with Oxendine dead," Keller said. "He said some of the cops reported to him. We need to get out of here."

"Only if I get to ride up front this time," Marie said. "That damn trunk gets pretty cramped, air holes or no air holes."

"You made her ride in the *trunk*?" Angela said, arching an eyebrow at Keller.

"Well, not the whole way," Keller protested.

"And he did reconnect the trunk release so I could let myself out," Marie said.

"He's a fun date, isn't he?" Angela said to Marie.

"He's never boring, that's for sure," Marie agreed.

"If you ladies are done discussing me," Keller said, "we really need to go."

"Is he always this grumpy in the morning?" Marie asked.

"Pretty much," Angela replied. "But he's been getting better." She opened the back door. "Saddle up, cowboy," she said. "Time to ride off into the sunset."

"Sunrise," Keller said, climbing into the driver's side.

"Whatever."

· · ·

The sun was rising over the desert, heat waves and dust devils swirling and shuddering in the rising wind. Keller stood by the burned-out, blackened hulk of the Bradley. He reached out a hand to touch the beast's metal skin. It was cold to the touch. He looked in through the blown out hatchways. The fighting vehicle was empty. He turned away and began walking into the desert, toward the light of the sun.

Keller opened his eyes. He rolled over and looked at the clock. Four A.M. He looked over at Marie's sleeping form under the blanket next to him. He reached over and wrapped his arms around her. He slept without dreams for the rest of the night.

Read on for an excerpt from the next book by
J. D. Rhoades

Good Day in Hell

Coming soon in hardcover from
St. Martin's Minotaur

The first blow split Stan's lip and knocked him into a stack of recapped tires at the back of the repair bay. He caught a glimpse of the bright sunlight and the road outside before his stepfather's bulk eclipsed the light like an evil moon. The second, third, and fourth blows were softer but more humiliating, delivered as they were by the hand holding the rolled-up magazine.

"This how you pay me back?" his stepfather bellowed, shaking the magazine in Stan's face. Rolled up, all Stan could see was part of a bare breast and nipple and a flash of thigh. "All I done for you?" He began punctuating his diatribe with blows across Stan's face from the rolled-up magazine, as if Stan were a puppy who had piddled on the rug. "I (WHACK) put a ROOF (WHACK) over your HEAD (WHACK), put FOOD (WHACK) on your PLATE (WHACK) and all . . ." He shook the magazine in Stan's face. "So you can sit around my business reading PORN?" He threw the magazine aside, and grabbed Stan by the collar of his t-shirt.

"I didn't . . ." Stan blubbered. "It's not . . ." He hated himself for the tears that sprang to his eyes. Stan was sixteen, almost seventeen, and he was almost as tall as his stepfather. But when the blows came, forehand, backhand, he was as helpless as a five-year-old before the older man's fury. He didn't even dare put his hands up to shield his face. Every time he had tried that, he had been beaten worse, once so badly he had lost a tooth. So he took the punishment, his guts twisting with fear and hate. He tried to make himself go far away, so it would all seem like it was happening to someone else. Sometimes he could make that happen. Those times were easier. It was easier if the loathing he felt was for some other weak, helpless pussy. This time, though, he couldn't do it. It stayed real. It was Stan who felt the collar of the t-shirt rip in his stepfather's hand, Stan who saw the rage double in the man's eyes, Stan who saw the open hand pulled back, closed into a fist, and ready to put the lights out. . . .

There was a tinny double ping from out front that signaled a vehicle pulling up. Saved by the bell, Stan thought giddily as his stepfather released him and straightened up. "I'll finish with you later," the older man snarled. He turned on his heel and walked out of the repair bay. Stan slid down to the floor and hugged his knees, willing himself not to cry. He leaned over to pick the wadded magazine off the floor. On the cover, a slim blonde girl who looked hardly out of puberty was looking back over her naked shoulder with what was intended to be a sultry look. She really just looked pissed. *Barely Legal*, the magazine title promised. He laid the magazine on the workbench and tried to smooth out the wrinkles where his stepfather had wadded it up. Suddenly, a crimson speck appeared on the girl's pouty face. He stared at it uncomprehending for a moment until the speck deformed and began to run down the arch of the girl's back, across the glossy paper, leaving a watery red trail. Stan put a hand to his nose, felt the wetness there. His hand came away red. "Shit," he said out loud. He looked around for something to stop the bleeding. All he saw was a pair of grease-stained rags draped over the back of the workbench.

He stumbled to the front of the repair bay, through the doors to the front office. He glanced at the gas pumps. There was a black Mustang convertible pulled up at the full-service pump. Stan's stepfather was pumping, wearing the obsequious grin he always used with customers. A man stood by the Mustang's front fender, his arms crossed across his chest, nodding and grinning back at whatever was being said. The man was tall, over six feet, and dressed entirely in black: jeans, shirt, even his boots. He wore dark glasses. His black hair was shot with streaks of gray and combed back from his fore-head. At one time, he might have been regarded as a handsome man, but the outline of what once had probably been memorably rugged good looks had sagged under the weight of years and hard living.

There was another person in the car on the passenger side, but Stan couldn't see them clearly. He snagged the restroom key off the hook behind the cash register and exited through the side door. The station's single working restroom was halfway down one side, past the door to the other restroom with the OUT OF ORDER sign that had been there for as long as Stan could remember. He fumbled the key into the lock and slipped inside. He glanced into the mirror over the cracked and rust-stained sink. "Oh, FUCK," he blurted. The area below his nose was a trail of crimson that led over his puffy and bleeding lip. There were spatters of blood on his light blue uniform shirt as well, the same color as the embroidered "Stan" over the pocket. Stan moaned in fear. The only thing worse than the beatings was the possibility that someone would find out, that the Social Services people would come back, that the whole round of questions and courts and lawyers would start over.

The first time it had happened, Stan had been twelve. He had thought then that they would take him away, put him someplace where he and his mom could be safe. And they had, for a while. But within six months, his mom went back and, eventually, so did Stan. His stepfather had made all the right noises, taken all the right steps. But all that had really happened was that he was more careful to hit Stan where it wouldn't leave marks. For a while. But after a while, caution receded. His stepfather had knocked one of his teeth out for spilling motor oil on the floorboard of the pickup. And the cycle had begun again. Questions, hearings, orders for anger management and parenting classes, and, in the end, Stan was back where he started. Only now that he was older, he realized that everyone knew. Everyone knew how weak he was. He hated that worst of all.

Stan rolled a handful of paper towels off the holder and blotted at his face. He managed to mop most of the blood off, but a steady flow still came from his nose. "Fuck, fuck, FUCK," Stan muttered. He looked up at the ceiling and pressed the paper towels against his nose. There was a knock on the door.

"Just a minute," Stan gasped, his voice breaking on the last word.

"Come on, hon," a female voice said on the other side of the door. "My back teeth're floatin'."

Stan closed his eyes. "Fuck," he whispered one last time, with feeling. He tipped his head back upright. The bleeding seemed to have stopped, but his nose and lip were still visibly swollen. He hurriedly stuffed the paper towels in the wastebasket. He turned to the door, took a deep breath, and opened it.

The girl waiting on the other side looked to be not much older than Stan. She was dressed in a pair of low rise jeans that looked about ready to slide off her bony hips and a thin tank top that hugged her upper body. There was an applique design of a daisy on the shirt between the slight bulges of her small breasts. She had a large shapeless bag slung over one shoulder. Her face might have been pretty except for her jaw, which looked too big for the rest of her features. It gave her a belligerent look, as if she were daring anyone to disagree with something she had yet to say. Her blonde hair was cut short and moussed into carefully plotted disarray, with a swoop of hair down over her left eye.

"Whoa," she said. "What happened to you?"

"Nothing," Stan said. "I, um, I fell down."

The girl swept the hair away from her face. Her blue eyes narrowed. "Huh," she said. "You fell." She looked back to the front of the station, where Stan could hear his stepfather guffawing over his own joke. Her jaw tightened, and she looked back. "I gotta pee," she said.

"Oh. Yeah. Sorry," Stan said. He stepped past her as she stepped into the restroom. As he started to walk away, she said "Hey." Stan looked back at her. She was leaning on the door, looking out.

"What's your name?" she asked.

"Stan," he said.

"That guy out there," she said, jerking her head towards the front. "He your daddy?"

"Stepdad," Stan said. She got a look in her eye that Stan hadn't expected. He had been dreading pity. What he saw looked like . . . determination. She closed the door.

Stan walked around to the front of the station. He reached the front door to the office just as his stepfather came out. "Make yourself useful," he said, handing Stan a plastic card. "Run this guy's credit card." He stood outside the office door, joking with the older man.

Stan went to the old credit-card machine and got out one of the carbon forms. The credit-card rep had been trying to get Stan's stepfather to lease one of the newer electronic credit-card machines, but so far he hadn't wanted to spend the money. He looked up to see the blonde girl coming around to the front. She was walking quickly, her hand stuffed into the bag over her shoulder. When she reached the spot where the two men were talking, she pulled a large handgun out of the bag and shot Stan's stepfather in the face.

He fell backward, blood gushing between his hands. A horrible bubbling sound came from between the fingers, as if he had tried to scream. Stan stood behind the counter, frozen by shock. He knew his mouth was open, but he couldn't make any sound come out.

The girl looked up at the man in black. "Like we agreed?" she asked.

The man nodded. "Yeah."

The girl handed the gun to the man in black, who stepped over until he was standing with one foot on each side of the body still writhing and flopping on the ground. He looked at the girl, a slight frown on his face. "You're startin' early," he said. He aimed and fired downward. The body beneath him gave one last convulsion and lay still. The man in black stepped over to the counter, where Stan was still rooted to the spot. He pointed the gun at Stan. "Open the register, kid," he said. Stan tried again to speak, but all that came out was a low moan. His hands were apparently smarter than his tongue; they seemed to move of their own accord as he hit the button to open the register. The girl stepped forward and pulled out the cash drawer. She was smiling at Stan. She looked back at the body on the ground. "I used to fall down a lot myself," she said. She poured the contents of the cash drawer into her shoulder bag, her eyes still on Stan, that scary smile still on her face. He felt as if his legs would give way any second. "Roy," the girl said over her shoulder, "hand me the gun."

He handed the gun over. She placed the barrel almost gently under Stan's chin. The barrel was hot, a circle of pain against his flesh. "Hey, Stan," she whispered. "You want to be famous?"

Stan finally rediscovered words. "Wh-wh-what?"

"We're gonna be famous," Roy said. He was grinning.

"Yeah," Laurel said. "And you can come along. If you want."

"Hey," Roy said. "That's not . . ."

"What about it, Stan?" Laurel interrupted him. "You wanna be famous? We can make it happen."

"Laurel," Roy said, "We've gotta get moving."

"Come with us, Stan," the girl said. "What have you got here? Some dipshit gas station out in the country? We're gonna be on TV. In the papers. Books, movies . . . you name it. Or," she looked a little sad. "I can put a bullet in you. Then Roy'll put a bullet in you, 'cause we agreed. Your choice. But you need to tell me now."

Stan swallowed hard. He cut his eyes towards the figure of his stepfather on the ground. It began to dawn on him that he wasn't going to have to get slapped around anymore. He looked back. The girl saw his eyes, and her smile got wider. She lowered the gun.

"Okay," he said.

"You sure you want to do this?" Keller said. He pulled the big car up to the curb and put it in park.

"*Si*," said the brown-skinned man in the passenger seat. He sounded calm, but the way he nervously stroked his thin moustache betrayed him.

"Don't worry, Oscar. This will be easy," Keller said. "This guy Olivera's got no record of violence, he just has a problem with showing up for his court dates. We find him, you explain the situation to him, we bring him back. No problems."

Oscar Sanchez regarded Keller with no expression in his dark eyes. He spoke with the precise diction of someone who had learned English in a classroom rather than in the street. "Of course. That is why you have brought a gun."

"I always do that," Keller said. "It doesn't mean I think the guy's going to get rowdy. It just helps to be prepared. I have an extra one in the trunk if you want it."

Sanchez smiled thinly. "*Gracias*, but no. I prefer to be just the interpreter."

"You're sure you're okay?"

Sanchez nodded. "I am sure, Jack. I have rested long enough. It is time I made myself useful."

"Okay, let's go then," Keller said as he opened the door. He stood up and tucked a stubby Glock 9 mm pistol into the holster at the small of his back. He waited at the curb, looking away uncomfortably as the other man retrieved a dark-colored wooden cane from behind the seat and struggled to his feet. He was in his mid-forties, but the pronounced limp and the cane gave him the look of an older man. Keller slackened his pace to allow Sanchez to keep up. When they reached the door to the small duplex,

Sanchez's face was shiny with sweat and he was breathing hard, as if he had climbed a flight of stairs. Keller knocked on the door. There was no answer. He knocked again.

After a moment, a teenaged girl opened the door. She was barefoot, dressed in a denim skirt and a brightly colored floral blouse. Her skin was the same shade as Sanchez's, but her eyes were hooded and unfriendly. "*Que*?" she said.

"*Buenos dias*," Sanchez said. "*Estamos buscando Manuel Olivera. Es él casero*?"

"*No sé cualquier persona Manuel nombrado*," the girl said.

"She says she doesn't know anyone by that name," Sanchez told Keller.

"Uh-huh," Keller said.

The girl made as if to close the door, but a boy of about seven or eight forced his way around one of her bare legs and blocked the door open. He stared at the two men in the doorway with grave interest. "*Porqué usted desea ver el Manuel*?" he asked in Spanish. The girl made as if to yank him out of the doorway, but the boy evaded her grip with the ease of long practice and shot past her onto the small concrete stoop. "Who are you?" he demanded in English, looking at Keller.

"Ramon!" the girl hissed. "*Consiga detrás en la casa . . .*"

"My name is Mr. Sanchez," the man with the cane

said to the boy. "You can call me Oscar. My friend here is Mr. Keller. Do you know Manuel Olivera?"

"Sure," the boy said. "He's been making out all morning with my ugly sister here." He raised his voice. "HEY, MANUEL!" he yelled. The girl shouted something unintelligible at her brother and tried to slam the door, but Keller stiff-armed it the rest of the way open. He shoved his way past the girl and into the apartment.

"You can't do that!" the girl yelled in English. "You got no warrant!" Keller ignored her. The front door opened into a tiny kitchen and an equally miniscule space that the landlord probably optimistically described as a breakfast nook. Keller moved past them and into the living room. The girl turned to Sanchez, her face dark with impotent fury. "He doesn't have a warrant," she said in Spanish.

Sanchez shrugged apologetically and replied in the same language. "He isn't a policeman."

Keller found himself in the living room. The only illumination was provided by a color television, which was playing a game show in Spanish. A sagging couch rested against one wall. Beside the couch, a darkened hallway led to the back rooms of the apartment. Keller pulled a pair of handcuffs from the back pocket of his jeans. He drew his gun from the small of his back with his other hand. "Manuel!" he called out. "Come on, man, let's make this easy on everybody." According to Keller's information, Olivera spoke no English, so Keller tried to sound as calm as possible, hoping Olivera would respond to the tone of voice, even if the words meant nothing to him.

It didn't work. Keller heard the slamming of a door at the far end of the hallway. He plunged into the darkness towards the sound.

"What do you mean, he's not a policeman?" the girl said in Spanish. "Why is he in my mother's house, then?"

"He works for Manuel's bail bondsman," Sanchez said. He leaned his shoulder against the doorjamb to take more weight off his knee. "Manuel missed his court date. If Senor Keller doesn't bring him back, the bondsman loses the money." Sanchez took a handkerchief from his back pocket and mopped the sweat from his brow.

"Hey, Mr. Oscar," the boy asked. "What's wrong with your leg?"

Sanchez hesitated. "Some bad men shot me in it," he said finally.

The boy's eyes widened in amazement. "Cool," he said in English.

There was only one door closed, the one at the end of the hall. Keller stopped short of it. He raised his right knee nearly to his chest, then shot it out parallel to the floor, pivoting on his left leg until his left heel pointed at the door. The heel of his boot smashed the door off its hinges with a shriek of rending wood. The door fell inwards, revealing a narrow bathroom. The window next to the toilet was raised. The room was empty. Keller heard a grunt as a body landed on the ground outside the window. He tried to reach the window, but stumbled on the ruins of the door. Keller cursed as he fell full length on top of the splintered wood. He could hear footsteps outside the window, growing fainter as his quarry got away.

"Did it hurt?" the boy asked. "When the bad men shot you?"

"I hope it did," the girl said spitefully. She sat down on the stoop and crossed her arms on her knees.

"You shouldn't be so hateful," Sanchez told her. "It will put lines on your face." The girl gave him the finger.

Sanchez heard the sound of running footsteps. He turned toward the sound in time to see Manuel Olivera come tearing around the corner of the house. Sanchez could see the whites of his eyes. He raised his hand as if to signal Olivera to a stop. Then he saw the knife in the other man's hand.

Keller heard the girl scream outside as he picked himself up off the ruined door. Then there was a sharp crack, like the report of a small pistol. He felt the blood drain from his face. Oscar, he thought. Oh, fuck. I shouldn't have brought him. I shouldn't have left him alone. He ran back down the hallway as fast as he could.

When he got back outside, the girl was sobbing, crouched over a prone figure on the sidewalk. Keller saw the glint of a knife in the grass a few feet away. There was blood on the girl's hands. There was blood on the face of the man on the ground. Keller looked him over, mentally comparing the face to the photograph in his file. It was Manuel Olivera.

"I think he needs a doctor," a voice said from behind Keller. He turned. Sanchez was standing there, propping himself against the house. He held up a dark piece of splintered wood. "And I need a new cane."

"You can buy one with your cut of the fee on Olivera," Keller said.

Sanchez looked surprised. "My . . . cut?"

"Why not?" Keller said. "You did the takedown."

"Ey!" the man on the ground said as he sat up. He held a hand to his face. Blood flowed from between his fingers. "That sonofabitch," he said in heavily accented English. "He break my fucking nose!"

Keller and Sanchez looked at each other. "You said he didn't speak English," Sanchez said.

"Outdated information, I guess," Keller replied. He opened the handcuffs with one hand. "On your feet, Manuel," he said. "We'll get you a doctor at the police station."

"I sue you, sonofabitch!" Manuel said as he staggered to his feet. "I sue your ass off!"

"We'll make an American out of you yet," Keller said as he put the cuffs on.